I0669360

DEAD GIRLS DON'T

DEAD GIRLS DON'T
MAGS STOREY

An imprint of ChiZine Publications

FIRST EDITION

Dead Girls Don't © 2015 by Mags Storey
Cover artwork © 2015 by Erik Mohr
Interior design © 2015 by Samantha Beiko

All Rights Reserved.

This book is a work of fiction. Names, characters, places, and incidents are either
a product of the author's imagination or are used fictitiously. Any resemblance to
actual events, locales, or persons, living or dead, is entirely coincidental.

Distributed in Canada by
PGC Raincoast Books
300-76 Stafford Street
Toronto, ON M6J 2S1
Phone: (416) 934-9900
e-mail: info@pgcbooks.ca

Distributed in the U.S. by
Diamond Comic Distributors, Inc.
10150 York Road, Suite 300
Hunt Valley, MD 21030
Phone: (443) 318-8500
e-mail: books@diamondbookdistributors.com

Library and Archives Canada Cataloguing in Publication Data

Storey, Mags, author
    Dead girls don't / Mags Storey.
Issued in print and electronic formats.
ISBN 978-1-77148-306-3 (pbk.).--ISBN 978-1-77148-307-0 (pdf)

    I. Title.
PS8637.T673D43 2015   jC813'.6   C2015-903032-3
                                               C2015-903033-1

CHITEEN
Toronto, Canada
www.chiteen.com

Edited by Sandra Kasturi
Copyedited and proofread by Tove Nielsen
Publishing Consultant: Christie Harkin

Canada Council   Conseil des Arts
for the Arts   du Canada

We acknowledge the support of the Canada Council for the Arts which last year
invested $20.1 million in writing and publishing throughout Canada.

ONTARIO ARTS COUNCIL
CONSEIL DES ARTS DE L'ONTARIO

an Ontario government agency
un organisme du gouvernement de l'Ontario

Published with the generous assistance of the Ontario Arts Council.

Printed in Canada

For the boy who forgot his pen
For the boy with the severed hand
For the boy who never left

Prologue

Some things in life are so bizarre, so insane, and make so little sense, you've just got to go with them and see what happens.

At least, that was the first thought that crossed Liv Munk's mind as she stared through the wrought iron fence at the fake-gothic monstrosity that was Rosewood Academy. There might be a certain twisted logic to spending your Saturday night breaking into the one place on earth you spent the rest of your life desperately wishing you could escape from.

But damned if she knew what it was.

The sixteen-year-old ran both hands through her long black and purple hair, then shot a sideways glance at Gabriel. His lanky form was slouched in the dark shadow between two pools of yellow lamplight in a stance that could only be described as lurking.

"Tell me you didn't just wake me up in the middle of the night so I'd come help you vandalize our high school."

Gabriel chuckled. "You know me better than that." He slid his body through the narrow gap between where the fence bars ended and thick hedges began. Then he reached back for her hand. "Brute force is hardly my style."

True. Or he'd have probably seen to it that the hallowed halls of Rosewood went up in some untraceable, "freak accident" ball of flames ages ago. The lovely "Zero Tolerance for Bullying" rules plastered in every hallway didn't seem to mean shit when it came to people like Liv and Gabriel, and what happened when the teachers' backs were turned. Not that Liv had ever expected the daughter of a waitress to fit in at a private school for the rich and self-important. She'd have thought the bullies would've had the sense of self-preservation not to keep beating down Gabriel— the one guy at school who (rumour had it) had hacked into the occasional major corporation or government website just for kicks.

She hesitated. "Promise me we're not going to do something stupid."

"Nope, we're about to do something really, really smart." Gabriel grinned. "And we're not going to get caught. Stay behind me, step exactly where I step and the security cameras won't pick you up. Hurry! I'm dying to show you something."

Liv grabbed his hand just long enough to let him pull her through the bushes. Then they ran along the tree line, all the way around the school until they ended up at a small utility door behind the auditorium. Gabriel pushed zero five times on the keypad by the door. It clicked and slid open. They stepped into the auditorium.

"Now, wait right here. Don't move. I've got to go up into the booth and do a thing."

Gabriel disappeared into the darkness to her right. She heard the utility door slam behind him. Moments later, the lights clicked on in the control booth above the balcony. Sometimes Liv suspected that the only reason he even deigned to attend Rosewood was for the hours he got to spend in the auditorium hiding out in a high-tech, state-of-the-art control booth and playing with video editing and projection equipment. The school had invested millions in its auditorium in the past year.

Liv shone her cellphone flashlight app slowly over the rows of chairs. To her left lay the huge curved stage with its built-in hydraulic platform that could lift actors halfway to the ceiling—and, of course, a hidden net underneath the stage in case anyone fell. There was whirring noise. Three retractable screens rolled down from the ceiling. Then she heard Gabriel running back down the stairs.

"I made something." He was practically rubbing his hands together. Gabriel led her down to the front row.

"A computer program. That lets you experience an event without actually being there. I've had the idea in my mind for ages, but it wasn't until the latest round of upgrades here that I actually had access to the processing power to make it happen. And it worked! I think."

"I don't get—"

"Just watch." He pulled a remote from his hand, pointed it up toward the booth, and pushed a button.

She heard water lapping on the shore. The rustle of trees. Then a fifty-foot-tall image of barrel-chested Rosewood jock (and all-around asshole) Brett Prosch sprung to life on the screen above them, standing in front of a huge cottage above a sundrenched lake. Brett swung both arms wide. A toothy grin spread across his huge face. "Welcome to the party!"

Then the cacophony of pictures started. Teenagers climbing out of cars. People randomly hugging. Arms carrying cases of beer. And an endless stream of selfies, interspersed with a few short videos.

Liv dropped into a chair. "How are we seeing this?"

"I call it 'Event Hack.'" Gabriel sat down next to her. "It's an algorithm that pulls together still images and video from dozens of social media feeds at the same time and compiles them. I hid it in a school-wide internet questionnaire I sent on behalf of the school about the prom video yearbook to get the maximum number of people to download it. I compiled a list of like a dozen or so people I knew who were invited to the party and then had the program cross-reference faces and locations, and add new footage as it found it. We're watching a time-compressed version. Obviously. But it'll catch up to real time soon."

Liv didn't know whether to be horrified or impressed. Either way, she couldn't look away. "Because you've always wanted to spy on parties we're not invited to?"

"Because knowledge is power." Gabriel pulled out a flask and took a swig. "How many of those people only get away with kicking the rest of us in the teeth because the school administration, or the alumni, or their rich mommies and daddies don't know how much they drink or get high or take naked pictures of themselves with anything on legs?"

Most of them. "So, you made this to blackmail people into leaving us alone?"

He glanced at her sideways. "I made this because I could." Then he leaned back and looked up at the screen. "Haven't decided what I'm going to do with it yet."

Well, right now "it" seemed to consist mostly of a string of pictures of the blonde, leggy Cynthia Maddox smiling like a supermodel in front of the setting sun, clutching random people in hugs.

Click. Cynn was cheek to cheek with Brett's fierce, dark-haired girlfriend Felix.

Click. Now she had one arm around mousy bookworm Emma.

Click. Now Cynn was with an unbelievably shallow redhead named Sharona, who'd somehow landed a small role on a sitcom. Their hands were cheekily placed on each other's breasts.

Click. Then a picture of all four girls with Cynn of course managing to end up front and centre.

"Odd collection."

"Try the four girls in the running for Rosewood prom queen. Emma's got the bookish image the alumni like. Sharona's got a tiny bit of local fame. Felix has top grades. And Cynn's actually going to take it."

Rosewood prom was all about the queen. The final vote didn't happen until prom night, but the campaigning leading up to that night was fierce. The school had apparently long since given up trying to get any of the guys to take running for prom king seriously. So instead, they tended to just hand a spare crown to the queen's date for the night.

Like the Rosewood equivalent of the Duke of Edinburgh.

"Now, here's your money shot." Gabriel pointed the remote behind his head. The screen froze. He flicked another button and turned on the remote's laser pointer function. "Right there. Face in the upper right hand corner."

He aimed the red laser dot at one face in the corner of the screen. The face in question was glancing back over his shoulder at the camera like he was hoping it wouldn't notice he was there.

Liv's breath caught in her throat.

Adam Clay.

Cute. Shy. With the kind of pale blue eyes a girl could spend way too much time thinking about. And a mess of dirty blond hair one might just fantasize about running one's fingers through.

If that girl had a death wish.

She forced her shoulders to shrug. "Adam is Cynn's boyfriend. So?"

The laser pointer moved so quickly that red lines slashed back and forth in front of Adam's face, as if Gabriel was trying to scribble him out.

"You got a thing for Adam you haven't told me about?"

Heat rose to her cheeks. Yup. One hundred percent. And she hated herself for it.

"No. I'm not stupid enough to lust after the guy dating Cynthia Maddox!"

The image didn't move. "You sure?"

"Would I lie to you about something like that?" Liv threw her hands up in the air and hoped that exasperation would double for sincerity. What? Had Gabriel noticed her looking at Adam a little too long in the hallway or something? "I've had exactly one conversation with Adam Clay. One. First day English class. He forgot his pen. I lent him one. It had *Never Forget Funeral Home* written on it, and he said he'd never met anyone who worked with dead people before." *I told him if he was interested I'd give him a tour.*

He asked me to meet him after class behind the school. He never showed. The next day I saw him making out with Cynn in the cafeteria. So the next time he tried to talk to me, I told him to go screw himself. "End of story."

Gabriel nodded slowly. He restarted the show.

The images kept clicking past. More alcohol. Fewer clothes.

A lot of gaps in the action.

The was a video of Emma the bookworm getting screamed at by a guy named Damien—whom Liv vaguely recognized as a driver for a corpse transport service her boss used. Emma looked terrified. But the video was too garbled for Liv to catch what the fight was about.

A disgusting jock named Eddy made a few half-assed attempts to hit on Brett's girlfriend Felix, which seemed to consist mostly of him trying to grab at her body and take selfies of the two of them together. But nobody's camera picked up the beat-down Felix probably gave him for that.

Cynn danced wildly in the middle of the living room. But the camera didn't pick up who her audience was.

Videos got blurrier and louder. Gabriel waved the flask in Liv's direction. She took a sniff. Whiskey straight up. She handed it back. After a while she found her eyes beginning to close. Her mother was working the night shift at the diner and wouldn't be home until nine in the morning. But still, her bed was more interesting than—

"Oh, god!" Gabriel grabbed her arm.

Her eyes jerked open. "What?"

"I don't know. Everyone just started running down the hill toward the lake."

She looked at the screen. Video was playing. The sky was dark. Trees filled the screen. The ground slanted steeply. People were screaming.

"What happened?" she asked.

"I said, I don't know!" Gabriel was almost shouting. "Whatever it was, nobody got footage of it!"

The lake came into view. Then a red car.

Adam's car.

Wrecked.

Nose first in the water.

Its hood smashed and dented.

"Oh my god, oh my god, of my god, oh my god . . ." Cynn sounded like she was crying.

The audio cut out again and the video disappeared.

Still images now. Blood on the passenger side window. Blood inside the car.

Brett's body. Slumped in the passenger seat. Hands tied.

Dead eyes staring at the ceiling.

Blood smeared down his bare chest to his boxers, from the slash across his throat.

Gabriel swore.

Wait a minute. Was this in real time? This couldn't be happening.

The video started again. Someone was stumbling around to the driver's side. Then Eddy pushed in front of whoever was filming and forced the door open.

Adam was slumped in the driver's seat.

No. He wasn't dead. He just couldn't—

Adam's head jerked back. He ran his hand through his hair, smearing it in blood.

His blue eyes filled the screen.

Wide. Terrified.

Adam's voice filled the room. "Help me."

Chapter One

They say the dead are smarter than the living. They say crossing over brings some kind of magical clarity that lets them rise above all the petty stuff and see the big picture.

They're wrong. The dead can be downright stupid sometimes. Especially when they want something.

Liv shoved open the heavy back door to Never Forget Funeral Home and looked out at the night. June rain pounded the pavement in the narrow alleyway. She bowed her head and braced herself for the sprint to the subway. Then she stopped and slipped back inside.

She walked over to the stainless steel prep table and looked down at Jake's body. Youngest corpse she'd seen yet since working at Never Forget. They'd met just three days ago. After he'd died of cancer.

Her fingers brushed his shoulder. "Hey, dead guy. So, I'm guessing this is goodbye."

Dark eyes gleamed as Jake's skin tone deepened

from the artificial tinge of mortuary makeup to a living, vibrant brown. "Don't worry. I already told you, I'm moving on to somewhere a lot better than this."

Liv had never bothered to say goodbye to a corpse before. She'd taken the job at Never Forget back in the fall because it seemed like a cool and even kind of peaceful way to make some extra cash without having to deal with all the noise and drama of a typical customer service gig. The first time she'd heard a dead body suddenly start talking to her, inside her own brain—the day after Brett's murder—she'd been too startled to even answer back. She'd talked to four more corpses since then, but most were so boring and cranky it was barely worth it. But Jake had been a lot nicer than most. He'd actually listened. Plus, he was practically her age.

"So you're excited?" she asked.

"Hell yeah. Cremation sounds like a blast."

She watched the teenager's corpse take a deep breath then tuck his hands behind his bald head. It was like watching a see-through projection of something she knew wasn't really there, and yet could still totally see.

It was weird.

Liv only tested her ability to talk to the dead when she was absolutely sure she was alone, especially since her boss, Tony, had walked in and almost caught her once. That had taken some awkward explaining.

"Oh, don't look so serious!" Jake said. "It's just my

body that's getting turned into ashes. Not *me*. Didn't hurt when you stabbed me with the scalpel, did it? Told you the dead don't feel a thing."

"I'll take your word for it."

Her abilities seemed to be growing, bit by tiny bit. Jake had been the first corpse who'd been cool with her experimenting on him to test the limits of what she was able to do. Nothing major or too creepy. Just keeping her one hand pressed onto his body to keep the connection open, while her other hand waved random objects around like some deranged post-mortem eye test to see if he could see anything else in the room beyond their immediate connection. (He couldn't.)

And, oh yeah, she'd stabbed him a couple of times.

He laughed. "So, what's my tombstone like?"

"Awesome." She waved one hand through the air and kept the other one on the corpse. "*Here lies Jake Azivi. Fought a truly epic battle with cancer.*"

"You're a terrible liar."

Liv smiled. "Honestly, I don't know what they're doing. Your nana asked us to courier your ashes up to the family cottage."

He smiled. "Yeah, Nana lives up there year round. We've got a family plot in a cemetery up there."

She glanced at the clock. "Okay. Well, I gotta go. Have a good one."

"You too."

Oh hell, one more final experiment couldn't hurt, right? After all, she was hardly expecting to see Jake again. Liv grabbed the neckline of her black t-shirt with her free hand and pulled it down just enough to flash him her bra.

"Purple lace. I approve. But you know boobs aren't really my thing."

Heat rose to her cheeks.

"I didn't think you'd be able see it!" Liv shifted her neckline up even higher than it had been. "You said you couldn't really see anything beyond my face!"

"I said it was all kind of hazy beyond your face. Like a bad video chat." He laughed. "You just boosted the signal. Try that trick on a straight corpse sometime and I'm sure he'll leap right off the table." Alright, he was totally teasing her now. "Are you like this with all the dead guys?"

"Nah, only the ones who let me stab them. And shut up." She smiled. "I'm leaving. I'm going to miss you. Enjoy being dead."

"Enjoy living."

"I'll try." Liv took Jake's hand in hers and backed away slowly, inch by inch, until her fingers were still barely touching him. Finally he slipped from her grasp. The moment they lost physical contact the mental link severed and his image faded. She sighed, then walked back to the corpse, pulled the sheet back over it and straightened it.

Couldn't have Tony finding out she'd been mucking about with the corpses.

Clutching her bag to her chest, Liv ran through

the storm. The subway station windows were cracked again. Fresh graffiti layered over old graffiti. Someone had wedged the bars of the turnstile open. She fed her pass through anyway.

Her phone was ringing. Gabriel.

"Tell me you're sitting down right now," he said.

"No, I'm just leaving work. Did I tell you we got one guy in who was only like sixteen?"

"You should really try hanging out with a real live boy someday."

"Yeah, I'll get right on that." The steps down to the subway were filthy. The platform was deserted. Her phone was down to one bar and she was surprised she hadn't totally lost the signal yet. "I'm about to hop a subway, so hurry up before I lose the connection. Or I'll call you back when I get out on the other side."

"Adam Clay escaped Meadowhurst."

"Don't even joke." Hell. It had been *three weeks* since Adam had been charged with Brett's murder and shipped off to the some jail-slash-treatment facility for troubled teens, called The Meadowhurst Youth Secure Detention Facility. Gabriel should be over teasing her about crushing on a killer by now.

"No word of a lie," he said. "It's on the news."

Liv's heart jumped. She backed up toward the staircase to keep the call from dying. Her eyes rose to the red news feed scrolling on the platform's electric sign half expecting to see "Son of J. Clay, Tory MPP, accused in grisly murder, escapes custody" or something equally dramatic and grammatically horrendous. It just showed baseball scores. "If you're making this up I'll kill you."

"Cross my cold black heart. Rosewood's favourite murder suspect is out and running loose."

The train pulled into the station. The screech of wheels against the rails filled the claustrophobic space.

"Maybe if you're lucky he'll swing by your work sometime for formaldehyde and scalpels," Gabriel added.

"I'll be sure to leave out cookies."

"Hilarious. I—" The phone finally went dead, cutting Gabriel off. Oh well. She was surprised the signal had even lasted that long. She walked toward the closest subway car. It was empty.

No, wait. There was a guy crouching on the floor.

She stepped onto the train. The guy jumped up and rushed for the doors. He stopped inches short of crashing into her.

Oh, hell—

It was Adam.

A feeling she couldn't identify filled his blue eyes. Fear? Panic?

Adam grabbed her. Hesitated. Hands on her shoulders. Mouth so close she could feel his breath. Then he kissed her. Awkwardly. But passionately too.

Nah, this wasn't real. This had to be some weird daydream. Insanely hot guys didn't just kiss her.

Ah, screw it.

She grabbed the back of his head and kissed him back. Hard.

Chimes sounded. The doors began to close.

Adam let her go and dove for the ever-decreasing gap, sliding his body out onto the platform just before the doors tightened around him.

"I'm sorry." He banged on the window. "I've gotta go see Cynn—"

Oh right, his *girlfriend*. "What the hell? You guys are still *dating*?"

"I'll explain later," said Adam.

"You'll what now?"

"If they catch me here they'll think I killed her too!"

"Killed her *who*?" Liv shouted back.

The subway was picking up speed, pulling her away from him.

"I'll come find you," he yelled. "I promise."

The train plunged into the tunnel.

She grabbed a pole and struggled to catch her breath. She stumbled over to a seat.

Oh crap.

There was a body on the floor.

Chapter Two

Liv remembered the first time she'd met Adam.

He was cute.

Which might not actually be important when it came to knowing somebody. But it was the first thing she noticed. He had dirty blond hair that was way too shaggy and a white t-shirt that looked far too big for his skinny frame.

The second thing she noticed was that he was late for English.

It was her first day, her very first class at Rosewood Academy and she'd chosen a seat halfway up the side of the classroom. Not too far forward. Not too far back.

Just the right place to be invisible. And here he was, walking in late, after the English teacher had already done attendance.

Adam Clay.

He had to be Adam. Nobody else had been absent when attendance had been called.

The boy she thought was Adam sat down in front of her, and the teacher started writing a list on the board of old books about the Canadian wilderness, probably written by dead guys.

The cute guy turned around. Blue eyes looked right into hers. "Hey, you got a pen?"

Who, me?

"Yeah, hang on." There were six or seven pens rolling around the bottom of her bag. She grabbed the silver one. The good one. The one engraved with Never Forget Funeral Home on the side.

She handed it to him.

"Thanks," he whispered. "I'm Adam."

"I'm Liv."

"Hey, Liv. So, how do you like Rosewood so far?"

"What kind of question is that? I haven't even been here an hour yet." She leaned her elbows on the table. "Why, how do you like Rosewood?"

He chuckled under his breath. But more like he was laughing at himself and not her.

"It sucks just the same as everywhere else I guess." He turned back to the front of the class.

Then he glanced at the pen she'd given him and turned back around.

"Oh, hey, I'm sorry. Did somebody die? I mean, did you lose somebody recently or something?" He ran a hand through his hair. "Sorry, that probably came out all wrong."

The teacher was scowling at them.

Liv's voice dropped even quieter. She leaned forward.

"No. Well, a lot of people died, actually. But nobody I know. I just got a job at there."

His blue eyes opened wide. A crooked smile curled at the corner of his mouth. "Whoa. That's kinda cool."

A flush rose to her cheeks.

"Can I come by sometime? You know, check the place out?" He blushed. "If that doesn't sound weird."

She could feel her smile spread up into her cheeks. "It's totally weird, but it's cool."

Why wouldn't it be?

A sudden lurch from the subway jolted Liv back to the present.

A funky leather boot. A leg encased in a black stocking. A hand. And a whole lot of blood.

Okay, she could handle this. Liv saw dead bodies practically every day. No reason to get freaked out about one now just because it was lying on the subway-car floor.

Though normally they weren't still oozing.

She stepped closer. The other leg, bent at the knee. A ridiculously short skirt. A stomach with a big knife sticking out of it. A whole lot of cleavage. A face—

Holy hell, it was Felix.

She inhaled sharply as sudden tears stung her eyes.

Sure, Felix was an ultra-ambitious bitch who treated Liv like crap. And considering her flair for the dramatic, lying gutted in a pool of blood was probably how she'd have wanted to go. But still.

Adam killed Brett. Now Adam's killed Brett's girlfriend too. . . .

The voice of logic whispered in the back of her mind.

Liv told it to shut up. Absolutely nothing about her life right now was anything close to logical.

Besides, she had to clear her mind if she wanted to open a link to Felix's spirit. She'd never talked to a corpse outside the funeral home, but now was as good a time to try as any. She dropped to her knees and laid her hand on Felix's.

"Hey, it's Liv . . . from school. You know—purple-streaked hair, black eyeliner? You called me 'skunky skank' like a week ago?" Among far worse things. "Anyway, you've just been stabbed, and I'm going for help. Hang on."

No response.

Okay, she was probably still processing. After all, getting killed had to come as a bit of a shock. Plus, Liv usually never saw corpses until they'd been dead long enough to have really thought things over.

She glanced around for a security camera. Dangling wires. Great, so, stolen then. Liv climbed onto the seat and pressed the emergency strip. A high-pitched siren filled the subway car.

Hopefully that had accomplished something besides permanent hearing damage.

The train was still rumbling down the tunnel, but the next stop couldn't be too far away. She jumped back down, crouched down next to the body and brushed Felix's hair from her face.

Hair extensions. Shocker.

"I'm back."

No response. Not even a flicker. Damn. How much did you have to hate someone to keep up the silent treatment after you were dead?

Jake said the dead didn't feel anything physically. But the dead still felt plenty when it came to emotions. And most of it wasn't much fun to hear.

"Look. I know we haven't been tight—" Now *that* was the understatement of the year. "But I'm here now and I'm probably your last chance to talk to someone."

The train began to slow.

"So, if there's anything you want to say, you better tell me now. Like, did Adam just kill you?"

Please say no. Otherwise the fact I just kissed him is way too creepy.

Still no response. She tried to pry the dead girl's hand open enough to slide her fingers against her palm. "Come on. You're dead. Got that? Over. Done."

There was a piece of paper clenched in Felix's hand. Liv reached for it then stopped.

What was she thinking? It was evidence.

The lights and the bright green tiles of the next station came into view. If she didn't look at it now, she'd never know.

The subway slowed. She grabbed the paper.

"Security," a voice called over the PA. "Miss, is everything alright?"

No. And I'm pretty sure you're going to want to call for some pretty major backup when you see all this blood.

It looked like the printout of an email. But the sender's address was too smudged with blood to read.

I know who took the knife Brett Prosch was murdered with and how they snuck it out of the party crime scene after without getting caught by the police. Meet me on the subway Sunday night.

"Stand back and put your hands where I can see them."

Get on at Summerhill. Last train going northbound. I'll meet you in the very back.

Guards were forcing the doors open.

Come alone.

Chapter Three

Liv dropped the note on the floor and raised her hands.

Okay, she could handle this. All she had to do was sound helpful and answer their questions.

Felix was dead when I got here. I didn't see what happened.

No, I didn't just make out with a killer—

They took her to the police station and called her mom, who came right away, even though her shift wasn't over. She hadn't even stopped to take off her uniform but just walked into the station wearing a turquoise poodle skirt and beehive hairdo, with a look on her face that practically dared the drunks in intake to snicker.

Had to hand it to Mom. She wasn't a wimp.

They were shown into a small room with metal folding chairs. On the wall was a poster of a chimp riding a motorcycle with a caption about wearing helmets. Seriously, if someone needed a monkey to tell them to protect their head, they had way bigger problems.

There was also a huge mirror. Were they being watched? Probably.

Well, she'd dropped the note onto the floor and saw the first officer on the scene pick it up. She'd been smart enough not to get any blood on her and it wasn't like they'd find her fingerprints on the knife. She couldn't have looked more cooperative if she'd tried.

Liv waved at the mirror. Then she flashed a grin at her mom, who managed a shaky smile back. There was a box of Kleenex in the centre of the table. Neither of them reached for it. If anyone thought that leaving her alone with Mom was going to make her start to cry and spill her guts, they were going to be disappointed.

She and the police went way back. Mom's bad luck with boyfriends had led to more than a few police station visits back when they lived in Vancouver. She didn't know which had been worse, trying to convince some uniformed stranger that her Mom's rich ex really had punched a hole through their door, or having to defend herself against some bogus trespassing thing the jerk had filed just to get back at them. Either way, tampering with evidence at a crime scene and kissing someone who'd just escaped jail were probably going to take things up a notch.

Mom sat down. Liv stepped behind her chair and started pulling the bobby pins out of her up-do. "You should've just finished your shift. I'm fine, really."

Mom squeezed her hand. "I know."

Liv closed her eyes. *Right, and if you get fired because of this, I'll never forgive myself.*

She heard the door open and someone come in. Liv opened her eyes. A slender woman with long dark hair that was pulled back in a French braid stood there.

"Detective Jasmine Prasad." She stretched out her hand and shook Liv's hand and then her mother's. "You can call me Jaz, if you'd like."

Detective Jaz sat down on the opposite side of the table. Liv sat down beside her mom, stared at a random spot on the table, and concentrated on telling her story like someone who had nothing to hide.

When she'd finished, Detective Jaz sat back and looked at her. "Are you sure there isn't anything else you're not telling us?"

She couldn't tell if the cop was fishing or if she already knew the answer. Liv ran a finger over her lips. They felt bruised. "I already told you. Felix was dead when I got there."

Something flickered behind the detective's eyes.

"Felix isn't dead yet, is she?" Liv guessed.

"What makes you say that?" Detective Jaz asked.

Because her corpse wouldn't talk to me. "I saw a lot of paramedics and no body bags."

Detective Jaz didn't blink, but her mother looked relieved. So, Felix wasn't dead. That was something at least. Liv rubbed her eyes and tried to look tired. It wasn't hard, considering it was probably close to two in the morning. There was no clock in the room, and they'd taken her cell phone along with everything else she had on her.

"And you think this young man you saw was Adam Clay?" the detective asked.

Okay, so maybe she hadn't told the police *everything*. Obviously she'd mentioned seeing Adam. It would've been stupid not to. Especially as there was a chance they'd managed to catch him on some security camera somewhere. The last thing she wanted was for anyone to think she was actually trying to help him. She still wasn't about to admit she'd kissed an escaped convict, though. Not in front of her mother.

"Right."

"Was this meeting prearranged?"

"Hell no. Until yesterday, everybody—including me—thought he was locked up at Meadowhurst."

"So you were aware he'd been charged with the murder of Brett Prosch?"

Like knowledge of a crime was the same as standing on the sidelines and cheering your ass off while the bloody deed was done.

"Of course I'm *aware*. The whole damn school is *aware*. You can ask anybody. Adam and I aren't friends or anything."

"Did he speak to you? Communicate with you in any way?"

Well, see he grabbed my shoulders and then I grabbed the back of his head. . . .

"He touched my shoulders, just for a second.

Honestly, I think he was trying to stop me from seeing Felix until he'd had a chance to run out."

The best kiss of her life so far and all because some guy had panicked about a bloody corpse on the floor. And she'd been the idiot who'd kissed him back. The thought landed hard, like fist in her gut, and for a second she had to press her nails into her palms to keep from letting it show on her face.

"Again, did he say anything?"

Why exactly was Liv protecting this guy? Protecting herself was one thing. But it was hardly like Adam had done anything to earn her loyalty. "Yeah. Sorry, he did. He yelled that he hadn't murdered anyone and that he was heading to see his girlfriend, Cynthia Maddox."

If police stormed Cynn's house, found them together and arrested them both, they probably deserved whatever they had coming.

"Had you been planning on meeting Felix Almon or anyone else that night?"

"No. That's just how I get home from work."

"Why did you touch her?"

"Instinct, I guess."

"What kind of instinct?"

"The kind of instinct that kicks in when you see someone you know lying on a subway floor covered in blood."

"Can you remember where you were the night Brett Prosch was murdered?"

Yup. See, Gabriel and I had broken into the school . . .

"No, but I know where I wasn't. He was murdered at some party at his family's cottage, and I'm not the kind of girl who gets invited to things like that. But since it turns out Felix isn't actually dead, why don't you question her? They'd been dating for forever. Actually, why don't you ask Felix who stabbed her?"

Not even a flicker of a reaction on the cop's face. Detective Jaz probably played a killer hand of poker.

"Can you think of anyone who might have had reason to kill either Miss Almon or Mr. Prosch?"

"No one in particular, but honestly, Felix's a power-tripping bitch and Brett was the kind of all-around jerk who spread crap on people's windshields. As a couple, they were a nightmare. She'd flirt with some idiot until she got his pants down, then Brett would beat him to a pulp. It's like they hurt people for sport. I'm sure the fact his super wealthy family owns a small airline makes his death seem more important than your average teen murder, but frankly, whoever stabbed them did the rest of us a favour."

So much for not saying anything suspicious.

"Thank you." Detective Jaz stood. "I'll be back in a minute."

She left the room.

Mom slipped an arm around Liv's shoulders. "You doing okay, honey?"

"Yeah." *Sort of.* "Did you know Felix wasn't actually dead?"

She nodded. "Yeah, sorry. Her mom messaged me

from the hospital. But the officer who called me said not to discuss anything about the crime with you until someone had taken your statement."

"How the hell do you know Felix's mom?"

Her mom gave her one of those mildly disappointed looks that said she should already know the answer. "We met in a single-parents' group online. She was the one who recommended we apply for Rosewood. Actually, I'm surprised you two aren't better friends. You have a lot in common."

"Lots of people have dads who flake out on them. That doesn't mean we all link arms and dance down the hallway."

"You're both at Rosewood on financial scholarships. You both work—"

"And she's a major bitch. And she's best friends with Cynn, who's the most popular girl in the school, even though she's a totally manipulative, evil witch, who people only like because she's great at *pretending* to be nice. And I'm a social outcast. I'm sorry Felix got knifed. Really. Just like I was sorry that her boyfriend got murdered. But that doesn't mean I'm going to be losing sleep over it."

Her mom sighed. Which didn't mean she was backing down, just choosing not to fight about it. "Can I ask you one thing? That boy who died? Brett? Was it his parents who're running the summer internship you applied for?"

Vitesse Airlines had decided to publically honour

Brett's death by giving one lucky Rosewood student the chance to travel the world visiting all the places they flew.

Liv looked at the table. "Yeah, only I decided not to go for it after all. It's mostly just a publicity stunt for them anyway."

"But—"

But, it's an unpaid internship. And the diner's cutting your hours. And I've kind of clued in that you're struggling to pay the bills sometimes even though you're trying to hide that from me. At least this way one of us is bringing in some steady money.

"I like my job at the funeral home. I know it's weird, but it's kind of cool." She squeezed her mom's hand. "Seeing the world might be fun, yeah. But it doesn't really make sense for me to quit my job just to go travelling. And it's mostly a social media thing. They're looking for someone who'll post smiling selfie pictures all over the place and hashtag them. Not my thing."

So, basically, a freak like me never really stood a chance, anyway.

"You sure?" Her mother's frown grew deeper. "I'm proud of how hard you work and how great your grades are. But all you do is work. And this is a chance to travel the world for free. You go for it if you can. You should be trying to balance work with some fun—"

Yup, and you should have a boss who isn't a total dick. And rent shouldn't keep going up. And I should have a school where bullies don't get away with beating on people.

Thankfully, Detective Jaz walked in again before Liv had to figure out what to say.

"Thank you for both your time," the detective said. "You're free to go."

Really? Why?

Liv and her mother stood up. Detective Jaz's dark eyes focused squarely on Liv's face.

"If you think of anything else that might help us in our investigation, please don't hesitate to call." She held out a flyer. Liv looked down. It was for Crime Stoppers. "It can be totally anonymous. I've put my name and phone number on it too. Anything you want to tell me, it can stay between you and me. Anything at all."

Well, I read the really creepy note that Felix was holding. I made out with Adam. I broke into the school with Gabriel the night Brett was murdered. And oh, I like to chat with corpses.

"Thanks." Liv took the flyer and stuffed it in the back pocket of her jeans. "But, really, I don't know anything."

Chapter Four

It was Monday afternoon. The long, dark shape of Gabriel was slouched against a lamppost, waiting for Liv to arrive at Never Forget. His hair was tied back in a ponytail and he was wearing dark glasses and a long black coat in defiance of the heat.

Two years ago, he'd just been some guy with a blog about zombies. He and Liv had chatted online a bit, then Gabriel ran a background check on Mom's boyfriend at the time—who turned out not to have so much as a parking ticket, let alone a secret wife or criminal record. Yay, Mom, for learning. Mom had moved them to Toronto last year so she could be with the guy. The boyfriend hadn't lasted, but Liv's friendship with Gabriel had.

Liv nodded to Gabriel then walked up the wide stone steps to the door. "Staking out a funeral home. How very you."

He grinned, detached himself the lamppost and followed. "You didn't leave me much choice. You hung up on me last night, and you skipped school today."

"Sorry. Believe it or not, I was at the police station all night so Mom let me sleep in. The police confiscated my cell phone."

"Ha ha."

"No, seriously."

He frowned. Normally, Gabriel was the undeniable source of all dirt worth knowing, master of collecting secrets for fun and profit. He just wasn't so great at keeping them.

Which is why she still hadn't told him about her chats with the recently deceased.

"What did I miss?"

She glanced down the street. A short woman in long flowing robes and way too much jewellery was watching them from the doorway of the pizza place. "Madame Delilah" was one of the regular kooks who hung around Never Forget, claiming the dead inside were calling out to them or that they could see dead people.

Liv's dead friend Jake had assured her the good Madame was full of it.

"Tell you inside."

Never Forget had been in her boss's family for four generations. Tony was an old-school Italian funeral director who still did his own embalming and restorations, as well as showing heartfelt sympathy to the grieving families. His daughter, Kiara, was a fashion designer who occasionally helped dress their richest clients. A nephew ran a hearse and limo service. Liv filled in paperwork, answered the phones and made funeral arrangements. Officially, that is. Unofficially, she also helped Tony with the bodies in a million little ways.

She walked into the building, flicking on lights as she went. The front entrance was wood panelled with walls full of calming nature scenes. Funerals and visitations were held in a long chapel-like room to the right. Down the hallway to the left was the display room for casket sales. Straight ahead through a nondescript door lay embalming.

Liv's paycheque was in an envelope under her keyboard.

There was a note attached—a new body was coming in later.

Liv turned to Gabriel. "Any chance you can quickly turn this into cash for me? My account's overdrawn, so if I deposit it the bank will just keep it."

"No problem."

Banks kind of liked to limit how deep in the hole you could get. Which pretty much screwed people like Liv and her Mom. But Gabriel always seemed to know a way around it.

He seemed to know his way around most things.

Liv handed the cheque to him. "Somebody tried to kill Felix—"

"I know." Gabriel slipped it inside his jacket.

"So, I found her."

He sucked in a breath. "Bloody mess in the subway?"

"Yup."

"How bloody?"

"Very. Take your sunglasses off. It's like talking to my own tiny reflection." She made a grab for them. He swatted her hand away.

"In a minute. Now, did you take any pictures for me?"

No. She'd been too busy trying to talk to the ghost of someone who wasn't actually dead.

"Of Felix? Right, because that would've looked awesome when the police confiscated my phone. I'm surprised you haven't hacked transit security footage yet."

"I tried. But it looks like there wasn't a working camera in that subway car. All I could find was some grainy footage of *someone* walking into Summerhill station." He stretched the word "someone" out for about six beats. So, did that mean he knew Adam was there? If Gabriel found out that she'd kissed him, he'd never let her live it down. "Though why Felix would choose to ride the subway alone at night is beyond me. Thought everyone from Rosewood was loaded."

"Hey, I—"

"Besides you." His smile was still a little smug—probably because he still thought he knew something she didn't. But she still wasn't about to rise to the bait.

"You've still got the social media mash-up you made of the night Brett died?"

"Yup. Why, do you feel like watching it again?"

Yes. No. Maybe.

The image of Adam sitting in that car, panicked and covered in blood had kept her up at night.

"I don't know. Did you ever turn it over to the police?"

Gabriel snorted. "It's all social media footage. There's nothing there the police couldn't find on their own."

Well, that was fair enough. She guessed.

"But have you ever tried digging around online into police files to see where they're at with the investigation into Adam?"

"Babe, I've tried hacking into *everything*. But I couldn't find anything we don't already know. About a dozen popular kids go to Brett's family cottage. People get drunk. At some point, people realize Adam's car's rolled down the hill into the lake and crashed into some big rock before it can go all the way underwater. Adam's drunk and high. Brett's dead. Bunch of drunk and stupid teenagers wade into mucky water up to their knees and contaminate the crime scene. Knife somehow goes missing. Everyone's best guess is that Adam killed Brett, freaked out, and tried to drive away somewhere with the body. Probably threw the car into drive instead of reverse."

Yeah, nothing she hadn't heard before either.

"I don't know if they'll even get anything conclusive from forensic tests," he added. "The whole thing is moving really slowly. Like the kind of slow that would happen if Adam *didn't* come from money. So, either his folks didn't bribe anyone to grease the wheels, or no one wants to upset Brett's family, or . . ." He frowned. "I don't know. Something's not right."

Damn right it wasn't.

"Well, they say Adam was apparently spotted at the subway station yesterday. . . ."

She tried to say it really slowly, like Gabriel would've. But couldn't keep a straight face.

"Do they now?" He leaned back against her desk and crossed his feet at the ankles. "First Brett, then Felix. Adam probably won't stop there. I'm thinking now that the Rosewood Psycho's gotten a taste for killing bullies, he might go for a complete set." Gabriel's tone was light, but not light enough to stop a shiver from running down her spine.

"Ten bucks says he'll kill Cynn next," he added. "If I were her, I'd have my rich daddy hire me some heavy security."

"That's one hell of a leap."

He held up his palms. "I'm just saying what everyone else is going to be thinking. Either Adam's back and trying to cover his tracks, or he's back to finish off what he started. You just be thankful he broke your heart before he got anywhere with you."

"Adam didn't break my heart." *Just dented it a little.*

"Anyway, I'm over it."

"Sure."

She tossed a cloth at him. "Come on. I need to dust. You want to hang out and talk, you have to help me."

He reached for the cloth. She snatched the sunglasses off his face.

He flinched. His right eye was bruised, purple and so swollen it wouldn't open all the way.

"Oh, God, Gabe!"

She dropped the sunglasses into his outstretched hand. Then, standing on her tiptoes, she kissed him gently on the temple.

He shivered.

"Who the hell did this to you?"

"One of the thugs from school." He didn't quite meet her gaze. "Eddy, actually. Did you hear he's got a thing with Sharona now?"

She shook her head.

"She posted a picture of them online yesterday. Which, of course, makes it official. Anyway, apparently she thinks I looked at her wrong, so he jumped me."

"Again?"

Gabriel gave her a dirty look. "Face it, babe. Some people just enjoy making other people hurt." He slid the glasses back on. True enough. Liv had never exactly been popular back in Vancouver, but she'd had some friends and didn't have to worry about being tripped whenever she walked down the hallway. Rosewood was different. She'd long stopped trying to figure out what she'd ever done to deserve half the crap she got. It wasn't like she was about to quit wearing black or dyeing half her hair purple.

Or hanging out with Gabriel.

Rosewood was a school for pretty boys and jocks. Not the kind of guy who flaunted being an outsider with every step. For a while there it seemed Gabriel had an inventive new bruise pattern on his body daily—mostly thanks to Brett.

Maybe Eddy was now taking over.

Gabriel walked back into the hallway. She grabbed cleaning spray and followed him.

"Tell me about finding Felix," he said.

"It was gruesome. I thought she was dead. And want to hear the really fun part? She had the printout of an email on her from some nameless person claiming they knew who had the knife Brett was murdered with, and how they somehow got it out of the party without it being spotted by police."

His eyebrows rose. "Well, aren't you full of interesting today? And here I always thought the knife had just gotten lost in the lake. Do you still have the email?"

"Of course not. I dropped it on the floor the moment the police showed up. I'm not an idiot."

"You know the sender's email address?"

"No. It was smudged."

He scratched his jaw. "Well, if what the email said is true, I don't know what's more intriguing—the idea someone could've just walked out of that party with the knife and didn't get caught by the cops, or the idea that there's someone out there who knows who that person is, and for some reason went to Felix instead of to the police. Any idea why the cops let you go?"

Liv shook her head. "No. But I'm pretty sure the detective who interviewed me believed that I was just some innocent bystander."

"Maybe someone else got killed while you were in there, and they knew you had an alibi."

Right after she told them that Adam was rushing over to Cynn's house?

Liv walked into the showcase room, sprayed the casket closest to the door and wiped the cloth across it. Gabriel walked in behind her and perched on a casket in the corner.

"Hey. No sitting on Big Ben."

"Don't tell me you name the coffins. I knew you were a freak like me, but still."

"Caskets, not coffins. Caskets are rectangular. Coffins look like something out of Dracula's castle. And the Benjamin is our only double-sized casket. Large enough to accommodate our plus-sized guests."

"*Guests?*"

"Get off the casket."

He hopped off. "Let me redeem myself. Let me take you to the dance on Friday and see where the night goes from there."

She hesitated. "What?"

He meant that as friends, right? He wasn't actually suggesting they try going on some kind of *date*? Sure, they'd flirted a little bit when they only knew each other online. Because that's what people *did*. But since meeting in person, it'd always been straight up friendship with zero messing around. It's not that Gabriel wasn't cute . . . in a dark, brooding kind of way. But you don't risk losing your best friend by dating him when you're not entirely sure you're into him.

Plus, she'd just kissed Adam yesterday.

"I'm going to be stuck up in the sound booth all night, anyway," he added. "You might as well keep me company. It's going to be epic. Huge screens. Hydraulic stage. Big-ass light show."

So, *not* a date then?

It was seriously *impossible* to figure out what Gabriel was thinking sometimes. It wasn't just that his cards were pressed right up against his chest. It was like he was actually holding more cards than the average person.

"You never know," he added, "You might even win prom queen in a surprise last minute write-in vote."

For some reason, the thought of that had him grinning like a Cheshire Cat.

But Liv sure as hell wasn't.

"Don't you even joke. Yeah, yeah, I know you're probably capable of finding some way of manipulating voting to make that happened. But if you even try it, I'll kill you." She rolled her eyes. "Honestly? I don't even get why you're helping with the prom anyway. Don't we spend enough time stuck in that place already?"

His mouth opened. Then he closed it again and shook his head like he was trying to reboot his brain.

She'd already dusted two more caskets before she realized he hadn't said anything. She glanced up.

He was staring at the floor.

Had she actually hurt his feelings? She couldn't handle Gabriel-related drama on top of everything else today. His friendship was the one thing helping her keep it together. "So, who's really going to be prom queen?"

"Nobody knows until people vote during the—"

"Like you haven't been through everyone's social media and found out who people are planning on voting for."

The wolfish grin returned. "Well, Cynn, obviously, but the three runners-up are Sharona the shallow, Emma the bookworm and Felix the big bloody mess. Right now, my money's on Sharona."

"Yeah, right. Over Cynn's dead body."

His grin grew ghoulish. "Exactly."

Chapter Five

Liv was still dusting when Tony came in. He was short, always wore a suit and walked with a slight bounce. Today his tie was green.

"I need you to run the refreshments room for Mrs. Jenkins' funeral. Keep the coffee hot and make sure everyone's got something to eat. I'll need you to manage clean-up, too. We've got a rough one coming in later."

A rough one usually meant bloody, bloated, dismembered or disfigured in some way. Tony had studied pathology as a young man back in Italy. He'd been a mortician so long that he'd become a bit of an amateur medical examiner when it came to identifying causes of death and he kept copious numbers of handwritten notes he'd given to Liv to transcribe. Normally, Tony let her see the bodies before they were embalmed and pointed out telltale signs of murder, suicide, and accident. Recently he'd been letting her help with restorations too—padding out sunken cheeks, adding the final touches of makeup. Sometimes she asked the dead what colours they'd like or how they wanted their hair parted. They usually appreciated that.

"Your school dance is Friday, right? Would you like the afternoon off?"

"Thanks, but it's not really my thing. Plus it's dead expensive. Dress, limo, hair, tickets. Stupid money."

"I'm sure my daughter Kiara has a dress that will fit you."

"Thanks anyway, but I'm good."

He was sweet. But that wasn't the same as actually understanding. After Tony left that night, Liv went into the prep room. The new body was laid out on the embalming table and covered by a pale blue sheet. She lifted the cloth and pulled it down to the shoulders.

Cynn.

How sick was it that she wasn't even surprised?

Long blonde hair fell loose around her shoulders. Neat stitches encircled her neck. Someone had slit her throat from ear to ear, just like Brett's. Really small blade, by the look of things. She checked Cynn's wrists. Bruised.

Liv took a deep breath, reached out and brushed her fingers along the pale cheek. "Cynn? Are you there?"

She had to say the words out loud, or Cynn wouldn't hear. She didn't know why. It just worked that way. No matter how many times she'd tried to just project her thoughts into her mental connection with Jake, it just hadn't worked.

"Of course I'm here, you freak."

For a moment, a vision of Cynn flashed in her mind: hands on her hips, eyes flashing, lips parted in a snarl. "Why am I talking to you? And why the hell are you touching me?"

Liv stepped back. The connection broke the instant her hand left Cynn's body. She stared at the corpse for a moment like it might jump up and strangle her.

It was kind of funny when you thought about it— Cynn acted sweet as pie when people were looking. She was *nice*. She volunteered for car washes, donated to clothing drives and shared her gourmet organic lunches. She'd been Rosewood's darling.

Liv took a deep breath and opened the link again.

"Where the hell did you go?"

"Sorry. If I let go of your body, I lose the connection."

Cynn sniffed. "What the hell is this? Some kind of séance? You and goth boy got a crowd standing around me right now with candles and incense?"

"It's not like that. It's just me. We're alone in a funeral home."

She almost looked disappointed. "How are you doing this then?"

"I don't know. It started a few months ago. I just kind of open my mind to someone's dead spirit." *And then they slip inside.*

Cynn's image closed her eyes tight. Emotions

flickered across her face, like she was looking for the right frequency. Then her eyes opened again. "Sorry. I'm just trying to get my head around things. Didn't mean to be rude or whatever. How'd I die? Tragic accident? Heart attack?"

Well that was a half-assed, insincere apology if Liv'd ever heard one.

So this was what it was like to have Cynthia Maddox playing nice to you.

"You mean you don't know?" Liv asked.

"I really don't."

Being dead didn't mean she couldn't lie, but why would she bother? "What do you remember?"

"Not much. Felix and I were trying on our prom dresses. Then she left and I had a smoothie. I was . . . tired, so I lay down. Next thing I know, I'm here, I'm dead and you're talking to me. Why? What happened?"

"You were kind of . . . murdered."

Cynn's eyes opened wide. Her face was pale, even for a ghost. If she was lying, she was a good actress. She actually looked hurt. "How?" She spoke so quietly Liv barely heard her.

"Someone, um, slit your throat."

"Who?"

"I don't know."

"But you're going find out for me, right?"

"I really wasn't planning on it."

Cynn's image crossed her arms. Static crackled through the link.

"You're going to go find out who killed me. You have to." Her voice almost echoed.

Wow. Never heard a corpse's voice do that before. Trust Cynn to try to be special even after dying.

"Tell you what. If I hear anything, I'll let you know."

There was another weird hiss in the air, almost like interference.

Liv clenched her jaw and focused.

It stopped.

"People are going to think it's Adam," Liv offered. "Have you seen him since he broke out of Meadowhurst?"

Cynn's smile twisted at the edges. "Maybe. I don't remember. But you're hoping it wasn't him. Right?"

Liv pressed her lips together and didn't answer.

Cynn snorted. "At least the funeral should be huge. What are they burying me in?"

"I don't know."

"So, go see. Please?" Cynn's lip actually quivered. "I'm dead. I'm helpless. I've been murdered, and you won't even help me with something that basic?"

Liv scanned the room. Tony usually left things like clothes and jewellery in the same cabinet where he kept his tools, but she'd have to borrow his keys to open it.

"You want to know for sure Adam's innocent?" Cynn added. "You'd want to help stop someone from going to jail for the rest of their lives for something they didn't do if you could, right?"

Right.

"Well, I can help you with that," Cynn went on, "but you've got to do something for me first. Find out what they're burying me in."

Tony kept a complete set of keys in a locked box under his desk. She wasn't supposed to open it, but she knew the combination.

"Okay, but I'll have to drop my link with you to go look."

"Whatever. Just do it."

It wasn't like Tony had ever specifically told her she couldn't open the embalming cabinet without permission. It was just, well, kind of assumed. Liv ran and got the key. The walls of the funeral home tilted and blurred around her like an out-of-focus movie. She hated dropping links that fast. The best connections always had a nice slow settling into the dead person's world and a gentle pulling out. Force it or leave it too fast, and things started getting freaky.

Sure enough, there was a long black bag in the cabinet, hanging next to the embalming aprons. She pulled the zipper down. The dress was hot pink, strapless, backless and gorgeous. Perfect for a prom queen. A velvet pouch dangled from the hanger. Inside was an antique pendant on a gold chain. Heavy, with flecks of jade weaving an intricate pattern up and down its length. Very cool, but way bigger and clunkier than she thought Cynn would like—not to mention it was all wrong for the dress. She felt around in the bottom of the bag and pulled out a pair of silver high-heeled shoes.

She came back to the table and reached for Cynn's hand.

"Okay, so we've got—"

There was a loud knock on the metal door behind her.

Chapter Six

Insistent banging filled the air. Like someone was pounding on the prep room door with both hands. Liv glanced at the clock. Way too late for this to be anything even remotely good.

"Hang on a sec." She dropped her link to Cynn.

The prep room only had one window, set up too high for anyone to see in. She kicked a stool over and hopped up.

"We're closed," she called out the window.

Eddy's blunt, ugly face stared back at her.

"You've got Cynn's body in there, right? Let me in. She's got something on her I need."

Yeah right. The only thing Cynn had on her right now was a sheet.

"Go to hell. I heard what you did to Gabriel."

She flipped him the finger, holding it up long enough to make sure he got it.

He returned the favour. His hands were huge. Hell,

his whole body was huge. Like a walking dump truck. "That freak deserves whatever he gets. Now let me get what I'm after before I break the door down."

"Sure thing, asshole."

She jumped off the stool. The prep room door was wickedly heavy. There was no way anyone was breaking in.

Eddy was still banging and swearing. Let him. He was used to pushing people around at school, but the funeral home was her turf. He wasn't getting in, no matter what he was after.

A loud scraping noise outside—like he was dragging something out of the alley toward the reception hall. She followed the sound. Through the stained glass windows, she watched him hoist up one of their industrial garbage cans. He threw it against the stained glass. One of the windows splintered.

Whatever that sick-ass thug thought Cynn had with her, he was done asking for it.

Liv ran into the office and grabbed the phone off her desk.

"Nine-one-one. What's your emergency?"

"I'm at Never Forget at St. Clair and Yonge. Someone's breaking in."

Another crash from outside.

"His name is Eddy Pyne. And he's a real violent asshole. Hurry!"

The stained glass windows wouldn't hold forever. They were pretty and perfect for a funeral home chapel, but hardly reinforced enough to take that kind of abuse.

"We've dispatched emergency vehicles to your location. Please stay by the phone and try to remain calm."

No way was she going to hang out by the phone while he broke in. The office door was mostly just a pane of frosted glass and would be far easier to break through than the stained glass windows. If she locked herself in, he'd probably throw a chair through it.

"Hey, bitch! I know you can hear me."

She dropped the phone, ran for the fuse box and threw the switch. The building went black.

"I swear I'm going to make you hurt," Eddy shouted.

There was a grunt. More breaking glass. A shout.

Liv sprinted down the hallway, felt for the display room door and yanked it open. She shut it behind her and pushed the lock in place. Hopefully it would hold him off until the police showed up.

"Hey! Get your ass out here."

Fumbling in the dark, she ran her hands along the caskets until she found Big Ben. Maybe she could wedge it closed from inside. She lifted the lid.

Someone reached out of the casket and grabbed her arm. Liv started to scream, but another hand clamped fingers over her mouth.

"Quiet!" a familiar voice whispered. Adam yanked her backwards into the casket, pulling her in on top of him. "And lie still."

He closed the lid.

Chapter Seven

Tension filled the space around Liv. Ragged breaths slipped from between her lips and into Adam's fingers. She was lying on top of him. His front against her back. His arm tightened around her waist.

"Told you I'd find you again," he whispered. "Listen, I'm not going to hurt you. I promise. You've got to lie still or they'll find us. Just nod to let me know you understand."

She nodded then let her body relax against this. At least the casket wasn't airtight. It was kind of disturbing how often random people tried to sneak away at visitations just to hop into a casket and see what they felt like from the inside. People were weird.

It wasn't like the fantasy of being alone with Adam had never crossed her mind . . . though maybe spooning in a casket wouldn't have been her first choice. But as long as Eddy was tearing up the place, fighting her way out wasn't going to make her any safer.

Adam peeled his hand away from her mouth and slid it down to her waist. "Who's out there?" he asked softly.

"Why? You going to bust out and murder him?"

His chest rose and fell against her back. His fingers brushed her stomach.

"Stop it."

"Sorry," he said. "Accident."

Liv could feel his breath on the nape of her neck. "It's okay."

She'd let him kiss her yesterday. And she'd kissed him back, hard. Huge mistake.

Whatever the reason he was here, she wasn't about to let him think he could get away with whatever he wanted.

"Umm . . . so, what was all that noise I heard?," he whispered.

"It's Eddy."

A splintering crack. Eddy must have broken into the prep room.

"I'm sorry," Adam said softly. "I didn't think anyone would come after me or even know I'd be here."

"I don't think he's looking for you. Cynn's dead—"

"I know."

Comforting.

Liv tried to minimize contact between her body and Adam's, but there wasn't much she could do in such close quarters. "Her body's in the prep room. Eddy said he's after something he thinks Cynn has with her. But the only thing I know for sure she's got with her are her prom clothes, which I guess are what she's being buried in. Whatever he's after, I don't know why he's searching here instead of at her place."

"Well, her room was pretty thoroughly trashed."

"You know this how?"

"I'm the one who trashed it."

Oh. Great.

"What's he looking for—"

"Shh." He pressed his hand against her lips again. "Listen."

There were several voices now. Lots of shouting. Sirens. The cavalry had arrived.

"Now what do we do?" he asked.

"You're kidding me, right?"

"No. I'm here for your help."

Whatever *that* meant. Now was so not the time to be arguing about this. While she'd definitely fantasized about Adam coming back, maybe even doing a little bit of begging, she hadn't really expected it—let alone like this. Plus, being this close to him wasn't exactly helping her think. At least whatever Adam thought he needed her for didn't seem to include slicing her open.

"Please, Liv." He sounded so sincere, his voice nearly cracked. "Help me."

Help me. The final image from Gabriel's media collage from Brett's murder filled her mind. Adam had looked so terrified, so panicked, so very lost.

● 64

"Okay. Fine. I'll tell them I didn't see anyone in here, but only because I want to know what the hell is going on. So, either you tell me when I get back, or I'll send the police straight to you, got it?"

"Fine." Something shook in his voice. Something vulnerable. Like he wasn't sure if he could really trust her.

Well . . . she wasn't sure she could trust him either.

"You going to let me out now?" she asked.

He reached up with both hands and shoved the lid.

She blinked. The power was back on. She climbed out onto the floor. "I'll come back when the coast is clear. May be a while."

Blue eyes looked up at her through a shock of shaggy blond hair.

"I'll be here," he said.

Sure he would. She'd make sure of it.

She shut the lid and closed the clasp, locking him in.

Chapter Eight

It was a different team of police officers this time. These ones took Liv's statement in five minutes flat. Apparently someone robbing a funeral home was a lot less important than someone stabbing someone on the subway, especially since it looked like all Eddy had done was throw Cynn's body on the floor and steal her prom clothes.

Besides, he already had a reputation at 53 Division.

Tony hovered behind Liv like some kind of protective bird.

"I know my Liv." He puffed out his chest. "She's a good girl and had nothing to do with this."

Liv glanced at the display room door. How long would it take Adam to realize she'd locked him in?

"Don't you worry," Tony said, "I know none of this was you. We'll do a full inventory of the place tomorrow and insurance will cover it."

"Eddy didn't go near the caskets. I was in there the

whole time and nobody came in."

"Doesn't look like he came into the office, either. He just trashed prep and somehow managed to get the cabinet open."

Oh crap. She'd left the cabinet holding both Tony's tools and Cynn's prom clothes wide open after unlocking it to find out what Cynn was being buried in.

"He stole her burial clothes." Tony ran his hand over his head. "What kind of pervert does something like this? I promised the girl's mother I'd bury her in that dress. Look, Livvy, this isn't the way I wanted to tell you, but—"

"It's Cynthia Maddox. I know. I looked in after you left."

He sighed. "I'm so sorry, kid."

"It's okay. Really."

She waited until he went to help the police put the body back on the table then slid Tony's keys back into the lockbox, hoping no one would put two and two together and realize she'd left the cabinet open.

"You should head home." Tony stepped into the doorway.

"No. I'm good. I don't mind hanging out here for a while," said Liv.

"Go. There's no reason for you to stay."

Well, except for the fugitive hiding in the casket.

But since Tony was practically shoving her toward the door, she went.

There was a pizza place across the road and a few doors down. Liv grabbed a random slice, sat in a booth and picked off the toppings. Her fingers couldn't stop moving. Cynn's question buzzed like a wasp in her mind. *Who'd killed her?*

A shadow fell across the table. She looked up. "So, you're stalking me now?"

"Funny." Gabriel slid into the seat opposite her. "What's happening across the street?"

She scanned the pizzeria. Madame Delilah, the wannabe Dead Whisperer, was sitting at a nearby table drawing in a notebook. Liv glanced at it. It was a sketch of a girl in a flowing sheet, drowning in sea of flowers.

Liv nodded in her direction. "Just give me a minute. I just need one moment of quiet to breathe before we launch into the next round of drama."

"Understood." He dropped a packet of potato chips on the table and tore it open sideways.

She popped one in her mouth without really tasting it.

"Got your cheque cashed." He pulled an envelope out of his pocket and handed it to her.

"Thanks. Mom found out I didn't apply for the social media internship thing at Vitesse Airlines. I don't know why I was thinking of applying for it anyway." She shrugged. "We both know that no matter how much they emphasised 'bright and articulate' they were going to go with someone pretty who'd look good in selfies. And I don't do pretty."

"You're something better than pretty." Gabriel pushed the chips around in the package as if really intent on finding the right one. "How'd your mom take it?"

"Not great. I actually ended up telling her while we were in the police station last night. We didn't get that far into it before we were interrupted. I'm guessing that while she hates the fact I didn't go for it, part of it is that she hates the fact we can't exactly afford for me to quit my job for an unpaid internship. I thought they were supposed to announce who got it already, so I was going to just pretend I didn't get it. Now I think she's disappointed."

"Money still tight?"

"Yeah, pretty much."

Madame Delilah picked up her notebook and walked out.

"You know, if you need to borrow any money—"

"Topic shift." Liv stuffed the envelope in her bag. "Do you really think Adam's capable of murder?"

"You do know I was just joking around earlier, right?"

"Answer the question."

He grinned. "So you know about Cynn."

She wasn't the slightest bit surprised he did too.

"Yup, how do you know? Police scanner? Blogs?"

"Social media."

Figures.

"Well, we have her body, Gabe. Now answer my question. Do you think Adam's actually a killer?"

He grabbed a handful of chips. The packet rustled. "Is it true she was knifed?"

"More like her neck was sliced with something thin and sharp."

"Was she tied up?"

"Bruises on her wrists, so probably."

"Heard she was found in her underwear, too. Should've bet on Adam doing her next."

Guess he'd answered the question.

"What if it *wasn't* him? Someone lured Felix to the subway. Why her? Why not go to the police? What if some killer is taking advantage of the fact Adam broke out of Meadowhurst? You telling me no one else had reason to hate these people?"

His hand paused halfway to his mouth. "You seriously want to play detective?"

"Aren't you curious?"

"You know, Brett's family issued a reward for tips leading to Adam's arrest. A few thousand. Plus Cynn's family's chipped in another ten for anything leading to the conviction of her killer. So, if there really is someone out there hiding evidence . . ."

She glanced back toward Never Forget. Red and blue police car lights still flashed across the building.

He followed her gaze. "Ready to tell me why the police are there?"

Nope. Because Gabriel would probably freak out and seeing him upset would make it harder for her to pretend she wasn't. But she'd put it off long enough.

"Eddy broke in."

He dropped the chips. "Are you okay?"

"Yeah. He just threw Cynn's body on the floor and stole her prom outfit. Totally bizarre."

"Messing with some dead chick's prom dress would hardly be the creepiest stunt that pervert's ever pulled." His hands reached across the table and rested on top of hers. "But are you okay?"

"I'm fine. Really. I just hid until the police showed up." She squeezed his hands then pulled away. Liv gave the funeral home another look. The police cars were leaving, Tony was leaving. . . . Just a few more minutes. "Never mind. It's cool."

The dark expression on Gabriel's face combined with his now purple bruises made him look almost sinister. "Sadistic asshat. If anyone deserves to get sliced up, it's him."

"Who?"

"Eddy. You *sure* you're okay?"

"Positive. Now he'll get arrested. Will you stand outside Never Forget and listen out for me? You know, come running in if I start screaming?"

"Why don't I just come in with you?"

"Because I've got to take care of something." She stood up.

"Something you can't tell me?"

"I'll probably tell you sometime, but not tonight, okay?"

He actually managed to look hurt.

"Don't do this," she said. "Please. It's not like you don't keep secrets from me, too."

She half-expected him to argue with that. He just shrugged.

She grabbed his sleeve and tugged. "Come on. Do this for me and tomorrow we can . . . I don't know . . . you can tell me again why I should care there's a dance on Friday."

Chapter Nine

Liv left Gabriel brooding on the front steps of Never Forget. The funeral home seemed colder than usual. There was cardboard taped over the broken stained glass windows. She entered the embalming room, barely glancing at the body on the table. Cynn was probably screaming for someone to talk to. Too bad.

Now to deal with Adam. The last two times they'd collided into each other he'd definitely had the upper hand. This time, she'd make it damn clear she wasn't about to let him be calling all the shots. Liv crouched down and felt around underneath the cabinet until her fingers brushed against the metal shaft of the crowbar Tony kept there. Kind of melodramatic as weapons went. But there were a limited number of ways someone could arm themselves in a funeral home, and it was either that or a knife. She grabbed the crowbar and headed for the display room, then paused in the doorway for a moment.

Silence.

She reached down and lifted the clasp.

"Adam? Everyone's gone."

The lid opened. He sat up. His eyes cut to the crowbar. "What the hell is that for?"

She held the crowbar with both hands and braced it against her shoulder like a baseball bat. Just let him try and grab her now. "How did you know Cynn was dead?"

He groaned. "Seriously? We're going to do this now? Stop waving that thing around and let me up."

She was *not* waving it around. Her hands tightened their grip. "Answer my question."

"When I got to Cynn's, there was some guy hiding in her bushes."

"What guy?"

"I don't know. It was dark. He was taller than me and had a ski mask on. He jumped me. I got a couple blows in and then I ran. I came back a bit later and she was dead."

"You don't exactly look bruised."

"What can I say? He wasn't much of a fighter! Look, why would I tell you I was heading to her place if I was going there to kill her?"

He probably had a point.

"I just went by to talk to her, only someone killed her before I got the chance. Okay?"

"The chance to talk to her or the chance to kill her?"

"Ha ha." He pulled himself up into a crouching

position. Liv braced herself and readied the crowbar.

"This is ridiculous," he said. "I have to go to the bathroom."

"Why were you in the subway with Felix?"

"What the—why was she in the subway with *me*?"

She blinked. "What?"

"Look, I'm not going to just stay here in a goddamn coffin while you threaten me. So, are we going to fight or are we going to talk? You choose."

"It's a casket, not a coffin." She stepped back and dropped the crowbar to her side. "And fine. We can talk. But don't think for one moment that this means I'm just going to let you walk all over me."

"Wouldn't dream of it." He climbed out of the casket and walked out into the hallway.

"Bathroom's right beside the front office."

"Thanks."

"And don't you dare try to kiss me again!"

"Wasn't planning on it!"

Her heart was beating so hard she could practically hear it. She closed the casket and followed him into the hallway. It was empty. She counted to twenty-five slowly then pushed open the door to the men's bathroom.

Adam was washing his hands. "Seriously? You felt the need to check that I hadn't climbed out a window? What the hell's your problem?"

"What the hell's my problem? Where do you want me to start? The escaped convict in my bathroom?

The dead prom queen wannabe in embalming? What happened on the subway? Or how about the fact you're acting like I should give a damn about you when you stopped talking to me and ignored me all year."

His face went really pale. "Crap. So those emails weren't from you?"

"What emails?"

"I had an email address in Meadowhurst. It was hardly private. The guards read all your email. But still, people could email me. And I got a whole bunch of them from someone who called herself DeathFetishGirl99."

"You've got to be kidding." She leaned back against the counter. "So you assumed it was me?"

He looked down at his feet. His ears were red. "Well, you do work at a funeral home."

"But why the hell would you even think I'd write you?"

His eyes snapped back to her face. "How about because I was locked up? Or because you felt sorry for me? Or because you knew I was innocent? We were friends!"

Except working in a funeral home wasn't the same thing as either having a death fetish or crushing after a possible psycho killer. And calling flirting with a girl once and then totally ignoring her for months a "friendship" was a bit of a stretch.

"Friends? You think we were friends, Adam?"

"Okay, fine, we were never friends. But we knew each other."

"You ignored me all year."

Adam looked . . . not exasperated, exactly . . . whoa—was he actually upset? "It's not like I planned to ignore you. It was just awkward, because I started dating Cynn, and Cynn didn't like you."

"Well, now don't I feel better?"

"Look, I'm sorry. It was crappy. Believe me, I've had a whole lot of time in the past three weeks to rethink everything that happened between me, and Cynn, and you. Can we maybe clear my name first? And then figure out this thing with us second?"

"There's no thing with us," said Liv. And there would never be. She folded her arms and looked at him. "But go ahead, tell me the rest of it."

Adam just looked at her for a minute and then finally continued. "Well, DeathFetishGirl99 emailed me and told me to get on that train. You and Felix were the only ones there."

"Wasn't me. And it wasn't Felix. Someone sent Felix an email telling her to meet them there too. She had a printout of it in her hand when I saw her. So what you should be asking is why anyone would lure both of you somewhere. Maybe these letters are from Brett's killer. Maybe your DeathFetishGirl99 is whoever stabbed Felix."

"Sure, then why would the killer have offered to help me?"

"Hello? To set you up for another murder?"

"Crap." He braced both hands on the counter and

stared at the tile. "I really am an idiot."

"Yeah, you are."

He gave her a dirty look.

"So, you kissed me because of some emails from someone called DeathFetishGirl99?"

"I turned down a plea deal because of them! Then I broke out of Meadowhurst and hitchhiked back to Toronto because of them. Dammit, someone's been writing saying their life's in danger because they have proof I didn't murder anyone. Now two more people are dead and—"

"Oh, Felix isn't dead. At least not yet."

Adam looked at her for a minute then sighed like an old man. "Oh, yippee. I mean, I'm glad she's not dead, but I have no clue who these are from or who's killing people or . . . Hell, let's face it. I'm clueless. Which could get me killed if you're right."

Liv hoisted herself up onto the edge of the bathroom counter. "Maybe the fact somebody lured Felix to the subway too means she knows something. DeathFetish might not be the killer. She—or, actually, it could be a *he* for all we know—could be a Good Samaritan. But if they really do have the knife Brett was killed with, why don't they just go to the police with it?"

"She, he, whoever, didn't have it. She just knew where it was and needed my help to get it. When I saw Felix on the floor, I wondered for a second if she was the one who'd written to me, but then you came in—"

And whammo. "Hmmmmm. If the killer followed

Felix into the subway, maybe your pen pal actually witnessed the stabbing then took off for his or her own safety. Did you ever exchange phone numbers?"

He shook his head. "No, and I shut all my social media accounts down first chance I got. I was getting so much hate. Really nasty stuff. Even some death threats."

"Well, then I'm guessing DeathFetish will try to email you again. Hopefully."

"Or she's been scared into hiding," said Adam. "Or the killer chased her down and sliced her up too."

"Or DeathFetish is off on a wild killing spree, as we speak."

"You're fun. The only email address DeathFetish has is my Meadowhurst one. I don't know if authorities can trace my location if I log into it."

"Well, then, whatever you do, don't log into it here. There's a dodgy internet café-slash-convenience-store a few blocks south on Yonge. Should be open in the morning."

"So, what the hell do I do now? Where do I sleep? Where do I go?"

"You mean you didn't try to figure these things out before you broke out of jail?"

"You ever been locked up somewhere with a bunch of teenage criminals?"

Liv shook her head.

"Then don't ask me why I bailed the second I could."

"How did you bail anyway?"

"My facility was low security enough it still allowed field trips and my folks never got around to emptying my bank account. So, I bribed an underpaid guard to look away when I jumped out the bathroom window at a truck stop, while I was on my way to an appointment at another medical facility that was supposed to run even more tests to figure out how screwed up I might be. I think my lawyer was hoping I'd eventually just break down and confess to accidentally killing Brett in a drugged-out haze." Adam's eyes locked on hers. "Try to open your mind for a second and see things from my perspective. I'm just going through life like a normal guy. I get drunk, not for the first time, and wake up in my totalled car, in the lake, covered in Brett's blood with no clue what happened. I get charged with *murder* and hauled off to a soul-destroying hellhole full of teenagers with criminal records and *serious* problems, where I've got to be on my guard every second of every day."

Liv reached out to him then caught herself midair and pulled back.

Of course, he noticed. "I realize how this looks, okay? But I haven't had a real night's sleep since Brett died. I don't know what to do. I don't know where to go. I don't have anybody to help me."

"You have lots of friends."

"No, I have lots of people I used to hang out with, who turned on me the second I was arrested, none of whom even bothered emailing me once I was dragged off to prison, and who posted all over social media that they hoped I'd rot in hell forever."

Fair enough. A big wave of social media sympathy had been going pretty strong for Brett.

Not so much for Adam.

Liv was going to hate herself for asking the next question, but not as much as she would for chickening out.

"What the hell happened in September? One day you want to hang out with me, the next it's the silent treatment. In between you stood me up."

"Huh?" He stepped back. "I told my friends I couldn't go to the game with them because I was going to hang out with you, and they reminded me I'd said we'd all sit in my dad's box. So a couple of the girls went to ask you to join us there instead. Then they came back saying you were really pissy about it and that I should give you some space until you calmed down."

"You actually believed them? It never crossed your mind your friends might be lying?"

"Why on earth would they lie? And anyway, when I tried to talk to you about it you told me to go screw myself!"

She didn't actually know what seemed more pathetic—his letting his stupid-ass friends manipulate him like that, or that a very tiny part of her still kind of wanted to make out with him. If just to show him what he'd lost.

"Plus, I sort of hooked up with Cynn at the game."

She groaned. "You're pathetic."

"Look, I'm sorry. I wasn't exactly thinking about it or planning for it to happen. Cynn just came onto me. If I could go back in time and have a do-over, I would."

Liv hopped off the counter. "Tell me again why I'm not supposed to be freaked out about you trashing Cynn's room?"

"Because I'm also the guy who called 911. And I trashed Cynn's room *after* she was dead, but before the cops got there. So yeah, it was a pretty quick search. I only had a few minutes. So I just tossed things all over the floor and stuff. I was looking for the knife she was murdered with, in case it was the same one that killed Brett. I couldn't find it but, believe me, Cynn's dead body looked a whole lot like the crime scene pictures they showed me of Brett."

He shuddered.

"And you thought trashing your dead girlfriend's room was a better option than just trusting that the police would find the evidence themselves."

"Like they found the knife Brett was murdered with? They searched everyone who was at that party. Yet somehow, according to DeathFetish, somebody smuggled it home from the party."

"Well, looking at Cynn's neck, the weapon was really small," Liv said. "Like a utility knife or razor. Pocket-sized or even smaller, if that helps." Although she'd have thought the police would've patted people down at least. "Now, there's some leftover food in the reception room fridge. When you leave, use the side door. It'll lock behind you."

He smiled. The same slightly crooked smile he'd given her back when he'd borrowed that pen. "You're a lifesaver, Liv."

Her limbs suddenly felt fizzy. Like there were sparklers in her blood. She looked away. Who cared if he was cute? He'd always been cute.

He was still the same guy who just did things without thinking.

"Yeah," she said, "but I'm not going to be saving your ass forever. So you'd better think up a better plan than hiding here."

She took the crowbar back into the embalming room, wiped the handle clean and stashed it back under the cabinet. Her temples throbbed. She pressed her fingers against her eyelids.

When she opened her eyes, Adam was standing next to Cynn. There was still a sheet over her, but her hand hung out like she was asking for something.

"She's under there, isn't she?"

She took Cynn's hand and waved it in his direction. "Want to say hi?"

Cynn sat up.

Oh, crap.

Chapter Ten

"Where the hell did you go?" Cynn asked.

Liv looked through her image to Adam. He hadn't even blinked.

Okay, now this was totally new. Every other time she'd opened a link to a dead body in the past she'd actually had to concentrate and focus. But this time, she hadn't actually intended to open the link to Cynn's ghost at all. She'd just touched her corpse, like she always did, and pretended to start a conversation. It was kind of like pretending to hit someone and actually knocking them down.

Okay, no more talking to bodies she didn't actually want to have a conversation with.

Because, apparently, she didn't realize the strength of her own abilities.

"I'm sorry," Liv said, kind of trying to look at both of them at once. "I really have to go."

"I know," he said.

"What the hell." Cynn spit out the words like bullets. "Your mommy too poor to teach you manners? You can't just drop me and take off like that."

Liv rolled her shoulders back. "Don't even go there."

"What?" Adam's eyes searched Liv's.

Cynn's face hovered near, mouth snarling, eyes glaring.

Liv blinked, hard. "I'm leaving now. I'll be back here tomorrow after school. I'll talk to you then. If you're here."

"You *trying* to piss me off?" Cynn asked.

"You sure you're okay with me staying here?" Adam asked.

"Yes!"

Cynn's expression took if-looks-could-kill to a whole new level.

"I mean, it's cool you're here. It's fine if you're not tomorrow."

She didn't even look at Cynn, because Adam smiled. It was a slightly crooked smile, riding higher on the right side than the left. A girl would be willing to do just about anything to have a guy smile at her like that.

He stepped around the table.

Her eyes followed.

"Hang on." Cynn snapped her fingers at Liv. "There's someone else here, isn't there?"

"Cool," Adam said. "Thanks for being so awesome about this."

"Who's there?" Cynn asked. "Let me talk to them."

His hand brushed against Liv's shoulder, sending shivers up her neck. A grin tugged at her cheeks.

"Holy crap," Cynn practically sputtered. "Don't tell me it's Adam—"

Liv let go of her hand.

Cynn vanished.

Liv tucked the sheet down firmly.

Gabriel was still waiting outside exactly where she'd left him, fiddling with his phone. "Got it sorted?"

She nodded. "Sorry I took so long. I can't believe you just sat around waiting for me."

He shrugged. "No worries."

The air smelled like rain. Nervous energy tingled down her limbs. Gabriel walked her home, talking away while troubling thoughts ran circles in Liv's head, like the fact Cynn knew Adam was there. She let that one go. Cynn could throw all the hissy fits she wanted, but she was too dead to do anything about it, right? Unfortunately, Liv's own reasons for helping Adam weren't all that clear.

She felt sorry for him. She felt like he was in trouble. And she'd rather let him run away than be the one responsible for throwing him back in jail.

Was that it? She'd just taken in an escaped convict like he was some poor lost puppy? It wasn't because she *liked* him or anything. No way.

They reached a concrete forest of crumbling, low rise apartments and weaved their way between the buildings until they reached hers. Liv and her mom had a rectangular two bedroom unit on the main floor. Gabriel tended to skip the hassle of buzzing in through the lobby and instead just knocked on her bedroom window if he knew she was home. He said it was because he didn't want the buzzer to wake up her mom. Liv suspected it was because he was wired to ignore how normal people did things and to take any shortcut through life he could find.

Still, he'd never managed to convince her that her life would be simpler if she just came and went through the window too.

Liv stopped outside the lobby door. "Can I ask a random question?"

"Always."

She forced her shoulders to shrug and tried to look as disinterested as possible in what she wanted to ask. "I was thinking earlier about social media, and the Event Hack thing you made of the night Brett died, and the fact that a bunch of our classmates are probably going crazy posting things online about Cynn's murder and Adam's escape. . . ."

Gabriel crossed his arms. One eyebrow rose. "And?"

She stared at a patch of cement by her feet. "And if you, or someone, logged into a website or email program while you were on the run from the police, and the authorities were on the lookout for you, would they be able to use it to track where you were logging in from?"

A peculiar smile crossed his lips. "Me personally? Of course not. I built a personalized IP masker and never surf without it. But if you mean Adam?" He snorted. "The moment that boy logs in online, he's screwed."

Chapter Eleven

Liv walked through the front door and into the kitchen. It was empty. She pulled two twenties from her envelope and stuffed them into her mom's tip jar.

"I told you to save your money for college."

She turned. Her mom stood in the doorway.

"I, um, borrowed some earlier. Just paying you back."

"Did you buy the peanut butter and coffee in the cupboard too?"

Liv shrugged. "I was grabbing lunch yesterday and they were on sale."

She was going to head to her room, but her mom sat at the table and nodded toward the chair across from her.

"Your boss called. He said there was a break-in tonight. A kid from school. Might have been on drugs."

"I'm fine, Mom. Gabe walked me home."

"Tony's worried about you. I know you've been working really hard. I was thinking I could take tomorrow off. We could hang out downtown. I could take you to the hospital if you want to see Felix."

"Mom, you've got to stop about her. I know you mean well, but I'm serious. Felix has plenty of friends, and I'm not one of them."

Her mom sighed and looked down. "Julie, her mom, is sweet. Her dad cheated, moved in with his mistress, got a really high-powered lawyer and took almost everything in the divorce. He even tried to have Felix arrested last summer over some stupid nonsense about her damaging his fancy car. Rich men are the worst."

Yeah, no wonder Mom had bonded with Felix's mom. Sounded like they had the same bad taste.

"Anyway, Felix has been working two jobs and studying like crazy to get scholarships," Mom added. "She even works the night shift loading boxes at some warehouse. Julie's worried she might be pushing herself too hard."

Liv reached over and squeezed her mom's hands. "You're a wonderful person to care about Julie's daughter like that, but *your* daughter is fine. I promise. Go to work tomorrow. I'll think about what you said about Felix."

Not that she was about to change her mind.

Liv looked at the clock on her bedside table. Three a.m.

She rolled over, punched her pillow into a ball and shoved it under her neck. She never should have let Adam stay in the funeral home. She should have gone to the police. She should have told Tony, or Gabriel or her mom. Anything. Something.

Instead, she'd helped him. Why? Because of that insane, random kiss on the subway?

She groaned, yanking the blankets up around her neck. No, she helped him because she was almost positive he was innocent. Someone set him up. He was running for his life. He needed help.

The look on Adam's face when he'd come to in his car, covered in blood, filled her mind as vividly as if she'd actually been there.

"Help me."

She drifted in and out of a weird, unsettled sleep. Like her brain was a television set and someone kept randomly switching it on without permission.

When she finally woke up for good the next morning, Mom had already left for work, but she'd baked cinnamon egg bread, folded into little pockets with syrup in the middle. She grabbed one for herself and one for Adam. She thought again then pocketed a bottle of juice for him as well.

Liv walked through the lobby. Gabriel was leaning against a wall outside her building. Today, the sunglasses were blue.

"You're walking me to school?"

"I'm worried about you. Plus, I got you something.

Kind of." He shrugged like he was trying to make it clear just how little of a deal it was. "Basically, I convinced the principal that I needed a bunch of extra spare time to work on the video yearbook for prom, and he gave me permission to skip any classes I needed to. So I told him you were my assistant and I needed your help too. So you're on the authorized absences list from like now until the end of school."

"Oh wow. Seriously? You're the best."

He smiled. "Thanks. It wasn't exactly hard. Principal was totally salivating over the idea of showing off what their fancy new system was capable of. And last week of school's a joke, anyway. Teachers just put on videos and hand back assignments."

Gabriel was a friend. A real one. The kind who'd been there for her every stupid day since she landed on the school bitches' hit list. He was the one who fished her phone out of the toilet when they threw it in there and Frankensteined it back to life. The one who met her outside class so she wouldn't have to walk the halls alone. Here she was hiding things from him, protecting a guy whose friends used him for target practice.

She handed him Adam's slice of toast. He finished it in two bites.

"They found Cynn's clothes in Union subway station," Gabriel said. "Eddy set them on fire and stuffed them in a garbage can. Totally smoked up the platform. They had to cancel the Yonge-University line trains for like an hour. Moron."

Typical. There was an actual killer on the loose, and

Eddy was busy pulling stupid-ass stunts.

"Anyone claim that reward yet?"

"Nope. Whoever wrote Felix that email is either full of it or holding out for something bigger than money. Which would also explain why they didn't come forward ages ago." Gabriel had gone a little too far ahead and waited for Liv to catch up.

"Ready for the random Rosewood fact of the day?" he asked.

"Always."

"If Eddy doesn't get tossed in jail this time, and he's still dating Sharona by Friday . . ."

"You're giving them a whole week? Wow."

Gabriel laughed. "*Then* there's a good chance our remaining prom queen contestants are going to have their dates throwing punches in the parking lot."

"Seriously? You expect me to believe Emma the book-bore and Sharona the shallow actually have duelling boyfriends?"

He grinned and threw his arm across her shoulders. "'Twas early April. Major league baseball. Blue Jays' opening game. Brett hosts a party—"

"In Adam's dad's box?"

"Probably. Eddy shows up in a Yankees' jersey."

"Ouch."

"So Brett yanks it over his head and proceeds to pound on him for a bit."

"Had to be done," said Liv.

"But Emma's there with a steady boyfriend, Damien Pike. This totally arrogant pre-med student—"

"I know him. Well, at least I've met him. He's a driver for a corpse transportation service that Tony uses sometimes. The kind that picks bodies up from the hospital morgue and drops them off at funeral homes."

"He's a corpse chauffer?" Gabriel snorted. "I didn't know that. Anyway, so Damien films the fight between Brett and Eddy, and turns it over to the police, claiming he saw a knife. So, Brett and Eddy get arrested and spend a night in jail, before the my-parents-are-loaded defence kicks in. Three days later, someone takes a baseball bat to Damien's car, inside and out. Totals it. I doubt they've made peace since then. And now, having their dates compete?" He whistled.

"Did anyone suspect Eddy or Damien of actually killing Brett?"

"Brett beat the crap out of a lot of people, and Eddy always kind of took his lumps and moved on. I always figured Damien was the kind of pampered, trust fund baby who'd just get his daddy to buy him a new one. Honestly, learning he's working for a corpse transport service kind of puts a bit of a new spin on it. But still it's a hell of a leap from transporting some corpses—or throwing some punches for that matter—to actually stripping someone down to their underwear and cutting their throat. We're looking for a real sicko."

The kind who skulked around girls' houses in a ski mask. Here she'd thought no one was sicker than Brett. Liv shivered. Gabriel's arm tightened around her. It was comforting.

"You ever hear any rumours about Cynn having a stalker? Say, like a Rosewood Peeping Tom?"

He rolled his eyes. "No. I guess anything's possible."

They stepped through the twisted iron gates of Rosewood Academy. The school's giant state-of-the-art LED board flashed: *Think you know who killed Cynn Maddox? Log on and vote now at www.who-killed-cynn. com.*

"Your handiwork, I presume?"

Gabriel tried not to smirk but he couldn't pull it off.

"But why just Cynn?"

"Had a better ring to it than 'Think you know who killed Cynn and Brett and stabbed Felix?' Besides, newly dead is a lot sexier than not-yet-dead or already-rotting-in-the-ground. Now, if someone breaks into Felix's hospital room and finishes her off, I'll reconsider."

"You do realize that the board of governors must be going insane. Especially if you've actually locked the school out of their own system."

"I thought you'd appreciate it. It's like inviting the whole school to send us their gossip."

"I just don't want you to get suspended."

Gabriel pulled a phone from his pocket and pushed a button. The board went back to wishing the student body a productive and respectful day.

She laughed.

He shrugged. "Babe, I could crash the whole power grid if I wanted."

The bell rang. Most students headed toward

classrooms. Liv followed Gabriel to the auditorium. He reached inside his coat, pulled out a wad of yellow flyers and started stuffing them in between the seats every few rows. Liv reached for one. The page was blank except for the who-killed-Cynn website URL typed along the bottom.

"Love how we're going for the low-tech approach."

"Why, thank you." He crumpled up the final few and threw them in random directions. "Always good to pique a person's natural curiosity by making them think they've found something. The end-of-year concert is bound to be a pretentious snore-fest. Might as well give people another reason to play on their phones. Tomorrow, all the seats come out and they lay down the dance floor for Friday."

"So, do I get to see your latest masterpiece?"

He snorted. "Hardly a masterpiece. Just a quick diversion between more interesting projects. Come on. I'll show you in the control room."

They crossed the auditorium to a small door in the back which led into a stairwell. It was a tight space. Claustrophobic. Dark. A skeletal black staircase spiralled up two stories to the even smaller door of the audio visual control booth, a wide box with panoramic sliding windows that looked out over the auditorium below.

"You're really going to spend the whole prom up here?"

"Probably. There are a lot of buttons that need pushing."

A lot of buttons? There were enough buttons and switches and dials to shame a nuclear submarine. Plus four computer monitors. One was on and appeared to cycle through the school's security cameras.

"Another little hacking project?"

To her surprise, his cheeks reddened.

"Something like that."

He slid into a chair, opened a browser and typed the address. The screen went black. There was a scream. Terrified and terrifying. Then the words, "Did Adam Clay kill Cynn Maddox?" appeared. The font dripped blood. Two buttons hovered underneath, one for yes and one for no.

Way to keep an open mind.

"You're not afraid it's a bit too subtle?" asked Liv.

Gabriel chuckled.

"What happens when you vote?"

"Either way, you get this."

More screams. Two animated figures appeared on screen. Adam and Cynn—Photoshopped, of course. He waved a bloody knife. Her head fell off. They danced like tweeny-pop wannabes.

The bad taste in her mouth was now bitter. Gabriel was enjoying this entirely too much.

"Of course, the website logs the votes." He clicked more buttons. "So far, 987 votes. Ninety-nine percent guilty."

"How many times did you vote?"

He stopped clicking and looked at her.

"What's gotten into you? Two chicks you always

hated get knifed and you lose your sense of humour?"

"Maybe I'd find it funnier if this didn't feel like a huge Adam hate-fest. You guys got some history I don't know about?"

His mouth said, "Of course not."

His eyes said, *don't go there.*

"Are you really convinced he's guilty?" she asked. "The truth, please. It's important, so look at me while you say it."

He shrugged. But then he glanced at her face, and Liv could tell that she had him.

"Okay," he said. "He had motive and opportunity and bedroom access, which taken together are basically enough for conviction. But I'm not a hundred percent sure he has the guts to actually kill someone—not while sober, anyway. Pay someone else to, maybe. Nah, not even that. He's more of a follower than a doer."

She had to admit that was fairer than most people.

She leaned back and looked at the screen.

So did he. "What if I changed it? Made it more of an online poll and listed a whole bunch of different suspects? *Killer or victim? Who killed Cynn? Who's going to get killed next?* People love ranking things online. They could vote our suspects up and down some kind of ranking list with killer at one end and victim at the other, depending on whether they think the person is more likely to kill or be killed. Like an online game almost. They could even take bets."

"It's better to piss off a bunch of people by calling them psychos?"

"Hey, one of them might be guilty."

"And the rest would be innocent."

Gabriel raised an eyebrow. "Ever searched our names online? They've called us worse, believe me. Besides, it's like safety in numbers. If we list a lot of people, no one can take it too personally."

That kind of made sense.

"You're the one who wanted to play detective." He pulled a keychain out of his pocket, uncapped a thumb drive and stuck it into the machine. "In fact, how about this? We watch the social media mashup of the night Brett died and then make a list of anyone we know was at the party, but who wasn't accounted for when he died?"

It was hard to argue with that.

Even watching it on a much smaller screen, somehow the video was even harder to watch the second time around. Gabriel had compressed the whole party down to half an hour. But still, it was like watching a slow-moving horror movie, building to the moment the camera zoomed in on the bloody wreck. He kept notes on a piece of paper, writing names down as people appeared and crossing them off again.

Finally, Adam's face filled the screen, pale, terrified. His blue eyes seemed to lock onto hers through the screen.

"Help me."

Gabriel switched it off, then leaned back in his chair.

"Alright, I noticed twelve different people at the

party, but we can rule out a few of them, because they never left the living room or front deck long enough to kill Brett and push Adam's car down the hill."

"How many people are unaccounted for?"

"Five. Eddy and Sharona, Emma and Damien, and Felix. Six if you count Cynn."

Whoa. So all of the prom queen contenders and their dates.

"So, which of them also have a motive?" she asked.

"I don't know. Let's start from the top. What motive could Eddy have for killing Brett?"

Eddy had broken into the funeral home looking for something he thought Cynn had. Something was buzzing in the back of her mind. It was almost like her link with Cynn was somehow still open. What did both Brett and Cynn have that somebody would want?

"Know how you said yesterday that Adam could've killed Brett to become top dog?"

Gabriel's pen twirled in his fingers. "I wasn't really serious about that."

"But what if you're right? What if this *is* all about the pecking order? Eddy's head bully now that Brett's gone. You said Brett beat Eddy up in public a couple months ago. Think about all the money floating around Rosewood. Maybe being top asshole has its perks—like you can deal drugs, or people pay you not to kick the crap out of them."

Gabriel's back stiffened.

She went on. "Plus, Felix and Cynn were attacked

the same night, which knocks the prom queen competition down from four to two. Eddy's dating one of the remaining contestants and he destroyed Cynn's prom dress. Maybe Sharona helped Eddy kill Brett and now he's helping her become prom queen?"

He snorted. "Unlikely. Because Felix wasn't much of a threat. She was barely campaigning. Probably doesn't think it's worth her time because the prizes are always crappy."

"She was Brett's girlfriend, though."

Gabriel's smile grew teeth. "So does that mean the same motive applies to all the prom queen wannabes? Say Damien the corpse chauffer assumed it was Brett who wrecked his car. So Damien killed him then embarked on a bloody rampage to get his love the crown?"

"Insane." Liv grinned. "But I kind of like it."

Gabriel clicked a small, grey box at the top right side of the internet browser and the browser screen turned black. "You asked about surfing the net anonymously? Well, now we're in untraceable mode."

"You even installed it on a school computer?"

He grinned. "Especially on a school computer. At least until my dad springs for some toys this nice at home. Don't worry. Nobody will ever notice it. I'm the only student with access to the A/V box. And it's not like the school staff don't have better things to do than play around up here." He opened the template to modify his WhoKilledCynn website and added Eddy,

Sharona, Emma and Damien to the suspect list. He thought for a minute then added Felix.

"Why? She was stabbed before Cynn was murdered."

"Stabbed but not killed. And, she's the last person on my list of people who aren't accounted for. Besides, it rounds out your prom queen conspiracy theory. Maybe Felix hired someone to kill Cynn and then they double-crossed her and demanded more money. Better yet, what if Cynn helped Adam kill Brett? Or Cynn dosed his drink with some kind of drugs, just for kicks, but then he went psycho? In which case Felix could've killed Cynn for revenge."

"Insane. But sure. It's as good as any other theory. Plus, factor in that someone lured Felix to the subway. We don't know whether that was the serial killer or someone trying to help."

Gabriel spun around in his chair and looked at her over steepled fingers. "I think I know where we might get an answer."

He reached into his trench coat pocket, slowly drew his hand out and uncurled his fingers like a magician.

It was a hospital pass card. Liv sucked in a breath.

The card belonged to Gabriel's father, a prominent surgeon. He'd stopped trying to buy his son's love years ago, and now instead just more or less bribed him to confine himself to antics that wouldn't land him in jail.

"Let's go talk to Felix," he said.

"Seriously?" As far as she knew, he'd never pulled

a stunt on his dad's home turf. "Is that a real key card or a fake?"

"Fake. I'll use it once then dump it. Say we meet in the hospital lobby after school and . . . hang on—"

He pulled out his phone.

"Your boss is calling me. Why is your boss calling me?"

"He probably tried my phone and knows I don't have it with me. I put your name down as one of my emergency contacts."

"Really?" He grinned. "Oh wait, it's gone to voice mail. Hold on."

He made a face and stared at the screen until the message icon flashed. He put the phone up to his ear. "Okay. Tony says he'll be coming in to work with the police this afternoon. They're going to do a thorough inventory and some major clean-up thing. So if you want to be—"

Liv ran for the stairs.

Chapter Twelve

When she got to Never Forget, the lights were off and the front door was still locked. Liv tossed her bag onto her desk, grabbed a dust cloth and went looking for Adam. She wiped down every surface he might have touched. Last thing she needed was for the police to search their database for mystery prints and find out she'd aided and abetted a murder suspect.

Not that she thought he was guilty, really, but there was only so much you could risk on a hunch.

Cynn's lifeless body still lay on the prep table. Even with the break-in, her parents wouldn't dream of moving her elsewhere. Tony would make her so beautiful every girl at the funeral would be jealous of a corpse. Shame she was so damn ugly on the inside.

Liv uncovered Cynn's face. For a moment she wished Jake hadn't already been cremated. Not that she could really expect his corpse to hang around

Never Forget forever. Still, he'd been different, less self-absorbed than most. Then again, he'd battled leukemia for ages, which had given him plenty of time to prepare for death. His having been religious had probably helped, too—he'd been convinced that his spirit was headed to a better place. She hoped he wasn't just hovering around a pile of ashes now. Liv's hand brushed Cynn's cold cheek as her mind opened a connection to her spirit. In a nanosecond, Cynn's eyes blazed with indignation.

Understandable, really. Liv had just started talking to her yesterday and then totally disappeared on her, leaving Cynn alone in whatever empty void the dead vanished into.

Hang on. Where had that thought come from? Was she actually feeling *guilty*? Screw that—

"You're back." Cynn's eyes darted around the room. "Adam still here?"

"He left."

"Where'd he go?"

"I honestly don't know."

Cynn leaned back on her elbows. "Do you have any idea how jarring it is when you yank my mind around like that?" she asked.

"My being gone wasn't about you. Eddy broke in last night and stole your prom clothes."

Cynn's image jumped, like someone shoved a dart into her spine.

"What did he take? Tell me, exactly."

"There was a pink dress, silver strappy shoes, a gold chain—"

"Hell no!" Cynn sounded so loud it was hard to believe she hadn't actually come back from the dead.

"First I'm murdered, then someone steals my favourite sandals."

So much for death giving you perspective.

"*And* a really expensive-looking gold necklace," Liv said. "Like an antique."

Cynn sniffed. "Was it ugly? Probably some old thing which belonged to a dead great-aunt. My mom's sentimental about crap like that. She's got a whole drawer of the stuff."

Must be nice.

"Well, I'm sure a lot of people are going through your stuff now. Everyone's talking serial killer because your death looked exactly like Brett's. You don't happen to know anything about that, do you? Like where the murder weapon went after Brett was murdered? Apparently somebody smuggled it out of the party, past the cops. It was probably really small and really thin and sharp."

Cynn rolled her eyes. "Yeah, I pulled it out of his corpse and hid it down my pants just for laughs. Don't be ridiculous."

"But you were there the night he died. Your boyfriend was arrested. So you have to know *something*."

"But I don't know anything." She inspected her freshly painted fingernails. Blood red.

Weird. Tony always did the nails last.

"Did you know Eddy is dating Sharona, who's also running for prom queen?"

Cynn shrugged and looked bored.

"How well did you get on with them? Like, should we be suspecting them of killing you?"

"We got on okay. Eddy was a loser. Sharona was kind of pathetic."

"How about Emma and her boyfriend Damien?"

"Damien was boring but hot. Definitely doable, though. Emma was just plain boring. What do you care?"

"Well, someone killed you and Brett—"

Cynn yawned. "Yeah, and I told you to go find out who."

"That's what I'm *trying* to do!"

"By throwing random names at me? If I knew who killed me, I wouldn't be asking you."

"Can't you at least tell me if you had any enemies?"

Cynn threw up her hands. "Look at me. When you're the whole damn package, everyone's your friend and everyone's your enemy."

Oh please.

"How are you doing this, anyway?"

"Doing what?"

"Talking to me."

"I don't know. I just can."

"Since when?"

"Honestly? Since right after Brett died—"

"Does Adam know about you doing this?"

"No. He couldn't see or hear your spirit."

Cynn snorted. "Because you didn't let him? Or because it's just a you-thing?"

"I'm not sure what you—"

"It's not a hard question. Can just anybody walk into the funeral home you work at and chat with dead people? Or is it all you? Can you do this anywhere?"

"I don't know," said Liv.

Certainly Madame Delilah seemed to think she could chat with corpses, too. But that didn't mean she could.

"How can you not know?" Cynn asked.

"Because I don't have a supply of dead bodies *anywhere* to practise on."

"Then why don't you go round up some friends, if you've got any, bring them here and see if they can do it too? Then you'd know if you actually have a gift or not."

Not for the first time, Liv wished Cynn would come back to real life long enough that she could kick her ass.

"Like, go get me Felix."

"You're in a funeral home," Liv said. "You get that? I'm not going to throw a party around your dead body just so you can find someone you like better to talk to."

Something vicious flickered in Cynn's eyes. She didn't even bother to hide it.

Liv looked through her to the clock on the wall. "Sorry, but I've got to cover your body back up."

"No! Wait!"

Suddenly Cynn stood in front of her, just inches from her face. Liv blinked.

She'd never seen a ghost projection get up off the table before.

"What was Adam doing here?"

The actual corpse was still lying on the table where it had always been. Liv could only take a tiny step back without actually letting go of Cynn's dead body. But Cynn's image was right up in Liv's face. "Come on. Don't lie to me now."

There was a new edge to her tone Liv couldn't interpret.

"He thought I could help him. I couldn't. So he left."

"But you wanted to." Cynn smirked. "You think he's innocent, don't you?"

Liv shrugged and tried to turn away, but her head didn't seem to want to turn. It was as if something was forcing her to look at Cynn.

"You *think*. But you don't know for sure." Her tone was sweet now. Soothing, like Cynn was trying to let Liv down easy.

"You think I didn't know you always wanted him? I saw the way you looked at him—even though he never really liked you. He's always known you were a little piece of loser trash. Now he's using you to save his worthless skin."

"I don't want him, Cynn, not that it's any of your business. But I do think he's innocent."

"What if you're wrong?" She raised a finger in front

of Liv's face. "What if he pinned me down on the bed, climbed on top of me and slid a knife across my throat?" Slowly she dragged a manicured nail across Liv's neck. "*Freak*."

Liv almost felt the nail on her skin. She closed her eyes. This wasn't real. The dead couldn't touch her.

"You think he'll fall in love with you if you save him? Or are you secretly hoping he'll kill you too? You got a thing for getting hurt?"

"Cut the crap. You actually think Adam could have killed you?"

"You actually think I'm just going to tell you?"

"I think you're a selfish bitch," said Liv.

The back door slammed. She jumped.

Adam was back. "What the hell?"

Chapter Thirteen

Liv dropped the connection. The image vanished. But her eyes didn't seem to work quite right, because when she looked at Cynn's corpse it was almost like she was seeing double. She blinked and tried to force the images to settle. Normally she came out easier than this.

"What the hell were you doing?" Adam said.

"Talking to your dead girlfriend. I asked if you killed her, but apparently she's not telling." She pushed her fingers up against her eyes and rubbed. "Where have you been?"

"I had to take care of something."

"How'd you get back in?"

"I found some duct tape under the counter and taped the latch down so it wouldn't lock."

Was there something different about his face? Had it changed since she'd seen it yesterday? His cheeks looked thinner, hollow. Dark circles stood out under fierce blue eyes. It was like the perception filters in her eyes were suddenly off.

He stepped towards her. She stepped back. The cold metal prep table dug into her skin. Her fingers brushed against a retractable scalpel.

"Found this in your floor drain, by the way." He dug in his pocket and pulled out the necklace. "Guessing Eddy dropped it."

Well, so much for hoping Eddy'd get caught trying to hock it.

"What were you doing with the drain?"

"Needed a shower."

So he'd taken it right here, in this room, next to Cynn's dead body? The tiled floor had a grate in the middle for when Tony used the hose to wash away whatever gunk came off the bodies. Even she never looked in it.

He held it out to her, and when she didn't take it, set it on the counter.

"I can't believe you were yelling at a corpse." He eyed Cynn, his face impassive. Then he picked up Cynn's hand and held it for a moment. He traced the bruises on her wrist. His fingers linked through her dead ones.

Cynn's nail polish was gone.

"So, what did you tell her?" he asked Cynn's body. "Did you faithfully stand by your man?"

Liv inched the scalpel along behind her back. She tucked it into her back pocket and pulled her shirt down over it.

"Did she answer?"

He looked at her. "Don't be ridiculous." He pulled the sheet back over Cynn.

"You don't seem to miss her very much. I thought you were in love with her."

"Not really. Just because she called me her boyfriend doesn't make it real. It's more like she thought I would do as a boyfriend. She never even tried to contact me after I got arrested. Not once. I thought she cheated on me, even before then, you know. She probably did."

The clock ticked. Tony and the police would be here soon, and if they found Adam here, they'd arrest him.

"You think I killed her?" he asked.

"No, but . . ."

Something flashed in the depths of his eyes. Frustration? Disappointment ? "I told you I didn't, Liv."

"Then who did? Some random dude in a ski mask?"

"Yeah. Probably."

"Then who the hell is he?" asked Liv

"You think I'd still be here if I knew?"

"Why *are* you still here?" she asked. "Why haven't you run?"

"Where am I supposed to go? I don't exactly have people lining up to help me."

"People around you keep turning up dead."

Adam's jaw tightened.

"What about your parents?" she pressed. "And you have a lawyer."

"Yeah. Hired by my father."

"But—"

"But nothing!" His voice rose so loud it cracked. "My father practically ordered me to accept a manslaughter plea. Especially when they searched my bedroom at home after Brett died and found a bit of pot. So, they want me to admit to being some crazy teenager with emotional issues, who drinks and does drugs, and accidentally killed Brett. My father even suggested I could say I was showing off some fancy knife moves I'd seen on TV, didn't mean to cut Brett, and then had been trying to save Brett and drive him to the hospital when I crashed in the lake. Oh, they worked damn hard to find ways for me to plead guilty. Best option for Dad's political career. Keeps Brett's family happy, which means Vitesse Airlines is happy, which means more nice little bribes for defence contracts coming his way. At the same time, it makes my dad look tough on corruption to voters, because he's making sure his own son faces justice. Even turns me into a sympathetic rehabilitation story, because I stay in a youth facility and there's no risk of some judge ever deciding to try me as an adult and toss me in prison. Just means five more years in hell for me."

He sounded sad. Worse than sad—he sounded wretched.

But Liv didn't much feel like going easy on him. "So, your dad thinks you're guilty?" she asked.

Adam sighed. "What's with all the questions?"

"I need to know."

"Not good enough."

He stepped toward her, closing the space between them. "I'll ask you again. Do you really believe I'm a killer?"

Liv shook her head.

"Or maybe this has nothing to do with guilt or innocence?"

He moved closer. He was testing her in some way she couldn't put a finger on. Her skin tingled. Her heart seemed to be beating in time to his breathing. Her whole body was practically aching to make out with him so badly she was almost able to forget how foolish that would be.

"Maybe," he said, "it's a more basic, physical instinct." Adam's lips were just a breath away from hers. Then he drew back just an inch. "Cynn always said you had a creepy lust thing for death and gore. . . ."

"What the hell?" Liv shoved him back with both hands. "Stop! You don't have the right to talk to me like that. This is seriously messed up."

His eyes widened. She couldn't tell whether he was shocked or impressed. Either way, she didn't care.

"A creepy thing for death and gore?" she said. "You mean 'death fetish.' Like Gabriel and I like to get it on in the cemetery? Are you kidding me? Look, whatever Cynn and the bitch-brigade said behind my back, I don't have a thing for killers. I didn't let you sleep here last night for some kinky thrill. I did it because you need help and I *want* to believe you're innocent."

Adam opened his mouth, but not fast enough.

"If you don't want to trust me, then don't. Whatever. Go find somewhere else to stay and someone else who'll play along with your weird games, but don't . . . don't mess with me like this." She pushed past him, burst into the hall and walked into the office. Her hands shook. Adam came up behind her and laid a hand on her shoulder. She shook him off. "I didn't ask for this. You have no idea the stupid crap I go through every single day at school. You think I want all that in my real life too?"

"I'm sorry. I . . . I wasn't trying to mess with you, Liv."

She turned and looked at him.

The bravado and tension had drained away.

"I'm sorry if it seemed . . ." Adam closed his eyes for a few seconds. "I just . . . I just want to know I can trust you."

"And you think I can trust *you*?"

He swallowed hard. "Good point."

For a moment he just stood there, looking at her. Like a kid looking in the window of a car dealership at some fast, red, convertible he knew he'd never be able to earn enough to afford.

"Okay. Maybe I haven't been fair to you. But I might be able to change that. How about this?" He reached into his front pocket and pulled out a digital, high definition camera video card. "I told you I was outside

Cynn's house last night and somebody jumped me? Well, he had a small, high def video recorder with him. That's why I took off. He dropped it while we were fighting, so I grabbed it off the ground and ran like hell. Figured I could use it to find out who he was. But I guess it broke when he dropped it, because I couldn't even get it to turn on. Plus, I kind of stepped on it. I managed to get the video card out though. Here you go." He dropped the card into her hand. "I'm trusting you with this."

Chapter Fourteen

Liv heard a large car engine purring to a stop outside. Tony.

"We have to get out of here," she said. "Now."

"What? Why?"

She grabbed Adam's arm and pulled him down the hallway and back into the embalming room. She pointed to the back door. "The police are coming. If we don't leave now, you're going to be arrested. Hang on—"

She grabbed the necklace off the counter, dropped it into a beaker and sloshed acetone over it. The smell made her eyes water, but it would dissolve pretty much anything if she let it soak long enough. "That'll clean off whatever finger prints you left. I'll just tell Tony I found it covered in grate gunk."

Liv ran back into the office, opened her bottom desk drawer and stuffed the beaker in under a sweater.

It would take a while for the acetone to work its magic. Hopefully no one would go looking in her drawers for anything.

Adam was waiting for her in the back alley wearing a nondescript grey sweatshirt she recognized from the lost and found box behind Tony's desk. He zipped it up, pulled the hood over his head and added a pair of sunglasses. They cut through a small park and jogged down a side street. Within seconds they were walking down Yonge, lost in the anonymity of an overflowing sidewalk.

"I didn't call them, you know," she said. "But we should think about turning that video card over the police."

"Screw that, I want to see what's on it."

"Look, I met a pretty decent police detective at the station the other night and she—"

"And you think she's going to invite us in to watch it with her?" Adam said. "How naïve are you about how the whole chain-of-evidence thing works? We hand that over to a cop, they pass it over to whoever's in charge of Cynn's case, it disappears into wherever police evidence is stored and we never get to find out what's on it. *Ever.* Unless at some point, years from now, some prosecutor or defence lawyer plays it in court. My own lawyer had to petition the judge to let him see any of the evidence against me in my own trial, and even that took forever. After what I went through when Brett was murdered, there's no way I'm just handing this over to the police unless I've seen it first and made my own copy. Besides, don't you want to see what that creep was recording?"

He had a point. As much as she wished that he didn't.

"Okay," Liv said, "but I'm not promising I won't hand it over to the police after we've seen it. Did you try opening it on my computer?"

"Yeah, but you didn't have the right kind of software, or video card, or drivers or whatever the hell it was missing to open high def video files."

Probably all three. Tony's computer was a total dinosaur.

"We'll have to take it to Gabriel—"

"No!"

"He'll definitely be able to open it and can maybe even trace DeathFetish's email address."

"Not Gabriel." Adam shook his head. "Please. You can't trust him with anything."

"Right, because Gabe's a loser and you're—"

"It's not like that. We just have a history, okay? There was an incident."

"An *incident*. What, like you helped throw him into a dumpster?"

"Hell no, Liv. I never laid a hand on anyone before I went to Meadowhurst. Ever."

She believed him. She didn't believe him. Of course she believed him. How *could* she believe him?

"Think. The guy who jumped me was tall—really

tall. So how do we know it's not him?"

"Don't you dare—"

"You know how Brett and those guys treated him. Maybe he snapped. Have you seen him recently? Has he been in a fight?"

So what if he had? Gabriel was always getting beaten up.

"Someone was lurking in Cynn's bushes with a video camera!" Adam added. "You can't tell me that doesn't sound like something Gabriel would do. Do you even know where Gabriel was the night Brett was murdered?"

"Of course I do! He was with me. He woke me up so we could watch this live social feed of Brett's party."

"Oh really? At what time?"

"Eleven thirty."

Adam howled in laughter. "Eleven thirty? Well, I hate to break it to you, but I was arrested around ten o'clock at night. Which means that Brett was murdered at nine something. Which would've given Gabriel plenty of time to kill Brett, drive back home, wake you up and get you to be his alibi."

No. She wouldn't let herself think of Gabriel like that. She couldn't.

Liv stepped right in front of Adam.

He stopped walking.

"Gabriel is my friend. The only decent one I've had since I moved to Toronto. He wouldn't use me like that. He doesn't attack people, he doesn't stalk people and he sure as hell doesn't *kill* people. You get that?"

"But—"

"You say one more word against him and I'm gone."

"Okay." Adam's shoulders sagged. "I just wish you had that much faith in me."

"I'm working on it."

They started walking again. "Alright, I've got another idea," she said, "but you're not going to like it much."

"Can't be worse than going to Gabriel."

"Ha ha." She stepped into an alley between two stores. He followed. "The school's got an amazing A/V suite in the auditorium sound booth. Gabriel's showed me how to get in after the school's closed without being seen. You can sneak in after school lets out, watch the video on one of the computers there and probably make yourself a copy." *Probably.* "Plus Gabriel's set up a special web browser thing on one of the computers there so you can even email DeathFetishGirl99. Gabe says the only person who's ever in there after hours is him, and I'll make sure he's with me and nowhere near the school."

"You're right. I hate that idea."

He turned to walk out of the alley.

"You came to me for help and I could've said no," Liv said.

Adam stopped.

"I'm not your saviour," she said, "and I can't make you trust me. Run away if you want. Go find someone else to help you whose ideas you like better. Or go back to Never Forget and stare at Cynn's body. I don't care. But you asked me for help, and this is the best idea I've got."

Adam opened his mouth as if he was about to snap back. Then he stopped and ran both hands through his hair.

"Alright. Fine. Show me how to break into the school and then go see Gabriel, and if I decide to go for it, I'll let you know how it goes."

She nodded slowly. "Okay, we'll pick up a thumb drive on the way over for you to copy the video onto. If you do get caught, don't tell anyone I helped you. Alright?"

"Of course!" he said.

He stood there for a moment in the alley, just staring at her, like there were a thousand words battling through his brain and fighting to come out at once. Then he just stopped and sat down on the dirty step of some store's back doorway.

"Look, I really am sorry, Liv."

She sat down beside him. "For what?"

"Last fall," he said. "For standing you up. For dating Cynn. For not ever talking to you after. Believing what those girls said. It was lame and stupid. But after Cynn and I hooked up, it kind of felt wrong to hang out with you while I was sort of her boyfriend, because she knew I kind of liked you—"

Liv slid her hand on his shoulder. "It's fine, Adam.

Whatever. Really. I'm over it." *Because it doesn't really matter if you liked me, if you didn't actually do anything about it, now did you?*

He looked at his feet. "I just wanted to say it, because you're cool. Okay? Not a lot of people would do this for someone."

"It's really no big deal."

"Yeah, it really is." He looked into her face. Then his fingers reached up like he was about to wipe a stray hair out of her eyes. But instead, he just tapped her lightly on the temple. And somehow, that felt even better. "And you're really smart to think of trying something like this. You've got the best brain of anyone I know. I'm sorry I didn't get that about you sooner."

She couldn't laugh and cry at the same time, so instead she stood up and walked out of the alley before Adam could see the look on her face.

If she was so smart, then why did she feel like an idiot?

Chapter Fifteen

A white marble angel stood inside the entrance of St. Michael's Hospital. One hand was raised to the sky. The other clutched a sword which he thrust into the enemy beneath him.

Gabriel gazed up into the angel's face, his eyes hidden behind sunglasses, his long coat draped around him like a shroud.

So what if the feed they'd watched of Brett's party wasn't live. It's not like Gabriel had ever explicitly said it was, right? Even then, would Gabriel really kill Brett then rush back to Toronto to use her as an alibi?

"You believe in heaven and hell?" Gabriel was still staring at the angel. "That we all get eternally rewarded or punished for what we do on earth?"

Of course Liv believed in some kind of existence after death—it wasn't like she had a choice. As to what kind of life exactly, and how you ended up where you did, she had no idea.

"I don't know." It was the safest answer she could think of. "Why?"

"Eternity is too long to wait for some people to get what's coming to them." He looked at her and smiled. "The psycho-killer website is getting a lot of hits, and no one's managed to track it back to me yet. The idea of betting on who's a murderer and who might get killed next is really pushing some people's creepy buttons. I've been playing around online, looking for other suspects or a clue as to who might be hiding evidence. I hacked into the school server and some social media accounts. I'll hit the heavy stuff later."

"What have you found?"

"A whole lot of nonsense. Sharona launched a huge last-minute campaign for queendom, which she'll probably get. Emma apparently cheated on Damien with someone, which might be why he was yelling at her the night Brett died. Can't even tell if it's a guy or another girl."

"Way to go, Emma."

"Cynn did the poor-me thing to the max after Adam was shipped off. Posted a lot of pathetic status updates. Even tried to write some terrible poetry. Cut a whole bunch of classes until she was getting D's in everything. Like she was trying to stay in high school forever, dead or alive."

Liv was surprised. Cynn, whatever her faults, was plenty smart. Maybe she'd just wanted to stay somewhere that she knew she was in control.

"Felix, on the other hand, is taking extra classes and fast-tracking her way to graduation. She was shortlisted for that Vitesse internship—and get this, so was Cynn."

"My mom says Felix works two jobs."

"Evenings she works at a warehouse. Total grunt work, too. Must be packing all kinds of muscle under those miniskirts."

Of course nobody ever thought of Felix as working class.

"Weekends, she's a photographer's assistant," he added. "Does weddings and stuff. She actually worked Eddy's brother's wedding a couple weeks ago. And Eddy tried just as hard to get into her pants there as he did at Brett's party. I can also tell you she hasn't flirted with anyone online since Brett died."

"Maybe she actually loved him."

"Or maybe she's just keeping her hook-ups offline," he said. "Eddy, on the other hand, is a busy boy and doesn't have a clue about privacy or decency. He's definitely fooling around with Sharona, but that hasn't stopped them both from swapping dirty pics with practically anybody. He's been suspended twice for drug use, but his family has money, so no one's in a hurry to expel him."

All of which could mean something—or absolutely nothing. Especially as the only link between the girls was that they were all in the running for prom queen, and the only reason Eddy was in the mix was because

MAGS STOREY

he'd probably be one contender's date and because he'd stolen another contender's burial clothes.

"I can't shake the feeling that all of this has something to do with Friday's dance," she said.

Gabriel raised an eyebrow. "People don't actually kill each other over proms."

"It does make the most sense."

He looked at her as if she were a child and he had to figure out how to explain something she was too young to understand.

Liv hated that look.

"Only if you leave Brett's murder out and you're desperately trying to prove Adam's not guilty."

"Come on. It doesn't take half a brain to go after someone as obvious as Adam," said Liv.

"Because it looks like he's guilty."

"So say all the lemmings."

"I can't believe you just said that." Gabriel grinned and started down a hallway. "You coming? Felix awaits."

By the time she caught up, he'd already jumped into an elevator.

"You know I wasn't being serious—"

"Shhh. Let me think." He reached out and pushed about twenty buttons. "When we get to the first stop, I'll jump out. You hold the elevator."

"But I—"

"Now!"

The doors opened. Gabriel sprinted down the

hallway, his coat flapping behind. Liv braced her foot against the door, but he was already running back.

"Wrong floor."

"How do you know?"

"Maternity ward."

"I thought you knew where she was."

"I do. She's somewhere in this hospital."

"And we're not just asking at the front desk because?"

"They won't tell me—I'm not a relative. So we find her the hard way."

"Why would they ban her from having visitors?"

"Oh, I don't know. Maybe because someone's trying to kill her?"

They were at the next floor. He darted out and nearly collided with a wheelchair-bound patient and a whole lot of balloons. Minutes later, he was back. "Not this one either."

The bell dinged again. Gabriel was gone a lot longer this time and strolled back looking smug.

"Found her. You ready?" He reached into his coat and pulled out a stuffed kangaroo. "Here. Give her this."

"What?" It was heavy and whirring faintly.

"Just do it. Trust me. It'll be a big hit."

"Whatever."

Now that she was here, Liv was starting to realize just how nervous she was. She'd spent months learning how to avoid bullies, and here she was about to go poke one of the biggest ones with a stick.

Felix was alone, in a double room, staring out the window. Her face was pale. Her hair hung stringy and dull around her face.

"Felix?"

"Crap! What are you doing here? How'd *you* get in?" She pulled the hospital blanket up to her shoulders. "If this is some kind of joke, I'm not laughing."

Liv put the stuffed kangaroo down on a table next to a French travel magazine. There was no chair. She thought about sitting on the edge of the bed but decided to stand.

"Oh, you know. Gabriel seduced one of the nurses. Anyway. How's it going?"

"How is it going?" Felix snorted. "Let's see . . . I've been stabbed. I'm in pain. I can't use the phone or the Internet or talk to any of my friends, or the press. They won't let me have any visitors. Then someone decides to let the two of you in?"

Wow, so they really were trying to cut her off from the outside world, then.

"I wanted to ask you about getting stabbed in the subway—"

"Awesome, so now I'm cheap entertainment for the Rosewood freaks."

Ignoring that.

"Did you get a good look at the person who stabbed you?" Liv asked. "Who were you there to meet?"

Felix turned her body toward the window.

"Go to hell."

"Hey! I'm the one who alerted the guards. I might've saved your life."

"You were there?" Felix's turned back from the window. Her eyebrows raised. "I didn't know that."

"You didn't?" Liv asked.

"No." Felix frowned. "Nobody's telling me anything."

Her dark eyes ran from Liv to Gabriel and back again. Liv could almost see the gears turning in her mind. Felix had never been a charming little master manipulator like Cynn. Blunt and direct had been more Felix's style. Felix didn't like them. She didn't want them there.

But Felix also needed something.

"I walked onto the subway, found you there and called security," Liv said. "I honestly thought you were dead at first,"

Liv stepped closer to the single bed. Gabriel didn't move from the doorway.

Felix looked down at her stomach. "I lost a lot of blood."

Liv risked perching on the very edge of the single bed, against the bed rails.

"I'm sorry," Liv said. "I can't believe that somebody didn't mention it to you."

"Who? Who exactly would've mentioned it to me?" Felix's snapped. "I might as well be in isolation. No friends. No internet. No social media. There was a guard standing around my door for the first day, but he wasn't exactly chatty."

Liv glanced back at Gabriel. He was looking over

his shoulder back into the hallway. Well, if any of the random people milling around were undercover cops none of them seemed eager to burst in and drag Liv and Gabriel out. For now.

"This detective came to interview me twice and both times she was really blunt and to the point," Felix added.

Liv nodded. "Jaz? Yeah, I met her too."

"Well, it's frustrating." Felix waved her hand toward the TV. "The news keeps saying there's a demented serial killer on the loose. They keep flashing Cynn's picture on TV and talking about how terrifying it is that a *beautiful* girl was tied down and murdered in her own bed, and how her escaped convict boyfriend is on the loose. Meanwhile, my best friend is dead, I'm in hospital, and it's like 'oh well, Felix doesn't matter.'"

Didn't matter? Or wasn't being allowed to have a herd of news cameras trampling through the hospital hallways, turning her into a media whore for some sensationalist story?

"Well, maybe they're trying to protect you," Liv said. *Or protect their investigation from being compromised by one loudmouthed teenage girl.* "Your boyfriend and best friend were both murdered. And you *were* hanging out with Cynn before she was killed, right?"

Felix's eyes opened wide. "How would you even know that?"

Liv glanced back at Gabriel. His eyebrows nearly shot up to the ceiling. His eyes met Liv's and he mouthed *What the?*

Oh right, Cynn's dead body had told her that. Not the easiest thing to explain away. "Lucky guess."

"Yeah, and they asked about that but that's hardly important." Felix rolled her eyes. "Like I told the detective, we hung out every day. That's what best friends do. Cynn wanted to show off her dress. I tried on mine. Then I left, and she was still alive when I got stabbed."

Which fit with what Adam said. He saw Cynn was alive after Felix was stabbed, and then got decked by Cynn's stalker.

"Maybe we can help you." Gabriel's smile was doing a big bad wolf impression. "You know what's the biggest website in the world right now on the topic of Cynn's death? Mine."

Felix blinked. Gabriel yanked his phone out of his pocket, opened the browser to the page, and then walked over to the bed and stuck the phone in front of Felix's nose. She tried to grab it. He didn't let her.

"It's anonymous of course. Launched it this morning. I'm running an online poll on who Cynn's killer could be and another on who the next victim's going to be. Congratulations, by the way, yours is the top named voted as 'victim.' Most visitors seem to think you're just a mid-afternoon shower or late night walk in the park from being sliced into tiny pieces."

A very small smile crossed Felix's lips. "Really?"

"Yup." And now, he was actually cocky enough to sit down on the very edge of the bed beside Liv. Gabriel stretched his legs out and crossed them at the ankles.

"It's been trending on dozens of social media sites. Getting some traction among people who like creepy gore. The voting aspect's big. Plus the shock factor of a pretty teenage girl dying tied down on her own bed. Add the fact it's prom season, and that she was a potential prom queen. Of course, a bunch of the coverage is denouncing how horrible and depraved it is. But it's still driving traffic my way. Hate clicks are still clicks. And the comments section is flooded with people who want to tell me just how sick I am. But there's nothing the internet likes more than a controversial freak show. I'm already over eight hundred thousand hits. You want a big long interview on my site, you can have it. You tell us what you know, and I'll make sure the whole damn world finds out."

Felix's brow furrowed.

Liv leaned closer.

"My mom is friends with your mom. She's told me all this stuff about how crappy the divorce was and how strong you were when your dad left. How you totally worked you ass off to be independent, get scholarships, make your own money. I respect that." Oddly, that part was true. "I know how bad you want that Vitesse internship. You think they're not watching the news too? Wondering what really happened? Wondering if you're even still up for it? You know the Vitesse people will probably be making their decision any day now."

And here she was, lying so hard she half expected her panties to burst into flames.

"You seriously going to let some psycho take that away from you? I saw what he did to you and I'm totally on your side here."

Felix was hooked. Liv could tell because she was trying to look bored.

Liv took a deep breath. "We have to make sure no one can search for Cynn, Adam or Brett online without seeing your side of the story. Now, we can do it all by ourselves, but isn't it better coming directly from you? Your perspective? Your words?"

"Fine." Felix sat up straighter, emitted a theatrical sigh and raised both hands as if surrendering. "But I want the record to show I'm only doing this because I want to help catch Brett's killer. I loved him. For real. I loved Cynn too. Now they're both dead and I'm afraid I'm next."

An impressively realistic tear rolled down her cheek.

Gabriel cleared his throat.

Liv ignored him. "Did they have any enemies?"

Felix shook her head. "Some losers were jealous of us. Obviously. But Cynn was a real sweetie and Brett was amazing."

Gabriel snorted. Then coughed loudly as Liv stomped on his foot.

Felix turned to him. "I don't give a crap what you think, asshole. Brett was way more man than you'll ever be. When he was murdered, it was like my whole world was over—which is why I've been killing myself to get this scholarship with his family's airline."

"Right." Gabriel stood up. "Completely selfless move on your part."

"Cut it out, Gabe." Liv's eyes met his. *You think I like this any more than you?*

She turned back to Felix. "Sorry about him. Now, I saw the email telling you to be on the subway. You know who it was from?"

Felix was still glaring at Gabriel. She looked back at Liv and shook her head. "No idea. Some freak calling herself DeathFetishGirl99."

"Did you get any other emails?"

"No."

"Who did you tell about it?"

"No one."

Gutsy. Or incredibly stupid.

"Weren't you scared?"

"Yeah, of course I was scared. I'm not a goddamn robot. But they said they knew who had the murder weapon. You think I wouldn't do anything to make sure Brett's killer paid for what he did?"

"Except, apparently, go to the police," Gabriel said.

"You mean the cops that swarmed all over Brett's murder scene, threw all my friends in handcuffs but somehow *missed* finding the actual murder weapon? Or the cops that showed up at my front door last summer after my crappy excuse of a father tried to have me charged with some crap about his car? The sheer stupidity of the questions they asked me after I got stabbed makes me so regret I didn't go running to them to begin with." She rolled her eyes. "Like I believe for one second you two losers would've trusted the cops to handle it."

Touché.

"Did you see who stabbed you?" Liv asked.

"Of course, but he was masked."

"What kind of mask?"

"Uh, ski mask? Duh. You know, one of those ones with eyeholes and a mouth hole? Plus jeans and a black hoodie. Anyway, he just ran in and plunged a huge dagger into my gut. I thought I was going to die."

"Only you didn't," Gabriel said.

Liv gave him a dirty look. Felix gave him a filthy look.

He ignored both. "Was it a knife or a dagger?"

"Who cares? It was big. It stabbed me. It hurt like hell."

"And the guy?" Liv asked.

"He ran away."

"Did he say anything?"

"No."

"And you're sure it was a guy?"

"Like I'm just going to let another girl stab me?"

Well, depended on the girl. Felix probably could have flattened someone like Emma with a single punch.

"How big was he?" Liv asked. "Taller than Adam? Shorter than Gabriel?"

Gabriel said, "Bigger than a breadbox?"

Liv turned toward him. "Knock it off."

Felix sighed, a real one this time. "This is pointless, and I'm done talking to you."

Liv looked at Gabriel. "Give me a sec alone, okay? I'll meet you in the hall in two minutes."

He grabbed the kangaroo from the table, stuffed it back under his coat and walked out.

She turned back to Felix. "Sorry. He's in a weird mood and his timing sucks. So, what more can you tell me about the killer?"

Felix looked up at the ceiling. "He was taller than me and thin. Not built like Brett."

So definitely not Eddy then. "Did you think it was Adam?"

"I don't know."

"How can you not know?"

Felix's eyes slid toward the empty doorway. "Yeah, I thought it was Adam. Seemed like him anyway. But Adam was still my friend and I'm not going to go blabbing a friend's name on that freak's website unless I'm absolutely sure."

Liv took a deep breath. "Do you think Adam killed Brett?"

"No. Maybe. I don't know. The Adam I know wouldn't kill anyone. Doesn't have the backbone for it. He's always been a follower, right? A total beta. But Adam was really drunk or high that night. Totally out of it. Like he didn't know where he was or what he was doing. So, if he did, it wouldn't have been on purpose.

But now that Cynn's dead, and I got stabbed, and he escaped Meadowhurst . . ." She shrugged. "Who knows what Adam's really capable of? Maybe he's not the person any of us think he is."

For a split second, Liv's mind darted back to what it had been like sitting next to Adam in the alley. Yeah, a few days ago she'd have agreed Adam was the kind of guy who just did things without thinking. Was he actually starting to grow up?

"Is there anyone else you think could've done it?" Liv asked.

Felix shrugged.

"Or do you have a theory about who killed Cynn?"

"I'm done talking. It's really none of your business anyway."

"Hey, I'm only trying to help."

"Who? Me? Yourself? That joker in the hall? You think I don't know there's a big-ass reward out there?"

"Why do I get the feeling there's something you're still not telling me?"

Felix picked up the nurse-call button and pushed it repeatedly. "Obviously I need to have a guard back on my door, considering my life is probably still in danger and this hospital apparently lets in any freak who walks past."

Liv's shoulders tightened.

"Kick out the person who's trying to find your attacker if you want, but I don't care how fierce or tough you are, Vitesse would be stupid to hand an internship meant to boost their image on social media to a total bitch. At least Cynn knew how to pretend to be nice."

"You stay out of my business."

"My pleasure. And, for the record, I hope the next time somebody stabs you, they finish the job."

I can't believe I said that! thought Liv. She walked into the hall. Gabriel was gone.

Chapter Sixteen

Liv sat in the hallway for fifteen minutes watching people come and go. Nurses. Doctors. Patients in hospital gowns.

People on gurneys.

Gabriel had disappeared. And what Cynn had said about her abilities earlier nagged at her. She was pretty sure other people couldn't come into Never Forget and talk to the dead. But could *she* talk to them if she were away from Never Forget?

Trust Cynn to suggest the one really cool thing about her wasn't that big a deal. It wasn't like she could run around looking for corpses to talk to.

At least, not normally.

There had to be dozens of dead people in the hospital right now. Lying in their rooms waiting to be transferred to the morgue. Lying in the morgue waiting to be transported to places like Never Forget.

Madame Delilah, the no-doubt crazy kook who hung around outside Never Forget, claimed she could feel the dead calling to her. Liv closed her eyes and tried to reach out with her mind for a link. She felt nothing.

Alright then. Now what?

It wasn't like she could just aimlessly wander the hallways, waiting to hear that long beep noise they used on television shows whenever somebody flatlined.

Then again, there was nothing to stop her from hanging around the loading bay hoping to spot a corpse transportation guy she recognized. She'd had to arrange the transportation of the recently deceased from the hospital morgue to Never Forget more times than she could count. It was kind of a specialized line of work and you tended to see the same faces over and over again.

Like having a steady mail carrier bringing you dead people.

She took the elevator back to the lobby and walked around the building until she found the loading bay. It was open and there were a couple of people milling around she didn't recognize. No gurneys. No corpses.

She grabbed a drink from the coffee shop across the street, sat on a low wall close enough to the loading bay so she could watch it without being obvious.

Half an hour passed. Then an hour. Then an hour and a half.

It was a total waste of time. People came and went. None she recognized.

Then a nondescript blue van pulled in.

A tall, skinny guy with slicked-back hair hopped out and started for the loading bay.

Damien.

The pre-med student.

The corpse transporter.

The angry boyfriend of Emma the prom queen contestant.

Unaccounted for during Brett's murder.

Liv hurried over. She caught up with him just inside the loading bay.

"Hey! Damien!" She raised a hand in greeting. "How's it going?"

He kept walking. She kept pace beside him as if she was meant to be there. Nobody stopped them.

"Do I know you?" He didn't even look at her. He just waved his hand in her direction like she was some insect buzzing by his ear and not even a person. There was something so cold in his voice it was creepy.

"Yeah, I work at Never Forget," said Liv. "The funeral home on St. Clair?"

Damien pulled out his phone and started texting. She followed him into a nondescript room at the bottom of what looked like a service elevator, and kept talking. "You bring me bodies sometime. I'm getting into transport now too. You know, how some funeral homes do all their own transport of bodies? Like that.

I'm here to pick someone up. It's my first pickup."

It was rather amazing how good she'd gotten at lying in such a short period of time.

Damien couldn't have looked less interested if he tried.

The elevator arrived. Damien didn't get on. Instead, a middle-aged woman in scrubs pushed out a gurney with a corpse in a body bag. Gurney woman must've thought she was with Damien because she didn't even blink. She pulled a clipboard off the side, and she and Damien stepped over to the counter and started doing what looked like some kind of corpse transport paperwork.

Neither of them was looking at her.

Liv looked down at the body.

Right, well, now she had a dead body. But absolutely no chance to talk to it.

She stood with her back to them and brushed her hand against the body bag. The zipper was open a tiny crack. She slid one finger in and opened her mind.

This might just be the dumbest thing I've ever done, but—

"Young lady! What on earth do you think you're doing?"

The voice was loud, male and pissed off. It belonged to the corpse now scowling at her from inside the body bag. He had a neatly trimmed white beard and wore a black robe with a round collar.

Holy crap. She'd just opened a connection with a priest.

He frowned.

"I'll thank you to not use profanity."

Hang on. How had he just heard her swear?

She'd never been able to connect with a corpse just in her mind before. She'd always needed to talk to them. And it was confusing as hell. Just how quickly were her abilities expanding? Just how strong was she getting?

First she'd been able to see Cynn's projection in ways she'd never seen a ghost move before. Now—

I can talk to corpses inside my own mind?

The priest's image convulsed, like he was trying to get away and couldn't figure out how.

"Let me go. I have to ascend."

To where? You think I interrupted you on your way to heaven?

She'd met quite a couple of those, but normally they weren't so cranky.

His nostrils twitched. "The living do not belong in the land of the dead. As it is written in the Holy Scriptures, 'between your world and theirs there is a vast gulf that none should pass.'"

The elevator dinged behind her.

Trust me. I'm not actually in the land of the dead. We're just chatting inside my own mind. That's how this works. I open my mind. On purpose. And your spirit slips in.

And, apparently, it didn't just work inside the funeral home.

His voice dropped to something that almost sounded like pity. "Then you are in danger, my child.

All humans are entrusted with one mind, one heart and one soul. When you let others invade them—"

Look. No one's invading anything—

"What the hell do you think are you doing?" Damien snapped.

She leapt back. Gurney woman had apparently gotten back on the elevator and left.

Damien looked angry enough to snap her in half.

"Nothing. I was just—"

"Get your goddamn hands off that body!"

She stepped back and raised her hands. "I wasn't touching anything—"

"Don't you even bother lying!" Damien's eyes narrowed. His voice rose. "You think this is a joke? You don't touch my bodies. You don't mess with what I'm transporting. Ever. You got it?"

The video she'd seen of Damien screaming at his girlfriend at Brett's party flashed through her mind. And suddenly she got why Emma had looked terrified.

"You want me to call your boss and report you?"

"Got it. Sorry. I didn't mean . . . I've gotta go sort something . . ."

Liv turned and scrambled back along the hallway, hoping Damien would forget she'd said she was there to pick up a body.

She could hear Damien rolling the gurney down the hall behind her.

"Don't you ever let me catch you around my pickups again until you learn some basic respect!" he yelled.

Liv rushed out onto the sidewalk and started

walking so fast she was almost running.

Her heart was pounding.

The air outside was thick with the threat of rain. Grey buildings rose up on every side. Dark clouds squatted low in the sky.

Liv pushed her way through the station doors and a subway rumbled in the distance.

The memory of Adam's hands filled her mind. . . .

She bit her lip so hard she tasted blood.

She found a pay phone and called voicemail. There were two messages. The first one was from Mom.

"Hey, Livvy. Just calling to let you know that on top of working the night shift tonight, I'm also gonna be working a double shift on Wednesday night. Won't be home until after nine on Thursday morning. Hope I see you tonight if you make it home before I leave for work."

The second one was from Tony.

"Everything went well with the police walk-through. Nothing else was stolen. If you get a chance, can you pop into the office and e-mail Cynthia's measurements to my daughter Kiara? She's making her a new burial dress, and I left the numbers on your desk. Thanks a lot. You're a saint."

Yeah.

The security tape around Never Forget was wet and twisted in the wind. Liv slipped into the alley and headed for the back door,

A pale light glowed in the prep room window.

What the—?

She opened the door. The room was filled with candles.

Chapter Seventeen

Someone had pulled the sheet covering Cynn's body down to the top of her cleavage and smeared pink lipstick on her lips. Her hair was decorated with rose petals. The air in the prep room was thick with incense. It was really, *really* creepy.

"You've got to get out of here." Adam was standing behind the door.

"Are you out of your mind?" Wow, just when she'd thought that Adam might be growing up, he'd gone and pulled a stupid stunt like this. "What the hell do you think you're doing?"

"I'll explain later, but right now, you've got to go."

"Like hell I will—"

"The girl may stay." The voice was high-pitched and whiney. Madame Delilah stepped out of the shadows, clutching a stick of incense. She wore purple robes, too much jewellery, and way too much makeup.

She looked at Liv. "The spirit of Cynthia has commanded you to stay."

Oh goody.

"You let her in?" Liv turned to Adam. "Are you kidding me with this?"

At least he hadn't gotten caught and wasn't in jail right now. Not that this was much better.

"She let herself in! I never fixed what I did to the backdoor, and I guess she got in that way. I got into the school, I copied the video and all of DeathFetishGirl99's emails onto a thumb drive and I left as fast as I could. When I got here, she was already inside."

"And you didn't kick her out?"

"She said that Cynn's ghost had a message for me!"

"And you believed her?" She shook her head. "What about the video file?"

"It's of Cynn. Someone was stalking her."

Madame Delilah was now humming. She waved her hands around like she was picking cosmic trash out of the air and tossing it over her shoulders.

The whole thing looked ridiculous. It probably was ridiculous. Right? Then again, Liv had never watched anyone else connect with a corpse. For all she knew, there were hundreds of people who could talk to the dead, and all of them used cheap scented candles.

"Liv, she already seems to know a lot about who I am, and who Cynn is, and that we were a couple, and—"

"Like anyone who has an Internet connection! Trust me, the internet is having a field day with Cynn's death. How do you know she's not going to run right to the police and turn you in?"

"Well, it's kind of too late to worry about that now! She's already seen me!"

"The spirit is ready to speak." Madame Delilah fixed her eyes on Adam. "You must follow my process fully and without question. Do you understand?"

He nodded.

"You are to stand by her head and take her hand in yours." She glanced at Liv. "And you? The spirit wishes you to stand at her feet."

Of course she did.

As much as Liv hated going along with something this stupid, she had to admit part of her was kind of curious too. Especially if this nut job turned out to be legit.

"Silence." Delilah's hands shot toward the sky. "The dead girl's spirit is present. Everyone must now close their eyes."

Liv was still halfway across the room, but no one seemed to care.

Madame Delilah waved her hands above Cynn's head, while her keen eyes scanned Adam's face.

His eyes were clamped shut. "Ask her who she was fooling around with."

"The spirit does not wish to answer questions."

Now, that sounded like Cynn.

"The spirit is giving me a memory. Something she wishes to relive."

"Yeah, alright. But then I need some answers, okay?"

Liv stepped to the end of the table.

"The girl wishes to reunite your spirits."

He shrugged. "Whatever."

"She wishes to remember the eternal, ethereal link formed the moment her body last united with the body of another."

His eyes opened. Irritation flashed across them. "What the hell?"

"Do you remember that moment?"

"Uh, no."

His eyes met Liv's. Then he quickly shut them again.

If Delilah noticed, she didn't let it show. "Then we shall remember it for you. I see it now. In a vision, unfolding in my mind. It is night. You two are standing alone." She was sort of dancing now, waving a pungent incense stick above her head. She didn't even touch the body.

Liv put her hands on Cynn's feet. A connection hummed at the edge of her consciousness. Cynn knew she was there.

"Your lips brush against hers," Delilah said. "Soft. Warm. Inviting."

Liv pushed the connection back and opened her eyes. Cynn and Adam going at it was one headspace she didn't want to get into.

"She shivers. She is frightened, like a pure white dove. You take her face in your hands."

Yup, sounded exactly like the sweet, innocent Cynn the whole rest of the world wanted to believe in and nothing like the real bitch she actually was.

"You're sure this is me she's thinking about?"

"Silence! You will disrupt the spiritual connection."

His eyes were still closed, but Liv could tell Adam was seriously pissed off. Good—he *so* should have seen something like this coming.

"Her shoulders quiver. She wants you desperately. You can see it hiding behind the shyness of her eyes. . . ."

Someone was really laying the whole virginal routine on thick.

The incense grew thicker. Liv blinked. The moment her eyelids closed, Cynn's face jumped into view. Liv opened her eyes again, and the image was gone.

"Desire burns between you like a flame. . . ."

Liv's eyelids were growing heavy. She blinked again, slower this time. Cynn's body wriggled on the table, but no one else seemed to notice.

"Your fingers brush beneath the edges of her shirt. . . ."

Liv gave up and let her eyes close. Cynn smiled, rolled sideways on the table and slid one bare leg out from under the sheet.

"Welcome back," Cynn said. "What's new?"

The air felt thick.

"Your lips trace down her swanlike neck. . . ."

Delilah's voice was growing faint. Liv wished they'd hurry up and get the damn story over with.

The last time Cynn got laid was really none of her business.

Cynn giggled. "Aw, come on. You trying to tell me you're not curious?"

Liv shrugged. *I don't care. I really don't care.*

The spirit laughed. "Of course you do."

First the crazy old priest. Now her? How were they reading her thoughts without her having to talk out loud? It was handy, yeah. But kind of unsettling too. Okay, whenever this whole mess with Adam was over, she'd have to seriously figure out just how deep this talking-with-the-dead thing could actually go.

"Come on. Admit it. You've always wondered what it was like."

Yeah, but I never wanted to picture it.

Cynn shifted her body on the table, like she was looking for company. "Our last time was incredible. We were at this cottage by the lake. We were both really drunk. He looked so hot. I just jumped him and started licking his neck."

The image of a room flickered in the back of Liv's mind. Huge windows. Wood beams.

"Dude was so surprised he spilled his beer. All over the carpet. He was wearing this gold chain, right? I wrapped it around my hand and dragged him to the nearest bedroom. . . ."

Delilah kept droning on. "You take her hand in yours and gently lead her toward the bed."

"My other hand was going for his pants," Cynn said.

"Hang on," Adam sounded really agitated. "Can we just stop this for a second?"

Yeah, can we?

"If you interrupt again, the spirit will depart."

Adam let out a hard breath.

"We were making out like crazy," Cynn said. "He grabbed me and threw me down on the bed so hard I bounced off and hit the floor—"

Charming.

"She stands before you. You embrace her tenderly and promise to be gentle—"

"I'm on the floor, and he orders me to stay there. There's this old boat rope hanging on the patio. He gets this sexy, dangerous look on his face—"

Oh, hell no . . .

"You stroke her skin gently, nervously. Your fingers tremble . . ."

"He starts flicking it at me. Growling at me like a wild dog . . ."

"Trembling fingers?" Adam asked. "This really doesn't sound right."

"Yeah, it sure as hell doesn't." Liv stepped back. The link snapped. She gulped in a deep breath. The air felt clearer. "Why is it what I'm hearing and what you're hearing are totally different? Apparently the spirit's giving you sweet chick-flick clichés, and all I'm hearing about is kinky cottage sex."

"Hang on," Adam opened his eyes and practically jumped back from the body. "Who said anything about kinky cottage sex?"

Delilah glared at her. "The spirit wishes her to

depart. She is disruptive to the psychic currents."

Liv stared her down. "Or maybe you're just making it up as you go along."

"Who told you we had kinky cottage sex?"

Delilah waved her arms wildly at Liv, like she was practically swathed in psychic toxic waste. "I insist this girl is expelled. She is trying to pollute the spiritual connection of your love."

Adam closed his eyes again. When he spoke, his voice sounded strangled. "Get out."

Liv raised her hands. "Now, hang on—"

"Not you." He opened his eyes. "Her."

"But the spirit—"

"Is full of crap. Cynn and I made out some, but I never actually slept with her."

Chapter Eighteen

Liv washed the makeup from Cynn's face, tidied the corpse then pulled the sheet back over the body. Adam and Delilah argued in the alley. She opened the back door and threw the candles into the dumpster. Neither of them looked at the body.

When Liv went back inside, Adam followed. "Hey. About that—"

"You're lucky I know how to wash a corpse."

She handed him a broom.

"If only one of us had considered the possibility Madame Delilah might have been getting all her mystical inner knowledge from the internet. I just hope that if she does go to the police, she's too loony for them to believe her."

Adam started sweeping up petals.

"You know, it's not just the media that are calling you and Cynn lovers. After you were arrested, there must've been at least twenty girls at Rosewood who claimed they'd slept with you too. How many of them were lying?"

"Are we really going to do this now?"

"You're the one who let some lunatic turn my work into a freak show."

"Believe whatever you want, but I never slept with Cynn. Or anyone."

"So everyone spreads lies about you?"

Adam ran his hand over his face, like he was trying to rub away a particularly nasty memory. "Look, why the hell are we fighting about this anyway? You know as well as I do what Rosewood is like. Spoiled, selfish little rich kids pushing each other down to stay on top. You and I were in the same boat—"

"Some of us didn't even *get* boats! You expect me to feel sorry for you because your friends were assholes? Because the parties you were invited to were lame or too many rich bitches claimed you were hot in bed? Can you even hear yourself? You were allowed to exist. You could walk down the hall without looking over your shoulder, or wondering when someone was going to shove you into a wall, or grab your stuff, or force your head down a toilet."

She turned her back on him and wrapped her arms around herself.

Adam put his arms around her shoulders from behind. "I'm sorry. I shouldn't have said that. I only meant—"

"Damn right you shouldn't."

"You always seemed so hard, you know? Like it all just washed off you and you didn't even care."

She leaned against him and stared at the floor.

"You don't get it, Adam. You coudn't."

"Maybe, I didn't. Not like I should've. But . . ." His voice dropped until he was almost whispering. "I was terrified at Meadowhurst. Like seriously shit-scared. It really *is* a hell hole. I'd gone from being Cynn's boyfriend to being the kind of guy the worst bullies picked on. And I'd . . ." His voice cracked, like he was trying not to cry. "I'd rather die than go back there. It's like I'm trapped in a nightmare and can't wake up."

Whoa. Okay, so maybe he did get it. Some. Even if he never had before.

She turned to face him. And for a moment his hands just stayed on her shoulders, until they were standing there, face to face, close enough to kiss if they'd wanted to. Then he just let his hands drop back to his sides.

"I'm sorry you were in a real bad place," Liv said. "I guess I never thought that a guy like you would ever have that happen to them. And I still don't get how. A few weeks ago you're this hot, rich son-of-a-bitch that everybody wants to be around. Then suddenly, what? Your lawyer isn't even trying? You've got no one to go to for help?"

"You really don't get it. You think I actually matter to anyone?"

"But . . ."

"But *what*, Liv?"

"You were popular."

"*So*? You think that means anything? My dad loves his career ten times more than me. The guys at school called themselves my friends because I paid for beer and let them use my stuff. You think Cynn could love *anyone* besides herself? The truth is, nobody actually cares about me."

"Well, *I* care about you! And look where that got me."

They were still standing so close that they could barely breathe without their chests touching.

"Yeah and I screwed it up. I let you down. I get that, Liv. Believe me, I do!" He looked up at the ceiling and shook his head. "What do you want from me? You want me to tell you again that I didn't kill anyone? You want me to let you read these stupid emails I thought were from you?" He yanked a thumb drive from his pocket and slammed it down on the counter. "Here. I copied them all onto this. DeathFetishGirl99 hasn't emailed me once since I left Meadowhurst. She's not even trying to help me now. If she's even still alive. The video's on there too. I saved it in a basic format Tony's machine should be able to open."

Liv stepped back and took a deep breath. Probably not a bad idea to get out of this room, anyway. It was like there was still something weird floating in the air. An intensity. An electricity hovering over her skin. Almost like Cynn's link was still open.

She picked up the thumb drive, walked into the office and switched on her computer. There was a long, black garment bag hanging on the coatrack. Presumably Tony's daughter had dropped off a burial dress for Cynn without waiting for the measurements. Wouldn't be the first time she'd sewn a corpse into clothes. Liv sat down and rummaged on her desk for Cynn's measurements, anyway, and emailed them to Kiara.

Adam appeared in the doorway.

Her eyes scanned his face. Nervous? Embarrassed? He flushed slightly and looked away.

She swallowed. "You ready?"

He dragged Tony's chair out from behind his desk and sat down beside her. He was so close, his knee was practically touching hers.

Like she wasn't distracted enough as it was. "Here we go."

She plugged the drive into her computer and opened the folder. Two files, one text and one video. She clicked on the video.

A girl stood in a window, half hidden by a veil of gauzy curtains. Cynn. The camera zoomed in closer. She was in her panties with a thin tank top that barely covered her chest.

Liv's stomach churned. This was so wrong.

They watched for a moment as Cynn picked up her prom dress, held it to her chest and frowned. She sucked her stomach in. Then she reached for a smoothie sitting on her dresser. It was green, thick and looked disgusting. She took a sip and grimaced.

Her movements were slow, shaky. She dropped the drink, spilling half of it on the dresser. Then she turned and started toward them, practically falling into the curtains.

Drunk? Probably.

Cynn opened the window and stared directly at the camera. Like she knew he was there. And that he was watching.

Liv clicked on the volume.

"I already tried that. There's no sound."

She sat back. "That sucks."

Cynn was yelling something at the camera and waving her hands like she was losing her temper. It looked like she was verging on going ballistic.

Wow. "I've never seen her lose it like that."

Adam's face was grim. "Me neither."

Cynn's eyes flashed. She looked like she was furious. No . . . Wait . . .

Then Cynn started taking her top off.

Chapter Nineteen

Liv could feel her face squinch up in distaste.

"Don't worry, she doesn't actually strip," Adam said. "She's more like teasing the guy."

Of course she was.

Cynn pulled her top back down and gave the camera the finger.

"And you've never seen her this out of control?"

He shifted in his seat. "I've seen her act really crazy in a manic kind of way. Like she's trying to have angry fun and doesn't care who gets hurt. But only when she's really drunk or really high. Now, watch this."

The camera was moving again. At first Liv just saw the fence. Then Adam's face appeared over the top. He hauled himself up, threw his leg over and jumped down the other side. The cameraman zoomed in.

She sucked in a breath. "He knew you were there."

Adam nodded. "Yup, and he wanted to get me on camera."

She wanted to know if Cynn saw Adam there too. But the camera never went back to the window. Instead it focused on Adam as he kept coming closer and closer, like some hapless victim from a horror B movie.

The camera moved back. A tree blocked their view. Then Adam's face appeared for a second, full in the shot. A gloved fist coldcocked him in the jaw. The video stopped.

Liv sat back and let out a long breath.

"Not my finest moment." Adam pushed the chair back and stood up. He walked over to the door, then turned around and came back. "This proves there was someone else there, and that Cynn saw him. She probably even knew who it was. Maybe the other guy she was fooling around with. So, yeah, when I saw Madame Delilah in the prep room trying to set up a séance I thought, what the hell, and went for it."

Liv turned off the computer and stood. "I don't want to have to explain to the police where I got this video from. But I'll email it anonymously from school to Crime Stoppers tomorrow."

"Liv, this proves I was there!"

"But if it would help clear your name—"

"Of Cynn's murder maybe! But not Brett's murder. Not the murder I was actually charged with."

There were tears in the corners of his eyes. She wanted to reach him and somehow take his pain away—

"I just wish . . ." He shrugged.

"You wish what?"

"I wish I could've talked to Cynn."

Liv hesitated for what felt like a long moment. "You can." Her voice seemed to come from somewhere far away, as if her mouth was just a speaker whose source was a distant radio station. This huge secret she'd been so afraid of ever trusting anyone with suddenly didn't seem so huge.

Maybe because Adam had even more to lose than she did.

"Come on." She walked back into the prep room and pulled Cynn's sheet back down to her shoulders.

He followed. "What are you doing?"

"I can either talk about it, or I can do it."

She grabbed Cynn's shoulder.

Her face swam into view. Her mouth opened, but Liv wasn't about to let her get a word in.

"Hey, Cynn." She spoke loud and clear, like she was trying to reach someone with bad cell reception. "I'm back."

Chapter Twenty

Cynn's image rose from her corpse like a phoenix. Her lips drew back. "Where do you get off disappearing on me like that?"

At least she wasn't trying to leave the table this time.

"What are you doing?" Adam sounded more than a little freaked.

"I'm talking to Cynn. She's pissed at me because she was making up some stupid sex story earlier and I walked off in the middle of it."

Adam's eyes opened wide.

"Go to hell, freak. Why should I say another word to you when you're a total bitch to me?"

"Will you just be quiet a minute?"

"This is seriously weird," Adam said. "It sounds like . . . are you actually—"

"Hang on." She grabbed his hand with her other hand. "Give me a minute."

She turned back to Cynn. "Adam's here. He wants me to ask you some questions."

Cynn laughed. "And you think I'm just going to answer?"

Liv looked at Adam. "Look. I've got a connection open. I'll ask her whatever you like, but don't expect her to be civil."

Cynn snorted.

Adam swallowed hard. "Just stop a second. Okay? This really doesn't feel right."

"What's your problem? Half an hour ago you were ready to do some weird psychic link with Delilah and Cynn. Now suddenly the thought of a little post-mortem chat is making you nervous?"

"That was different. She's a random crazy lady. I know you. We were in the same English class. And she'd let herself in. So I just kind of went with it and didn't stop her."

Because just going along with what other people were doing had always worked so well for Adam in the past.

Liv linked her fingers through his. "You're the one who suggested we try trusting each other."

"Just . . . just get that this is weird for me. Okay?"

Right. And the feel of his warmth on her skin wasn't distracting in the slightest.

"You were willing to believe Madame Delilah could talk to Cynn's ghost but not me?"

His fingers tightened in hers. He looked down at

the body. "Maybe. I don't know. I'm almost hoping you really can't. Because, Cynn might be dead, but she'd still hurt you if she had the chance."

"I'm not going to give her the chance." Liv turned her attention back to Cynn again. "Adam's trying to prove he's innocent. We think the same person who killed you also killed Brett and tried to kill Fe—"

"You think I'm just going to let you use me so you can cozy up to my boyfriend?"

"It's not like that."

"It's exactly like that."

Liv looked at Adam and rolled her eyes then homed in on Cynn. "You want your murderer to get caught, don't you?"

"Uh huh." She crossed her arms. "And, of course, you're just helping him to make sure my killer is brought to justice."

Okay, choosing to ignore that. "Adam thinks you cheated on him, you know."

"Screw you."

"Speaking of screwing, we know someone was filming you through your window the night you died. Real classy how you offered him a peep show."

"What? Where?"

She actually sounded surprised. Or at least confused. Maybe she had actually been high or blackout drunk.

"On a video camera, in the bushes outside your window. You actually yelled at the guy and gave him the finger. You don't remember?"

Cynn frowned. Her forehead wrinkled.

"Look, were you cheating on Adam with anyone? Or even just started to see someone after he got arrested? If you were, he could be who killed you. If not, someone else could have been stalking you. Either way, it matters."

Cynn was quiet.

Oh, come on bitch, just admit you were messing around with somebody else, so I don't have to pretend to feel guilty about wanting some other girl's guy.

What the hell?

Hang on, Liv thought. That did *not* sound like herself.

Sure, she liked Adam—maybe a lot—but she wasn't that shallow. It was like ideas kept popping up in her head that she wasn't actually thinking.

"What's happening?" Adam asked. "Are you talking to her? Is something happening?"

"You can't see anything different? Nothing happening?"

"No."

Not that surprising considering Tony couldn't either.

"Yeah, I'm talking to Cynn, but her mood is weird right now," said Liv.

"Oh, I've got plenty to say." Cynn's image grew larger and brighter, her colours more vibrant, as if something was bringing her into focus. "You really want me to do some three-way chat with you between him and me? Fine, but we play by my rules. You've got to promise to repeat every single word I say back to him, exactly like I say it, or I'm leaving."

"You can't leave."

"Try me."

She vanished. Liv closed her eyes and pressed in deeper. The image floated back.

"Okay. I'll do it, but only because I don't want to waste energy fighting you."

Cynn smiled. "You will repeat what I say. Word for word. No changes."

"Got it." Liv turned to Adam. "Before you ask questions, I've got to do something for her first. I've got to repeat what she wants me to tell you, word for word."

To his credit, he didn't roll his eyes.

She closed her eyes again and strained her inner ear for Cynn's voice. She was whispering. Her words came slowly and steadily. Words Liv didn't want to repeat.

"She says she knows you're just using me. She says you might be a coward and a dickhead, but even you wouldn't stoop so low as to mess around with a girl like me unless you were getting something really major out of it."

"Aw, come on . . ."

Liv shushed him. "Correction, a *filthy skank* like me."

"Stop it. Now. I believe you, okay? I believe you." He took a big step back without letting go of Liv's hand.

Her other hand slipped off Cynn's body. "There's only one reason I know why you'd have that look on your face. I hated seeing it when Cynn was alive. I'm not going to just stand by and watch her hurt you now."

The link broke. Cynn vanished. The voice stopped.

"What the hell do you think you're doing breaking my connection like that? Do you have any idea how pissed off she's going to be now?"

"I don't care," Adam said. But he didn't sound defiant. He sounded almost . . . well . . . *protective*.

She didn't need his protection. Liv reached out to reform the connection.

"Don't." He squeezed her hand. "Please."

"I have to."

"No, you don't. She's not going to admit she cheated or say anything I haven't heard before. She hates you, you know. Big time. Now that she knows I'm with you, she'll punish you every way she can think of."

"Why?"

"She always thought I liked you better than her." He wouldn't look at her. "She probably thinks I still like you."

They stood there a long moment, his hand holding hers.

"Is she right?" Liv was jittery as hell.

He snorted. "Yeah, I like you—when you're not treating me like a serial killer. But there's no way she's going to help if she thinks we're together."

"So, does this mean you actually believe me now

when I say I was talking to Cynn's ghost?"

"Maybe. Yes. I don't know." He let go of her hand. Then he groaned. "It definitely felt very real at the time. Only now that it's done it feels kind of crazy to say—"

She reached out her hand again toward Cynn.

"Okay, I believe you!" Adam almost shouted. "Don't talk to her again. Please. I believe you. Just . . . how far do your powers stretch? Like what can you actually do?"

She crossed her arms. "I can open a link between my mind and the spirit of someone who's dead. Like there's a room inside my imagination I can invite them into."

"And then?"

"And then we talk. In my mind. I see like a projection of the ghost's spirit. No one can see it or hear it but me. But my powers keep growing. Like the more I connect with dead people, the better I get and the more I can do."

"How long have you been able to do this?"

"Started right after Brett was murdered," said Liv. "Like I told you, Gabriel and I watched Brett's party through some social media hacking thing he put together. I saw Brett's dead body. I saw you in the car. Maybe that jumpstarted something in my head, I don't know. But the next day, I was at work, working on a corpse. She was old. Her name was Jane. I was brushing her hair off her face and kind of telling her about Brett's murder." Actually Liv had been crying, wondering out loud if being dead might not be better than another day at Rosewood. "All of a sudden I sensed her talking back. Inside my mind. She told me school sucked for a lot of people, but life generally got better when you got to choose who you hung out with." She shrugged. "But it still took a couple more corpses before I could figure out how to have an actual conversation with one. It's like my powers keep growing."

Adam's jaw moved under the skin, like he was trying to digest something he didn't want to. "Do you have a car?"

"Uh, yeah, I can borrow my mom's. She's working a double shift tomorrow and taking transit to work. Why?"

Adam turned and walked to the corner of the room, then back again, like he was trying to get up the courage to say something.

"When Brett threw that party at his family cottage up near Gravenhurst, I actually missed most of it, because I had a fight with Cynn and then went outside for some air. Sat in my car for a while getting drunk. Passed out. Woke up to find the car had somehow rolled down the hill. Brett was beside me, all dead and bloody. See, my problem is that my memory from that night is a total mess. Like I was crazy hallucination-level high or blackout drunk—even though I don't remember taking any drugs. And my lawyer was making it sound like none of the also-drunk-and-stupid witnesses remembered anything to help clear me. But just because I can't remember anything useful, and none of my former friends in Toronto do, doesn't mean there isn't someone, somewhere who can. I'm thinking if we go back up there, to where this all happened, I might be able to find someone who can help me. Maybe even look for some evidence. Just let me check out some stuff and I'll fill you in on the ride up. You can read the emails then too, okay?"

"Okay."

"Seriously?" He stopped. "Are you absolutely sure?"

"Yeah, I said okay. I mean, it's okay."

It wasn't okay. Not really. Tomorrow felt too late. There was this need to know things now. A need ringing in her mind like a phone she couldn't answer.

Who? How? When?

Why?

Liv picked up the broom and walked back to the office, pulling rose petals out from between the dusty bristles as she went. She stuffed the flowers into the garbage can then wiped the dirt off on her jeans. The candlelit séance flickered in the back of her mind. Even dead, Cynn was still the centre of attention. Her funeral would probably turn out to be an even bigger event than the prom. Maybe that was reason alone for someone who hated Cynn to wreck the prom queen dress she was supposed to be buried in.

She reached for the designer dress bag and pulled

the zipper down. Smooth silver silk flowed into her hands. The dress was dazzling and delicately beaded. Probably worth a couple thousand, easy.

Cynn's dress gets stolen and she scores an even hotter upgrade. Typical.

No, wait. There was a note pinned to the hanger.

Dear Liv, My dad said you might need a dress for your dance on Friday. I thought this would be about your size. Enjoy. Kiara.

She let the fabric fall slowly through her fingers.

Damn.

It's not like she was really going to the dance. Sure, she might hide in the booth with Gabriel. But she didn't belong down on the dance floor. No dress was about to change that.

Still . . . what would it be like to wear a dress like that? To see heads turn as she walked through the crowd? To dance to the music in the middle of the dance floor with Adam's hands on her waist? To be queen? Static fizzled through her mind again like her brainwaves couldn't quite figure out how to turn themselves into thoughts. She'd never cared about proms, or dresses, or crowns, or anything like this before. Why would she? But somehow now it felt logical to want that. To need that. To even be willing to kill for—

Where was this train of thought even coming from? It was almost like there was a second brain inside her head.

"Hey, you okay?"

She blinked.

Adam stood in front of her.

"Yeah. Sure."

He looked worried. "You've just been standing there for like five minutes without moving."

"No. What? I was just . . ."

"Yeah. You just zoned out. It's like your mind went somewhere else."

"I'm fine. Probably just tired."

"Okay then." He let out a sigh and rubbed his eyes. "Me too."

"I still think this whole thing ties back to the dance. Cynn and Felix were both in the running for prom queen. Which meant either you or Brett would have probably been their prom-date-slash-king."

He frowned. "Except Brett died weeks ago, and killing Brett has nothing to do with who becomes prom queen."

First Gabriel dismissed her. Now him. Sure, she might have agreed with them a couple of days ago. But who's to say this didn't all come down to what Cynn had said about people being jealous of her? Sure, destroying her expensive prom-cum-burial dress would be pretty petty. But jealousy made people do petty things.

"How do you know that? Maybe Felix was always jealous of Cynn. Maybe she got someone to stab her and destroy the dress so she could hog the limelight."

"That sounds like something Cynn would say," he said gently. "Look, if Felix wanted to be popular, she'd have fought her for head cheerleader in the fall, and she wouldn't have been dating Brett."

"How do you—"

"I asked her out once, okay?" he said. "Last summer. Weeks before Cynn and I hooked up. We were at a bonfire on the beach. She and Brett had been fighting. She totally stood up to him, and he stormed off. It was kind of cool. I was really drunk, so I told her I thought she deserved better and almost kissed her. She had this whole tough warrior-chick thing going and I thought it was hot—"

"You're kidding right? I've seen Felix's tough side, and it's not hot!"

Adam looked at her. "No, you've only seen her bitchy side. It's not like she's a bitch with her friends 24/7. You don't exactly know the real Felix. Besides, there's something kinda hot about a girl who can stand up for herself. But anyway, she laughed at me. Told me I was a dumbass skinny boy. Told me popular didn't trump dumb."

"You *are* a dumbass." Liv shook her head. "And the fact she said that to you doesn't mean anything."

"Maybe not. But please, let's take a break." His arms spread apart like he wanted to hug her, but wasn't sure that she'd let him. "I need to eat. You need to sleep. And whatever you do, don't try to talk to Cynn again until she's calmed down. A lot. Because I don't want to see you get hurt and she *will* try to hurt you."

"She's dead, Adam. She can't do anything to me."

Chapter Twenty-One

Liv's mom was waiting for her in the kitchen when she got home. Her waitress uniform was already on and her purse was in her hand, ready to go to work.

"I'm glad I caught you. Got your bag and stuff back from the police," Mom said. "It's on your dresser. Julie told me you popped into the hospital to see Felix. That was really nice of you." Her arms twitched like she wanted to hug her daughter, but didn't know if she should.

Liv squeezed her shoulder. "Maybe you're rubbing off on me."

"Did you know her dad's not even flying up to see her? His daughter's in the hospital and he can't be bothered. I told you her dad actually called the cops on her after his car was vandalised?"

Vandalised?

When her mom had mentioned it before, Liv'd figured Felix had just scratched the paint or dented it or something.

"Vandalised like how?" Liv asked.

"I don't know. What kind of monster tries to get his own kid arrested?"

"I really have no idea."

Her mom left for work. Liv went down the hall to her bedroom.

She closed the door, lay on her bed and stared at the ceiling. Despite her mom's regular warnings about stalkers and thieves, she'd left her window open a crack. A warm, wet breeze filled the air, making the whole room smell like rain.

Her eyes shut. The memory of seeing Adam and Cynn together last fall filled her mind. The smile on his face when he looked at Cynn. The way he slid his arms around her shoulders and ran his fingers through her long blonde hair. The sickening feeling that had pooled in the pit of Liv's stomach as she watched him plant a kiss on Cynn's eager lips.

He wasn't really happy with her. He wasn't in love. It wasn't what he really wanted.

Liv's eyes snapped open. She blinked back tears. Who cared if that was what he said now? The pain in her gut had been real enough.

She got up, walked to her dresser and double checked her wallet and phone, before stuffing them back into her bag. The police had probably gone through them, but nothing looked out of place. The scalpel she'd slipped into her back pocket earlier when Adam was being weird was still in her jeans. She pulled it out and rolled the metal shaft between her fingers. The retractable blade slid up and down smoothly. There was really no reason to carry it now. It looked like whoever was picking off her classmates was limiting their blood lust to the popular kids. She trusted Adam well enough. Yet, there was a troubling something in the back of her mind, nagging. Something she couldn't pin down.

Suspicion? Doubt? Premonition? Fear?

Whatever it was, it wouldn't let her rest.

Something tapped on the window. She turned, but all she could see in the darkened glass was her own frightened face looking back. A hand slid onto the window ledge. Long fingers with dirt-stained nails grabbed the bottom of the window frame and tried to edge the window open.

Impulse swept over her, like someone had thrown a switch in the back of her head. *Survive.* She didn't pause. Didn't even scream. Just drove the scalpel toward the hand, barely catching the tip of the prowler's middle finger before he managed to pull away.

"Shit!"

"Gabriel?"

She retracted the blade and shoved the window open. Gabriel stood outside, sucking his finger.

"Oh God, are you okay?"

He glared at her. "You stabbed me."

He held out his finger. She'd barely nicked it.

"You were breaking in my bedroom window."

"Um, no. I was walking by. I saw you through the window, so I tapped on it and said 'Hey Liv.'"

She shook her head. "I'm sorry. I didn't hear you. My head must have been somewhere else."

"Somewhere stabby." He rolled his eyes. "I would've called first, but last I heard the police had your phone."

And it was true. This wasn't the first time he'd shown up at her bedroom window. Gabriel had never seen the point of walking around to the front lobby, punching in the code to call her apartment and potentially waking up her mom if she'd come off a late shift, when the window was right there.

"Well, I have my phone now. Do you need to go to the hospital? Or a Band-Aid?"

He sighed and leaned his arms on the window ledge. "Believe me, I've done worse to myself."

Fair enough. Only, her heart was still beating so hard she could barely breathe. "You want to come in?"

"Nah. I just dropped by to say sorry for disappearing earlier." His face was mostly hidden in the shadows. "I just popped outside to give you a minute and then I couldn't find you."

Something in Gabriel's tone made her wonder if he was telling her the whole truth. She wasn't sure how to push the issue without admitting where she'd been, though.

"You sure you're okay?"

"Yeah, I think this whole people-getting-stabbed thing has me more on edge than I realized." Liv walked over to the dresser and tossed the scalpel into her bag, then went back to the window. Then she walked back to the window. "Your website turn up any new interesting theories?"

"Emma's mother emailed threatening 'immediate legal action' for suggesting her daughter's a psycho killer," said Gabriel. "'Cause apparently some teenagers still have their parents fight their battles for them. Rumour has it some of the school governors suggested cancelling the dance this year. But the students and their parents revolted, saying they deserved a chance to have fun and celebrate life, or something—probably because they've shilled out thousands for dresses already. So the principal struck some compromise that there'd be extra chaperones and extra rent-a-cops. Because nothing says party like having even more adults watching your every move."

The students were irritated enough that Rosewood held its prom on the last day of school, after exams were done. The private school claimed anything earlier would detract from "a serious learning environment." If they cancelled the dance altogether, they'd likely have a riot on their hands.

"Did it ever strike you as dumb that they elect a queen on the last day of school?" she said. "And that they just give the king crown to whoever her date happens to be?"

"A lot of things about Rosewood strike me as dumb." Gabriel stretched one arm through the open window. "Don't forget, the prom queen also gets a feeling of superiority and a $500 gift certificate to Yorkdale."

Liv leaned her head against his arm. "Nobody would kill for that."

The fingers on his other hand tousled her hair. "I never claimed anyone would."

"Why else would someone kill Cynn, and during the last week of school?"

"She's really annoying."

Now that was the truth. "Seriously though? We can't come up with anything better than that?"

"Fine. How about jealousy, revenge, lust, money or good old insanity? The field for motives is still wide open, babe."

He looped a strand of her hair through his fingers and tugged at it lightly.

She'd gotten used to play-fighting with him— almost like a brother, but there was something a little bit gentler in his tone than she was used to. It was super-comforting and yet weird all at the same time. Liv moved away. Gabriel pulled his arms back through the window.

"If Cynn's murder has nothing to do with the prom," she said, "then why destroy her prom dress? She was going to be buried in it."

He shrugged. "Eddy's an idiot."

"And Brett?"

"He was a major dickwad who beat the crap out of people for fun. The real question is why someone framed Adam?"

Good point—why hadn't she thought of that?

"We're also no closer to knowing why someone lured Felix to the subway. It's not like she has money. Plus Mom says her dad sued her."

"Huh." He stepped back from the window. "See, if I wanted to hurt Felix, I'd have started with blackmail. She and Brett got up to some really kinky stuff. I've got the pictures to prove it."

The night breeze turned colder. A shiver ran up Liv's spine.

"Gross. You've got them why?"

"They were stupid enough to upload them to a public server."

"And?"

He chuckled and took another step back. His form disappeared in the shadows.

"And baby, I'm a hacker."

Liv picked up her mother's car after school on Wednesday and drove to Never Forget. She checked to make sure Tony's car wasn't parked at the funeral home and then pulled into the alley behind it. She opened the back door to the prep room.

A hand grabbed her throat from behind.

"Hey, bitch. We got something to finish."

Oh, crap. It was Eddy.

Chapter Twenty-Two

Liv clawed at Eddy's arm as he propelled her into the prep room. His fingers clenched her throat. The door slammed. She tried to scream, but he tightened his chokehold before she could get out a sound. She clutched at his arm. Eddy took another step forward and his grip loosened again. Just enough to let Liv gasp for breath. But not enough to let her turn around.

Where the hell was Adam?

There had to be some way she could trip the alarm or grab something to defend herself. The scalpel was still in her bag, under the front seat of the car. Which she'd foolishly left there, thinking she'd only be popping into the funeral home for half a second. Her mind scrambled for a weapon. There were knives on the prep table and the crowbar under the cabinet, but they were all too far away for her to reach.

She didn't know if Eddy had a weapon or not. He wouldn't need one.

"Where the hell's the necklace?"

"You mean the one you dropped?"

He cuffed her on the side of the head with his other hand.

She saw stars. "It's in the office."

Soaking in a beaker full of acetone.

"Show me."

That wouldn't be all he wanted with her. Not Eddy. He was too mean and too stupid to let her go just like that—

"Move!"

He forced her into the office. Then he let go of her long enough for her to open the bottom drawer and pull out the beaker.

"What the hell is this?"

She slid a pencil into the acetone and pulled out the necklace. It glistened. "I was just cleaning it, okay?"

She dropped it into his hand. He looked at it. Then he poked it with his finger.

Liv threw the acetone in his face and ran.

He bellowed like an angry, wounded animal. The acetone wasn't strong enough to permanently damage his eyes, but it would definitely sting like hell and buy her time. She'd barely made it back to the prep room door when Eddy shoved her hard and sent her sprawling. She fell forward onto her hands and knees. He landed on top of her. She screamed, struggled and swung her elbow back, hitting him hard in the jaw. Eddy swore but didn't let go. He leaned his full weight on her back and pinned her to the floor.

"What the hell did you do to me, bitch?" He grabbed Liv by the hair and yanked her head back. "I'm so going to make you pay for that—"

There was a loud crack. Eddy fell off of her. She rolled over, then looked up. Adam was standing over Eddy, clutching a giant wine bottle—probably left over from a wake. One side was sticky with blood.

Eddy blinked. His eyes darted from Adam's face, to the bottle then back to his face again. Like he didn't know whether to be more surprised Adam was standing there or that Adam had actually hit him with something. He touched his fingers to his temple, then stared at the blood on his fingers. "What the hell, Clay?"

"Get the hell away from Liv." Adam tightened his grip on the bottle. "Leave her alone, and get out of here."

Eddy's lip curled up into an ugly sneer. He wrapped the necklace around his fist. "No way I'm just letting you have this."

"Like I care." Adam snorted. "Take it. Go try your luck hocking it. Just get the hell out of here and don't come back."

"Or what?" Eddy glared. Then he stood. He was half a foot taller than Adam. "You think you can stop me?"

Liv got up slowly and slid along the wall until she reached the security alarm. Her finger hovered over the police call button.

"Or stay here and you two can keep throwing punches while I call the police."

While I pop into the prep room and grab the crowbar and swing it right for your head.

She didn't exactly want to call the police right now. But it would do as a distraction and it definitely beat the nightmare this could turn into.

Eddy paused a long moment. Then he walked backwards to the door.

"Next time I see you, Clay, you're a dead man. And trust me, bitch, that goes double for you."

"Whatever." Thankfully her voice sounded a whole lot stronger than her legs felt.

Eddy disappeared out the door, back into the alley.

"Well that was uncharacteristically heroic of you." Liv let out a long breath. "Thanks."

Adam's hand brushed against her arm. "But are you okay?"

"Yeah."

She stepped back and slowly ran her fingers through her hair, then down over her clothes. Her legs were shaking. "But . . . he saw you."

Adam shrugged, but his eyes looked anything but confident. "So? It's not like he's going to tell the police he was here."

"No, probably not."

"Though, honestly, when I heard you scream like that I didn't exactly stop to worry about Eddy seeing me. Stopping him from hurting you was more important."

Liv didn't know what to say to that. Besides there

was still that reward out for Adam's arrest. Eddy could still call in and say he'd seen her with Adam somewhere else. Last thing she needed was for police to drag her in for even more questions. Or even worse, decide to start following her.

"Judging by the weight alone, that necklace must be worth hundreds," Adam added. "Maybe even thousands. I'm not really that surprised he came back for it."

"Well, I never did tell Tony I'd found it. So as far as the police know, he's always had it."

She went into the bathroom and splashed cold water on her face. She wanted to call the police. She wanted to hear someone with a badge and gun tell her they were going to throw that ugly, creepy slimeball behind bars and make sure he never touched her ever again. She wanted . . .

She wanted this whole thing to be over.

Liv walked back through Never Forget, turning off lights as she went. Adam was waiting in the alley with a big black bag. He tossed it in the trunk. It clunked. "You want to talk about what just happened?"

And say what exactly? That she felt angry? Scared? Vulnerable?

And helpless.

So. Goddamn. Helpless.

She forced her face into the tried-and-true "I Don't Care" facial expression that had gotten her through the worst Rosewood had been able to throw.

"I'm fine."

"You're not fine," Adam said gently but firmly.

"Eddy's a thug. He got what he was after. He's gone. You're driving." *And while I'm glad you came to my rescue, I'm not about to let you try and be the hero here.*

She walked over to the passenger door, got in and slammed the door behind her.

Adam paused for a long moment. Then he walked over to the driver side and got in. "I forgot to ask how things went with Felix."

"Bitchy."

He started the car. "She tell you anything?"

"No. Not really. She said you got really drunk the night Brett died."

"Yup. I did that."

"And that you wandered around in a potentially psychotic stupor. She said her email—the email luring her to the subway—came from DeathFetishGirl99. But she couldn't actually tell me anything helpful about your secret friend."

He pulled the car out of the alley and onto the street. "She tell you what her attacker looked like?"

Liv sighed. "Like you."

"Are you serious?"

"Tall, skinny and wearing a ski mask."

"Dressed all in black?"

"Yeah. How did you—"

"So was our mystery cameraman."

It took three hours to drive from downtown

Toronto to Gravenhurst. Adam had printed out the emails from DeathFetishGirl99 and she read them while he drove.

Hey Adam,

First off, I'm so sorry about everything that's happening to you. I can't believe you had anything to do with Brett's murder. And I hate the way everyone is talking crap about you now. I think you're really awesome. And brave. And smart. The way you held your head up high when you were arrested, you looked just like a movie hero.

Second, I hope it's okay I'm writing this without telling you my real name. I don't want anyone finding out I'm talking to you. But I feel I don't have anyone else I can talk to about Brett's murder or what happened that night. I totally believe you're innocent, but nobody else does.

I want to help you and do the right thing, but I don't know how.

One of my closest friends is being really weird and creepy about Brett's murder, and dead bodies in general, and what happened, and saying he knows stuff about what happened. I feel so scared. And so alone.

In a weird way, I feel like I need you. I

MAGS STOREY

hope you need me too. I feel like we have a connection.

Maybe, hopefully, you'll be able to guess who I am.

I'm hoping you will.

xoxoxoxoxo
DeathFetishGirl99

Yeah. So that wasn't creepy at *all*.

"Yeah, so DeathFetishGirl99 has a huge crush on you." Liv looked up. She hated just how irritated her voice sounded but couldn't figure out how to hide it. "Not that I'd pick an accused killer in a troubled youth facility to be my knight in shining armour. I'm guessing you figured Gabriel was the 'weird friend.'"

"I won't lie. I thought it could be him."

"What about Emma? How well did you know her?"

"Not well. We went to a few of the same parties. Why?"

"I get the impression from something Gabriel said that Emma's kind of passive and used to having other people fight her battles. And her boyfriend, Damien, is kind of weird and creepy. He transports corpses for a part time job—"

"*You* work in a funeral home—"

"Fair enough. But he also has a pretty nasty temper. He and Emma could be our killers."

Adam snorted. "Except, they're like peace activists. Emma and Damien protest against animal violence.

They're both militant vegans."

"Vegans kill people. They just don't eat them. At least Gabriel's making an effort to think up other suspects."

She went back to reading.

After a while she said, "Whoever wrote these is really obvious."

"Yeah?"

"Yeah. Listen to this: *I'm dying to know what the police think your motive for killing Brett was. Do they suspect anyone else? Do they have any idea why the knife wasn't found? I mean, the search was supposedly really thorough. They searched and checked everyone. And knives don't just disappear into thin air. My friend says someone probably just walked out with it. But I don't know how. Do you have any idea? Who else do you think could've killed Brett?* Most of these letters are just different ways of digging around for the same info."

"DeathFetishGirl99 is trying to solve the crime?"

"Or trying to cover his or her tracks. Or protecting someone else. Maybe she knows who the killer really is. Or thinks she does."

Adam nodded. "Interesting."

"You can't really tell if it's a girl or a guy who wrote these. But if it was a guy, I'm positive it wasn't Eddy."

He grinned. "Because of the writing? Or because they asked for a picture of my ass?"

She laughed. "I haven't gotten there yet. But no, any email Eddy wrote would be full of typos. I don't think he even knows how an apostrophe works. Someone covering up for him, maybe."

"Like Emma?"

"Possibly," she said. "Though why would Emma protect Eddy? Felix could have written them, but I don't know why she'd bother. And I don't think Sharona would bother writing an email using real sentences when she could just use text speak and emojis."

"How about Cynn?" asked Adam.

Liv's heart skipped a beat.

"Now that's dark. What if Cynn wanted to communicate without letting you know it was her for some reason? You did say the guards were reading your emails and that you didn't get any messages from Cynn?"

"Nope. Like I said. After that party, it was like I never existed."

Yet, he still went running back to see her when he escaped Meadowhurst.

"Maybe we're looking for *three* different people. DeathFetishGirl99 who wrote these letters, Cynn's stalker who attacked you and videotaped her, and the actual killer. I'm having a hard time thinking of one person who could've done all of that. Plus, even though it's not impossible to stab Felix at Summerhill station and still beat you to Cynn's house long enough to hide in the bushes and make that video, it's really unlikely. God only knows, though, if any of these people are actually working *together*. What did you tell DeathFetishGirl99 about the case?"

"Not much. I told DeathFetish my lawyer wanted me to take a stupid plea deal that would mean five years of custody, probably in Meadowhurst to start, but maybe eventually I'd move into a halfway house after a few years if I could prove good behaviour. And that I was thinking of turning it down because they never found the knife. I mean, that alone was enough to create doubt, right? But Dad's lawyer said they could take years to get to trial and they could still find me guilty without it. Showed me stories of a whole bunch of court cases where people were convicted without the weapon ever being found. Said even if the knife did turn up in the lake, and there were no prints on it, they'd just say I chucked it there to destroy evidence. And I'd lose the chance at the deal. So I should hurry up and take a plea bargain, fast, because there'd be a whole lot of underpaid cops and juries full of underemployed people eager to see a rich politician's son suffer."

Yeah. And she could even sympathise some on where they'd be coming from.

"Then DeathFetish told you she'd found the knife for you," she said.

"Pretty much, yeah."

Liv kept reading. Once you got past all the flowery crap, the letters were actually pretty boring. Sure, there were flirty parts, but they were only window dressing for the same questions, over and over again. Who do you think killed Brett? What evidence is there? What do you think happened to the knife? Why don't you think it was ever found?

Then, two weeks ago, the tone took a dramatic shift.

I found out for sure who has the knife! But I need your help to get it. I'm too scared. I can't do it on my own. Please help me.

"Laying it on a little thick, don't you think?" Liv said. "Might just as well have addressed it 'to big strong man from helpless female crushing on him.' Why didn't they go to the cops? Why is an accused killer the only person they can turn to? Had you thought of breaking out before they told you to?"

He looked at her sideways. "I *thought* about breaking out my first night there, the second I realized how much money I was going to need on a regular basis for bribes to keep some of the bigger, meaner assholes in there from tormenting and hurting me. There were some seriously screwed up monsters in that place. Not to mention bribing some of the guards. The thought of begging my dad for it month after month, year after year, was just . . ." He stared at the horizon. "I started actually *plotting* how to escape once I realized Dad was planning on just leaving me there."

"What would you say if I told you I thought someone lured you out of there so he or she could kill Cynn and Felix—and blame it on you?"

"I'd say I've wondered the same thing."

Dark clouds hung over the lake. The water was choppy and grey. Adam drove fifteen minutes past the turn-off to Gravenhurst, past a small cemetery ringed by a simple wooden post fence, then stopped the car on a dirt track by the water's edge.

"You do realize we've stopped in the middle of nowhere."

"We're a five minute walk from where we're going," he said. "I didn't want to park where somebody could see us." He unbuckled his seat belt. "What's the matter? You still think I'm dangerous? And don't forget crazy. I'm a *psycho* killer."

He flashed her some bizarre grin—which he probably thought made him look insane, but actually just made him look kind of goofily adorable. Then he got out of the car.

She followed. "You want to hear crazy? Yesterday, after seeing Felix, I snuck into the hospital morgue loading bay and talked with a scary old dead guy that Damien was transporting, just because Cynn said my abilities might not be portable. Only he kind of freaked me out. Well, they both did. The dead guy and Damien. The dead guy told me the dead could scramble my brain. Damien just yelled at me for touching the corpse."

He laughed. "You're amazing. I wish we'd done this sooner."

"Driven around crime-solving together, or gone somewhere isolated for a creepy conversation?"

Adam just stared at her, like she was a picture he'd seen lots of times before that was only now coming into focus.

"You're funny," he said. "Like, actually funny."

He said it like he really meant it. Not like he was trying to be sarcastic.

"Uh, thanks?" Her chest felt weirdly light and she didn't know what to say to that. So instead, she shoved her heel onto the bumper and hopped up to sit on the hood. "Now, no more secrets. What happened the night Brett died? Everything you remember."

Adam stared up at the menacing clouds then looked straight at Liv. "I didn't want to go to the party. Cynn and Felix bitched at each other the whole way up. Really stupid. I picked up Felix first, and the skirt she had on was short even for her. Then when I picked Cynn up, she told Felix to move into the back seat, and Felix said no way. Cynn accused her of trying to flash me her panties, Felix said she could have me if she wanted, and Cynn said she could steal Brett . . . I'm sorry, this all seems so stupid now."

"It's okay," Liv said.

"They were taking pot shots at each other the whole damn ride up. Bragging like guys in the locker room over who they'd fooled around with, or who they could screw if they wanted—like I said, stupid."

"Um, girls brag about fooling around just as much as guys," she said. "Maybe even more. Anyway, what did you say?"

"No one wanted my opinion. Anyway, Cynn was in a really weird mood at the party. Drinking too much and dancing like—I don't know. It was crazy. I just grabbed a six-pack and went outside."

"How long were you out there?"

"A long time. I just sat in my car and drank. There was another kid outside too. He walked over and sat in the passenger side for a while and we got to talking." Adam climbed up beside Liv, leaned back and looked at the sky. "He was Brett's cousin or something. Hated being there as much as I did, but it was his family's cottage, so it wasn't like he had anywhere else to go. After a while it sounded like this major fight was breaking out inside."

"Fight between who?"

"I don't know. I turned on the radio to tune it out. I was in a pretty bad mood. I remember Brett coming out all worked up, but he handed me half a bottle of booze and told me I was a decent guy. He left. I drank. Then I think I passed out. I really don't remember anything else until the car had crashed and Brett was dead. Even then, it's all blurry."

"What do you remember from the car?"

"Blood. Lots and lots and lots of blood." He took a deep breath. "I don't know how much of that was from him bleeding to death, how much got spread around by the car crashing and how much was me freaking out and trying to figure out how to get out of the car. It just felt like it was everywhere." He shuddered. "I just kept thinking it had to be a nightmare or something. They said it looked like both Brett and I had taken something like GHB. But my lawyer said toxicology isn't always conclusive for certain types of drug and they tend to leave the system pretty quick, so they don't always show up in urine tests. Even when the drugs do show up, the tests don't always stand up in court. I mean, they could always say I took GHB myself for the fun of it. Brett used to take it for fun. I don't remember taking anything, so I'm guessing it was in Brett's whiskey."

"Was Brett trying to drug you or was someone trying to drug Brett? Or both of you?"

"Hell if I know. Maybe Brett was getting high anyway and thought I wouldn't care. He was the kind of guy who took stuff like that for kicks, and bragged about slipping it to other people he wanted to mess with. Bottom line is this: I passed out with the keys in the ignition and Brett is the kind of guy who could've easily hopped in the passenger seat of my car, to search through the glove compartment and accidentally knock it out of park. Heck, he might have put it in drive just to scare me. He was *sick*. He might have even wandered around in nothing but boxers if he was drunk enough. A whole bunch of kids went skinny dipping that night and Brett was hardly shy. It was *that* kind of party.

"You know as well as I do the media has made this whole thing look like some teenage sex and drug orgy. Now the prosecution wants to make an example of me. They figure I chucked the knife in the lake, or the woods, or something, knowing it'd cost the police thousands of dollars to dredge the place for it. The country's in economic free fall, and here I am as the freaking poster child for spoiled, rich politicians' kids thinking they can literally get away with murder. So yeah, there's no way one missing knife is going to stop them from taking this to trial. They'd rather lose at trial than be accused of going easy on me."

Liv shook her head. When Adam was first arrested everyone had said it wouldn't stick. Everyone said his dad would pay some bribe and he'd be out by the weekend. So, when he was shipped to Meadowhurst instead, people didn't really know what to think.

No, they did. They'd thought he was guilty.

"But still, the forensic tests—"

"Will take months and might not show anything that'll help me! The car was a *mess*, Liv. There was water, and mud, and blood, and people everywhere. Even the prosecution can change their theory to fit whatever they find." His voice rose. "My lawyer kept saying, I only got to be in a place as 'nice' as Meadowhurst, because we were 'cooperating' with the police. So, why should I lose a huge chunk of my life waiting for some evidence, which might not even clear me, when he could get me a really good plea deal *immediately*. One that would keep me out of somewhere even worse and keep some prosecutor from thinking it might be a bright idea to charge me as an adult."

"By you pleading guilty to murder."

"Manslaughter. Not murder. My lawyer wanted to push the theory I went 'dissociative' and accidentally killed Brett in some druggie haze and blacked out the details. Then again, he works for my dad, who's never given me the benefit of the doubt on anything. The fact I might be innocent doesn't seem to register with anyone."

"You can see why they think you did it, though."

"Thanks. That's great. Real supportive."

"I'm just talking about how it looks, okay? Now, what else happened? Someone got really pissed off with Brett, so they waited until he wandered into your car and then slit his throat? That's some heavy duty hate."

"Yeah. But like you said—for me or him or both of us?"

Her hand brushed against his. He looped his fingers through hers.

"There was this moment when I was looking at the plea bargain papers my lawyer drew up and . . . I considered it. Signing. Told myself it'll take years for my case to get to court, where I could be found guilty anyway. Then he handed me the pen, and it hit me— why should anyone else fight for me if I won't even fight for myself?" He squeezed her hand, let go and jumped off the hood. "Lots of people hated Brett. I find it hard to believe someone hated me enough to frame me for murder. But a whole lot of them probably thought I was too chicken to do anything about it."

"So this is you fighting back?"

"This is me trying. It's kind of new for me." He glanced at Liv, still perched on the hood. "Let's just say I'm grateful you're around. You're the kind of person that makes people want to be strong."

A breeze brushed in from the water. Shivers ran across her skin. "What can you tell me about Brett's cousin?"

"His name was Jake. I don't know where he lives. I think the cottage belongs to his grandmother."

Now the shivers got into her stomach and knotted things up in there. "Was he about our age? Black? Bald?"

"Yeah, and the bald thing totally didn't suit him."

"He had cancer, you moron."

Adam winced. "Hell, I'm sorry."

"He died about a week ago. Was cremated on Monday. I didn't meet him until after he died, and I had no idea he was related to Brett. Different racial backgrounds. Different last names. Opposite personalities."

"I think he said they were step-cousins."

"He was really nice." She sighed. "I don't meet a lot of nice people, alive or dead. So it kind of sucked when he was cremated."

He walked back and slid his arms around her. Her head fell against his shoulder. "I'm really sorry, Liv. He seemed cool."

"He was, and I'm sure he told the police everything he could."

"Yeah, me too. That's why I wasn't actually trying to track him down." He let go of her and walked around the car to the trunk.

Liv hopped off the front and followed.

He popped the trunk, reached for the big bag, set it on the ground and unzipped it. There was a shovel inside.

"We're here to talk to Brett."

Chapter Twenty-Three

"What is *wrong* with you? He's dead, Adam. Really dead. Extremely dead."

"You talk to dead people all the time."

"Not like this! What were you thinking? We're going to go dig him up?"

"Well—"

"Adam!"

He hoisted the bag up onto his shoulder. "You only need to touch the corpse, right? I figure we dig a hole straight down six feet and you reach in and touch him. The graveyard Brett's buried in is just on the other side of the trees. You just admitted to sneaking into a hospital morgue and—"

"That's so not the same." She looked back to the car. "I'm sorry. I really am, but this crosses a line."

"Come on, Liv. I can't exactly do this without you. I need you, and you know it."

"And what if I won't? You planning to haul me there and hold me down over his body?"

"I was kind of hoping it wouldn't come to that,"

If he was trying to make a joke there, he'd just failed big time.

"Oh, ha ha." She leaned back against the car. "You actually think this is funny?"

"No, of course I don't. I think the situation is sick and stupid. I think that you might be the only reason I'm even still alive."

"And what if I can't do it? Did you even think about that? What if I try and it doesn't work? Or what if something bad happens? What if I connect with his corpse and . . ." Her voice trailed off.

"And what?"

"And I don't know." She wrapped both arms around herself.

Adam dropped the bag on the ground and took a step toward her. His voice dropped. "You're the bravest girl I know. Screw that, the bravest *person*, period. You've got serious guts and you don't back down. If you don't want to do this, we don't do it, okay? But I totally believe you *can* do whatever you decide to do."

Liv looked down at the ground for a moment, not even knowing what to think.

Then she looked up.

Adam was still looking at her intensely.

"Don't look at me that way."

"What way?"

Like you're waiting for permission to kiss me. "Like you're pretending I'm not just here because you need me."

He shook his head. "You ever thought that maybe I like spending time with you? That maybe I think you're interesting? Or if I actually get my life back, we might go out and do things besides tracking down a serial killer?"

"So, I help you talk to the dead and this time you'll take me to movies?"

"Definitely. I can't wait to trade some grave robbing for popcorn." Before Liv knew what was happening, Adam leaned forward and nipped her lips with his teeth. Then his tongue flicked against hers.

Her eyes closed. *Hasn't he had plenty of chances to be with me before his life was on the line?*

So what? Adam was kissing her now. Like he wanted her. Like he'd always wanted her.

Then why did he date Cynn?

Shut up. Just shut up and let me have this.

But, it's not like he dumped Cynn. They only broke up because she died.

The buzzing in Liv's brain was back. Loud. Insistent. Painful.

She could see Cynn's body on the stainless steel table. The stitches that encircled her neck. Someone had killed her. And stabbed Felix. And killed Brett. And would probably keep on killing unless someone stopped them.

The pain in her head was throbbing so hard she could barely think.

She pushed Adam back and pressed her fingers hard against her temples.

He let go and stepped back. He stuffed his hands in his pockets. "Okay, so I guess I totally misjudged that."

"I just want it all to stop."

"Which means what?"

"I want Cynn out of the funeral home. I want the killer caught. I want everything to go back to normal."

Friday was only two days away. Cynn would be buried that night.

Then there'd be the dance—

"You're zoning out on me again."

"Sorry." She blinked. "I haven't slept. Not really. Not in days. It's like . . . like I know I'm not going to sleep again until we know what really happened." She stood up straight. "Let's go get this over with." She pushed past him and picked up the bag.

"Hang on! What the hell just happened here?"

What's happening is I want to believe you like me. I want to believe you've changed. I want to believe any of this actually meant something. And I don't.

Liv pulled the strap of the bag over her neck. "You said we were going to dig down to Brett's corpse, and I'm going along. But digging up a grave is a crime, okay? If we're caught, my mom and I can't hire some fancy lawyer. So, if I'm crossing this line, know that this means no more clever misunderstandings. We're in this together. I guess we're leaving the car here and walking to the cemetery to help hide the fact we'll be in there digging up a grave??"

"Just wait a minute, okay? You're not making any sense. One minute you're kissing me back. The next minute you're freaking out."

Adam tried to take the bag from her.

Liv yanked it back. "Maybe I just remembered you have a freshly murdered girlfriend who hasn't even been buried yet."

"That doesn't change the fact I like you. I told you, I like you more than I ever liked Cynn."

"But you're only here because you need me. You said so yourself."

He walked to the hood of the car, turned around and walked back. Like he was stuck in a cage and trying to find his way out.

"I don't know what to say." He shook his head like there was water trapped in his ears. "It's like there's something in your brain that hates you—or hates me—and it's trying to screw you over from the inside. Maybe this whole digging up a grave thing is a bad idea—"

"I thought you weren't a lazy-ass rich boy who never did anything to fight for himself anymore."

Liv couldn't believe she'd said that.

Yeah, she did want to know whether Adam was trying to be the kind of guy who stepped up and actually took responsibility for his own shit. But she'd have normally found a nicer way to say it. It was almost like she was possessed or something. Like there were two different voices trying to talk out of her mouth right now and two minds thinking inside her skull, both fighting to make themselves heard.

And one of them really, really wanted to hurt Adam. And dig up Brett.

He stopped. Turned to face her. Narrowed his eyes. "Yeah? So?"

Liv threw the bag against his chest.

He caught it.

"Prove it."

Chapter Twenty-Four

A thin, narrow shovel slid into the soil. Thunder rumbled in the distance. Hopping the wooden cemetery fence had been a breeze, but the shovel Adam had brought was a joke for digging up something as big as a casket. But once Liv explained they didn't need to dig up the whole thing, just make a hole large enough for her to reach down into it, they'd raided the cemetery toolshed and come up with a corkscrew auger and a long narrow clam shovel. After all, she'd connected to the priest with just one finger. Now, Adam stood neck deep in a conical hole.

"Just a couple more feet oughta do it." He grinned. "Ground's soft. Thank God it's been raining."

Liv concentrated on holding the flashlight steady in the tiny cemetery. If there was a God watching, she doubted they'd want credit for this.

Adam pulled off his sweatshirt and tossed it onto Brett's tombstone. The car keys fell out.

She stuck them in her pocket.

Down went the shovel, then up again, splattering the surrounding grass with mud.

"So, how's it feel to know the answer to the big question?" he asked.

"Which is?"

"What happens after death."

"I'm not sure I really know anything. I've never seen anyone who's been dead very long. None of them know what's going to happen to them next."

"Switch." He handed her the shovel and she passed down the auger. They'd been alternating between the two, using the auger to dig straight down and the shovel to remove the dirt. He pressed one end of the corkscrew shaped tool into the ground and turned the handle, screwing it deeper and deeper into the ground. "What are they like?"

"The dead? Distracted, mostly. Some want to figure out how to come back. Others are in a hurry to move on somewhere else."

"Where else?"

"I don't know."

He ran a gloved hand over his head, streaking his hair with dirt.

"I can't promise this'll work, you know," she said. "Brett's spirit may not still be hanging out with his body. Or if it is, he may not want to talk to me. The dead are just like the living, only more extreme."

"Brett was a lunatic. A really evil bastard when he wanted to be, which was most of the time. He probably deserved what he got, but Cynn didn't. Not like that. Her whole death scene was kinky as hell and set up like something out of a slasher movie." A shovelful of dirt flew over his head. "If it really was the killer who caught Felix in the subway, she should be thankful she got away with a quick stab to the gut. Looking at this sicko's record, who knows what he'd have done with her if he got her alone."

Liv wrapped her arms around herself. Adam grew silent. He kept shovelling. The hole was almost as tall as he was now. The temperature was dropping as a wind came up.

"Ever wonder why the killer decided not to murder you, too?" Liv asked after a long moment.

"All the damn time."

A crack split the night.

"Now all I've got to do is open this thing so you can reach your hand inside, right?"

"Right, but it'll be sealed."

"Yeah, but I can use the auger like a corkscrew." Adam stabbed the top of the casket with the point and practically jumped up and down on it. "I've made a tiny hole in the top. Like small enough you might be able to squeeze your hand into. You want to try it?"

"Sure. But I can't promise this'll work."

He passed the tools up to her. Then he climbed back up onto the grass.

Liv looked down at the narrow hole. "You want me to climb down there?"

"Yeah. But I'll hold your hand the whole time and won't let go. I promise."

Right. One hand on Adam and one hand in Brett's casket. That was going to be fun.

Liv slid down into the narrow hole feet first. Earth rose higher than her head on either side. Adam lay on his stomach beside the hole and reached down as far as he could, until practically his whole torso was hanging in upside down.

Liv crouched down. She couldn't begin to imagine how ridiculous they must look right now. "Don't you dare fall in on top of me."

"I'll try not to."

She reached one hand up above her head and grabbed hold of Adam's fingers.

"I won't let go of you," Adam added. "I promise."

"You'd better not."

Then she crouched down, gritted her teeth and slid her other hand straight down inside the casket, trying to forget the fact she was now feeling around for a three-week-old corpse.

She couldn't feel a thing.

"I don't think this is going to work. I can't even feel Brett's corpse—"

Screams shook the air around her. Cold, wet darkness poured like water into her eyes.

"Have you connected with him?"

Sticky tendrils slid up around her body. They wound their way around her neck.

A voice licked at the edges of her mind: *Nobody wants you. Nobody likes you. Why should they? You're crap. Pathetic. You need to die. You'd be better off dead.*

She opened her mouth to scream. But the darkness poured into her throat, filling her lungs, freezing her voice in her throat.

"Are you okay? Nod if you can hear me."

She was going to die. But it didn't matter.

She didn't matter.

"Liv, you're starting to scare me. . . ."

She was nothing.

Her body went limp.

She was standing in a dark room. Wood beams crisscrossed above her. There was a lake outside the window. Something rustled in the trees. She'd seen this room somewhere before.

She turned to go, but Brett blocked the door. He took a swig from a bottle of booze, then held it out towards her. "You can't leave. The party's just starting."

"Liv? Come on. Snap out of it."

She reached for the bottle, but it dissipated through her fingers like smoke.

Brett laughed. Cynn and Felix appeared from the darkness behind him. Brett snaked one hand around each of their bodies. His arms wrapped around and around their waists like rope. One huge fist slid around each girl's throat, choking them until their faces turned blue. They didn't seem to care. They were laughing at Liv, calling her ugly, filthy, worthless.

There was something hanging around Brett's neck. Heavy, gold, like a chain.

Curiosity overcame fear. She stepped forward.

Cynn slapped her in the face. Felix punched her in the stomach.

She tried to fight back but couldn't move.

Tried to argue but no words came out.

She fell onto her knees.

More laughter. The girls disappeared.

Brett knelt.

The gold chain around his neck uncoiled and raised itself toward her. It wasn't a chain—it was a snake.

A door slid open behind her. Someone was coming.

She turned.

Brett grabbed her throat and turned her face toward him. There was something in his hands.

Gabriel's severed head.

The gold snake slithered down around the bloody neck. Gabriel opened his eyes and looked at her.

Her stomach heaved.

Someone stood behind her now. A hand landed on her shoulder. A voice spoke her name.

Adam!

"Adam!" Her voice escaped from her throat. It echoed in her ears like thunder. "Help me!"

Adam shrugged. He turned and walked away.

Chapter Twenty-Five

Adam yanked her upwards.

The link to Brett peeled away like duct tape.

Liv screamed.

Adam hauled her out of the hole, pulling her back up onto the grass.

She opened her eyes.

Adam looked terrified. "Holy shit, Liv. What just happened? You were shouting."

She looked back. The hole had begun caving in.

"You did nothing."

"What?"

"You. Did. Nothing." She sat up. "Back at Rosewood. You saw what was happening at that school to people like me, day after day after day, and let your friends do whatever they wanted to people. Didn't matter how they treated me, or Gabriel. You just stood there and did nothing."

Liv pulled herself to her feet and ran back toward

the car. Snatches of what she'd seen in the grave flashed through her mind. Gabriel's severed head. Adam watching. She'd been so stupid. Adam was one of them. He'd always been one of them. She yanked open the door and fell into the driver's seat, jammed the key in the ignition and threw the car in reverse. Something bumped under the wheels. She hit the brakes.

Adam jumped in. She'd been so lost in her own head she hadn't even realized he'd been following her. He dropped the flashlight on the floor.

"What did I run over?"

"The shovel. We've got to go back and fill in the hole."

"You can if you want to," Liv said. "But I'm not going back there."

She tapped the break just long enough to see if he was going to try to get out of the car.

He didn't. She kept driving.

"What happened?"

"It was dark. And violent. And scary as hell. And I couldn't even speak or fight back."

"Well, maybe it was like a dream. You can't always talk or fight back in a dream."

"It wasn't like a dream." She jammed her foot down on the accelerator and clenched the wheel so hard her knuckles hurt. "There was so much anger and hate. Maybe it was his spirit. I don't know. But when I opened my mind, he tried to reach inside it and mess with me."

She was speeding. She didn't care.

Adam fumbled for his seatbelt. "Maybe people's souls decompose after death, like their bodies, or something. He didn't give a crap about—"

"Like you're any different."

She swerved back onto the highway, turning so hard it took all her strength to keep the car on the road. Thunder cracked in the sky.

"I saw you there, in whatever place Brett made me go. Gabriel was dead. Your friends were beating on me. And you weren't doing a damn thing."

"Hey, it wasn't *real*."

"The place wasn't real. What I saw wasn't real. But the way Brett acted, the way you were, the way it felt to be laughed at, and hurt, and made fun of while you just ignored me? That felt real. That felt just like how I've felt a thousand times before. You just don't get it, *can't* get it because you coasted past all of it while you let the bullies do whatever they wanted to us."

"No! God no. How can you think I'd actually let someone hurt you?"

"Because you *did*."

Rain began to drive against the windshield.

"This is getting crazy. Stop the car so we can talk."

"The hell I'm—"

"STOP THE DAMN CAR!"

Liv ignored him. The tires spun on gravel. She swerved back onto the road.

"Okay," he said. "I didn't want to go here, but you're so off-base, I have to. Did you know Brett duct-taped

Gabriel to the front of a car a few weeks before he was killed?"

"No, he didn't. Gabe would have told me."

"Yeah, he did. Bastard threatened to drive him around the parking lot playing bumper cars."

"Why are you telling me this?"

"Because I'm the one who got him down," said Adam.

"You what?"

"I paid Brett a thousand bucks to let your friend go and leave him the hell alone."

"I don't believe you."

Where had the highway road gone? She must've taken a wrong turn and ended up on an unpaved country road. The ground was mud beneath the wheels.

Liv slammed her foot on the brake.

The car spun sideways. Then slid to a stop. They were in a field, a few feet from a barn.

"Now, let me see if I've got this straight," Adam said. "I may or may not be a serial killer, but I'm definitely a spineless wimp. I'd never do anything good for anybody and I didn't help your friend—I only said that because I'm also a liar."

"Adam—"

"But I *did* pay Brett to back off Gabriel. Maybe it wasn't all that heroic of me. Maybe using money to stop Brett was the coward's way out. Maybe it doesn't begin to make up for everything I should've tried to stop. But I did it. Because he'd taken it too damn far that time. I'm not that do-nothing guy anymore."

"So you went to jail the kind of guy who throws his daddy's money at bullies to make them go way, and came out, what, a superhero?"

"I came out of jail terrified, but then I found you again. And it's pretty hard to be spineless around you."

Something was prickling inside her chest, making her breathing go funny. "You had your chance with me, and you blew it."

"I know that now, and I'm sorry. Maybe I wanted to believe those emails were from you because I wanted another shot. You think I'd have kissed just anybody like that?" He reached out and brushed his fingers through the hair that fell beside her face. "I really like you. Why can't you see that?"

A tinny rock song began to play under his feet.

"My phone!" said Liv.

She pushed Adam's legs out of the way and pulled out her bag from underneath his feet.

"Don't answer it."

"It's Gabriel." She grabbed her phone.

"I said, don't answer it. Please."

"We should have included him sooner. He's already digging into this, and he'll be able to find out things we can't." She opened the phone. "Gabe?"

"Where the hell are—"

Adam grabbed the phone from her, hung up and threw it in the backseat. "Please! Not him, not now."

"What *is* it between you two?" She was practically yelling.

So was he. "Why are you so sure he's not the killer?"

"He's just not."

"How can you possibly know that? He's into weird, dark stuff. He doesn't have a real alibi for when Brett died. He could've easily been the guy who filmed Cynn. He hated Brett, Cynn, Felix and me."

"Gabriel doesn't have a violent bone in his body."

"Oh yeah? After I saved his ass, I asked him if you were single or if you guys were a thing. And he freaked out. Said if he ever found out I was even talking to you, he'd get his dad's gun and shoot my balls off."

"Gabriel would never say that in a million years."

She threw the car into reverse and pressed the accelerator. The tires spun. The car didn't move.

"What's this?" Adam had the scalpel in his hand.

"Where'd you get that?"

"It was on the floor." He looked at the blade. "Is that blood?"

She'd been so distracted by stabbing Gabriel, she hadn't even checked the blade for blood before retracting it.

"I accidentally stabbed Gabriel with it."

"What? When?"

"Last night. He was opening my bedroom window. I mistook him for a stalker."

"Jeez. You're still worried *I'm* going to hurt you, but you're trusting Gabriel blindly."

"He's my friend."

She gunned the engine again. The car was stuck.

"And I'm your enemy?"

"No." She said it softly. Rain now pounded the roof.

"I just admitted I liked you. Can't you at least be honest about whether or not you like me?"

Adam acted like it was easy. Like all she needed to do was open her mouth and say she liked him too, and nothing else would matter.

"I like you, too, dammit. But if you liked me enough to ask Gabriel if I was single then you should have dumped Cynn. Asking if I was single while dating her was a wimpy, cowardly thing to do. Or did you figure you'd just be with us both while you made up your mind?"

"That's not fair."

"The hell it isn't," said Liv.

There was a fork of lighting in the rear view mirror. A few seconds later, thunder rumbled then boomed.

"I can't do this anymore, Liv. I said I was sorry. I said I liked you—"

"And I *want* to trust you, but—"

"Either you do or you don't."

He shoved the door open. Rain rushed in. "This car isn't going anywhere until the rain stops and the mud dries. And I'm not about to randomly hitchhike to the next town and risk getting recognized. I'm going to find a dry place in the barn and get some sleep."

He stepped out into the storm, taking the flashlight with him.

"Adam."

He turned back, already drenched.

"Look, you don't have to go. Why don't we both just sleep here?"

He stared at her, then gave a short laugh that sounded more like a bark. "You think I'm ever going to be able to sleep in a *car* again?"

Chapter Twenty-Six

Adam slammed the car door behind him.

She fished around in the backseat for her phone. Gabriel answered on the first ring.

"Sorry about that."

"Where are you?"

She stared through the windshield. Not that she could see anything through all the rain.

"In a field. In front of a barn, off Highway 11, in the middle of nowhere."

"Very funny. So, get this. You know how someone smashed up Emma's boyfriend's car with a baseball bat? Well, last fall Felix's dad actually sued Felix and Brett for doing basically the same thing. Story goes, a week after dad moves in with hot mistress, two masked teenagers beat the crap out of him. Then they trashed his car so bad he had to write it off. Said his own daughter broke his leg with a baseball bat. Apparently he tried to press charges, but police said there wasn't enough evidence."

Huh. So the story of how Felix's dad tried to press charges against her was way worse than it had sounded. Maybe Mom hadn't known about the assault part. Liv leaned back and looked out the window, letting his words wash over her. "Felix beat up her own dad?"

"Allegedly. But yeah. Remind me to tell my dad how good he's got it. Of course, she was with Brett. Trust me, he was one sick son of a bitch."

"Did Adam save you once when Brett taped you to the hood of a car and tried to play bumper cars with you?"

She practically heard his throat tighten.

"Who told you that?"

"It's true, isn't it?"

He didn't answer. He didn't need to.

She couldn't even begin to imagine how terrified he must have felt.

Or how humiliated.

Her voice dropped. "Why didn't you tell me?"

"Adam is an asshole."

"I know. But he asked you if I was seeing anyone, didn't he? And you threatened to shoot his balls off."

"Yeah? So what?"

"So . . . everything. So . . . I don't know. Never mind. Sorry, I have to go."

"Wait, Liv, how do you even know—"

She shut the phone, tossed it onto the passenger seat and got out of the car. Without headlights, the rain pelting her seemed black. She sloshed through the deluge and groped along the side of the barn until she found the door. It was open a crack.

"Hey, Adam?"

She wouldn't have thought it could get any darker, but she stepped into pure black, feeling her way with her feet over soft wood that creaked gently. Something rustled. A light flashed on and off. A sepia image of a pile of hay and some scattered tools came into view before everything went black again.

"Adam?"

He moved. The flashlight flickered on again. His face shone pale in the yellowy beam. His hair dripped over his forehead. He'd stripped down to his shorts.

She stepped right up to him, wrapped her arms all the way around him and ran her fingers up into his wet hair.

She kissed him.

She kissed him without letting herself stop to overthink it. Kissed him because of every time she'd fantasized about being with him. Kissed him because she wanted him so badly it almost made her body ache—

He didn't kiss her back. His body stiffened. His back arched away from her, as if her skin was on fire.

She stopped. She'd been wrong. Stupid. What was she thinking? Here she'd gone and thrown herself at him and—

Then his hand crept up her back. His fingers curled around the collar of her shirt, pulling it back from her neck. His face brushed against hers in the darkness, his lips floating just above her skin.

He wanted her. She felt it. He wanted her every bit as much as she wanted him, but he wouldn't drop his guard.

She kissed him again. She traced her lips along the edge of his jaw, down his throat. Teasing him. Daring him.

He groaned. The flashlight clattered to the floor, throwing a slash of light across the wooden boards at their feet.

His hands grew firmer, pulled her closer, and slid down around her waist, over her hips and back up. She gasped. Then he kissed her, until her knees buckled. The rain whipped at the sides of the barn. Thunder exploded in the air. Adam lifted her off her feet and down into the hay pile. She expected him to start peeling back her clothes.

Instead, he traced his finger over her face and down across her lips. "I . . . don't have protection."

She smiled. "That's okay. I wasn't exactly planning to have sex with an escaped convict in a barn."

"But you're okay making out with one?"

"Well yeah, once he stops talking."

She covered his mouth with hers.

And they lay there, side by side, in a tangle of arms and legs, taste and touch, as the storm rolled around them.

Chapter Twenty-Seven

Sunlight filtered through the slats of the barn door. Liv stretched and rolled over in the hay. And smiled as she reached out for Adam—

No one was there.

She pushed herself up onto her elbows and looked around. The barn was smaller than she'd thought. Older too, with random car parts and rusted farm equipment in the corner. She ran her fingers through her hair, pulling out straw as she went, replaying moments from last night.

Adam burying his face in her hair . . . twisting the strands in his fingers . . . pulling them up off her neck . . . leaving a trail of kisses down her throat . . .

How many times had she imagined what it would be like to make out with him like that? The reality had been different. More awkward. More real.

Definitely more fun.

"Hey, Adam?"

She slid off the hay, found her shoes, then shoved the barn door open.

The car was gone too.

He'd taken everything—her mom's car, her keys, her wallet, her phone.

What kind of asshole spent the night with a girl, then took all her stuff and left her in the middle of nowhere?

No. That wasn't right. He wouldn't just leave her here. He must have been murdered or kidnapped or—

By someone who decided not to murder or kidnap *her*?

Yeah, right.

Liv waited around for a while in the hopes that Adam would show up with a really good explanation and a *great* apology. Not having a phone meant not having a clue what time it was or how long she was actually standing around waiting. But finally, after what felt like forever—though was probably more like an hour—she gave up and started walking. She hated him. Hated herself for making out with him. Hoped that, for his sake, he was tied up in some psycho's trunk right now. Otherwise, she'd murder Adam herself.

Eventually Liv found a little highway gas station with fake neon orange trees out front. She used the gas station phone to call Gabriel.

"Hey Gabe? I'm in trouble. Someone stole my car and I'm stuck at a gas station on Highway 11, maybe three hours north of the city. Just south of Gravenhurst."

"I'm on my way."

Gabriel made the drive in less than two hours, in a black SUV he'd lifted from his father's garage. He got out and opened his arms.

She stepped into them and started to cry. "Please don't hate me."

"Never."

"I let somebody . . ."

"Adam."

Damn.

"Oh, I'm a real good guesser." He let her go, then sat on top of a picnic table. "In fact, I'm *guessing* he came by your work and needed a favour?" His jaw was tighter than she'd ever seen it before.

Sure, let's go with that. "He said there was something up here that might prove his innocence. Then he stole the car and all my stuff."

He cracked his knuckles. They were white.

"And you look like you've been rolling around in the dirt because . . ."

"I slept rough."

"Right."

He was staying pretty calm. Which wasn't necessarily a good thing. "You called the police?"

She shook her head. "I didn't know what to tell them."

His eyes locked on hers. "About Adam? Nothing.

Not one damn thing. You're not getting in trouble over that piece of crap. We're going to say we drove up here separately and your car was stolen. Okay? We'll nail Adam later in some way that doesn't connect back to you."

She swallowed hard. "You'd say that for me?"

"I'd do a hell of a lot more than that."

They climbed into the SUV, Gabriel in the driver's seat. Liv could still smell Adam on her skin. She wanted to shower it off.

Gabriel handed her his cell phone. "Better call your mom."

"Thanks."

She checked her voice mail first. Hopefully the lack of panicked message from Mom meant that since Mom was working a double nightshift she wouldn't even realize Liv hadn't made it home last night.

She left a vague voice mail telling Mom she was with Gabriel. Then she called Tony and told him she wouldn't make it in that night.

"Jake Azivi's ashes came back from the crematorium yesterday," Tony said, "so I went ahead and sent them up to his grandmother by overnight courier. I received notification that she signed for them this morning." He sighed. "That's two weeks in a row we've had a young one in. This morning I got a call about another teenager."

Oh no. Liv held her breath.

Tony sighed. "I hate to turn anyone away, but they

wanted me to take the body today and I just didn't feel right about it."

"Who was it?"

"Kid named Edward Pyne."

"Eddy?!"

She grabbed Gabriel's arm. The car swerved.

What? he mouthed.

"Yeah," said Tony. "Same kid you think broke into the place a few days ago and frightened you. I know his parents say he's innocent and it was all some big misunderstanding. But under those circumstances, I just didn't want to put you through that."

"I have to go. Thanks Tony. I'll see you tomorrow." She hung up. "Eddy's dead."

"Hell."

Gabriel pulled to a stop on the shoulder, took out his phone and scanned the internet. Eddy had been found by a maintenance man in Rosewood's football field, with his hands tied, his pants undone and throat cut ear to ear.

"You know I kind of wondered if he was the killer," Gabriel said.

"Maybe he was part of it and now his partner is tying up loose ends."

"Literally."

The news was reporting that Eddy had been killed "sometime in the night or early morning." So even if she had felt like telling people she'd spent the night with Adam, that wouldn't necessarily give him an alibi.

She sighed. "I'm guessing all our suspects were home in bed?"

His fingers flew over the phone. "Nope. According to social media, Damien was hours away at a water polo match in Montreal. Took Emma with him. The photos are pretty convincing. Not that it's totally impossible to fake those things. Felix is still in the hospital."

"That just leaves Sharona? Who decides to kill her own boyfriend two days before the prom because he's been helping her cover up a murder spree?"

"Guess so."

"But she's the one with the flimsiest motive. Eddy had more reason to kill Brett than she did."

Gabriel pulled back onto the road.

An idea flickered in the back of Liv's mind. "What if we go check out the first murder scene? It can't be that far from here."

"You just curious or you got a hunch?"

"Trust me. There's something there that I'm hoping can help."

Chapter Twenty-Eight

The cottage was huge, with giant arching windows and a wraparound deck. There was no car in the driveway. Looked like Jake's grandmother wasn't home. Liv stood by the deck and carefully looked down the very steep hill towards the lake. A cluster of wreaths sat around the shore. Some had Brett's face on them.

Gabriel hopped over the railing, onto the porch and tried the sliding patio doors. They were locked. He dug a utility knife from his pocket.

"Since when do you carry a knife?"

He looked at her sideways.

"How else am I supposed to splice wires and jimmy open casings?" He flicked out a nail file. "Got a corkscrew and a toothpick in it too." He crouched down and slid the file in the gap under the doors. "Oh, and a really big blade for murdering random classmates."

"Ha ha."

He moved the nail file back and forth.

She glanced over the lawn and tried to guess where Adam's car might have been sitting before it rolled down the hill. "Did you ever meet Brett's cousin Jake Azivi?"

"No . . ."

The syllable hung in the air, like it was asking her something.

"He's really nice."

"And really dead, right? Cancer kid you told me about? Cremated a couple of days ago? You didn't ever tell me you knew him before he'd died."

She didn't know quite how to answer that.

The lock clicked. Gabriel slid the door open. Liv stepped into the room. And froze.

She'd been here before. Tried to run out that door. Fallen on this floor.

Brett's dead spirit had dragged her here.

She turned back toward the porch.

Tall windows on either side of the sliding doors. Wood beams. She closed her eyes and pressed her fingers to her temples.

His spirit hadn't been the only one.

"I think Cynn made out with someone here."

He coughed. "Where the hell did that come from?"

"It wasn't Adam." She pointed. "They started out on that couch. . . ." She closed her eyes, remembering the story Cynn had told her about her last hook up. Her finger moved through the air. "Then they went in a room over there. It has a door out to the patio."

There'd been a rope hanging on the patio.

"And you know this how?"

"Would you believe gossip in the school bathroom?"

"So Cynn was cheating on Adam."

"Yeah, and I don't know with whom. I think she had a stalker, though. Adam said there was someone lurking in her bushes the night she died. Filming her even. What if this guy is a real sicko who saw his chance to get both Adam and Brett out of the way? Then she turns him down, so he slices her up too? "

"So Adam was at Cynn's house the night she died?"

"Really? That's where you're going with this?"

Gabriel sighed. "Just tell me what we're here looking for, exactly."

"An urn."

Hopefully if Tony had shipped it up by overnight courier yesterday it was still here. Jake had said his grandmother lived there year round.

"Understood."

"You take the bookcases. I'll hit the cabinet."

She ran her eyes along the shelves.

Where are you, Jake? And what do you remember?

There was a wooden box wedged at the end of a row. She opened it. Empty. Dammit.

"Hey, Liv, you gotta see this."

She turned.

A thick silver snake curled around Gabriel's neck.

Just like one did in her vision from Brett's grave.

"They collect antique jewellery," Gabriel said.

It was a necklace. Shivers ran up her shoulders. "Take it off."

She turned back to the bookshelf and felt around until she found a stone container hidden behind some books. She opened it. Beads.

"Oh wow. Weapons."

"Gabriel, focus."

"They actually have nunchucks and throwing stars. Looks like somebody's Nana is a serious badass, and . . . here we go . . ."

"What?"

He held up his finger. "There's a syringe in this ring. Very secret spy."

"Were you injected with poison?"

"It was empty."

"Tell me if you find something with ashes inside."

This was nuts. Sure, her powers were growing at super fast speeds. But she'd never opened a link to ashes before. She might not even be able to do it. Something clicked open behind her. Gabriel must've given up on the weapons and opened the door to the bedroom. She didn't turn. There was a silver vase on the top of the shelf. She reached up and gently pulled it toward herself.

"Uh, Liv?"

"Just hold on a minute." She stretched up on her tiptoes. Her fingers clenched the edges of the vase. "I've almost got it."

"You have to turn around. Now."

"Hang on a sec, will you?"

Then came the sound of a hunting rifle bolt clicking behind her.

Liv's hands slipped. The vase tipped forward.

Ashes spilled out all over her.

Chapter Twenty-Nine

An old woman in a housecoat was standing in the bedroom doorway, pointing a shotgun at Gabriel.

Oh crap.

Liv took a deep breath, raised her hands and started babbling, hoping she'd manage to come up with some plausible reason for being there if she talked long enough.

"Hey, you must be Jake's grandmother, right? I'm really sorry. Like, so, so sorry. I didn't mean to spill his ashes—"

Nana Azivi raised the rifle and levelled Liv in her sights. "Get out. Now."

Tears of frustration were building in Liv's eyes. She was here in the very place where Brett had been murdered and Adam had been framed. She'd come this close to being able to try to talk to Jake's ghost again. And now she was just going to turn tail and run?

Gabriel was already walking backward out onto the patio. His eyes met hers. One eyebrow rose with a look that implied the only thing that had kept him from hauling ass was not wanting to leave her behind.

And here she was, her dead friend's ashes on her hands and everywhere, still trying to talk down the old woman whose home she'd just broken into.

"Please, I know how crazy this must look.—"

The old woman's finger didn't even quiver on the trigger. "I'm counting to three. And then I'm shooting first and calling the police second."

"But, but if I could just have five minutes with Jake's ashes—"

"One. Two—"

"Come on!" Gabriel lunged across the room, grabbed Liv's arm and yanked her toward the door. They ran across the front porch, clambered back over the porch railing and ran around the side of the cottage. The sound of shotgun blast rippled through the trees behind them in what Liv hoped was meant as a reminder not to come back. They sprinted back to his vehicle, Gabriel practically dragging Liv behind him. He opened her door and pushed her inside, before running around to the driver's side and leaping in. The engine squealed.

"That was insane!" Gabriel was laughing. And speeding. Trees flew past the window. "And here I thought I was the delinquent in this relationship. I don't know where the hell good-girl Liv has gone. But the new you is a trip."

Liv leaned back on the seat. Tears of frustration were building in her eyes, but she didn't let them fall. Her fingers traced through the faint remnants of Jake's ashes on her skin, drawing patterns on her palm

Well, Jake, I'm sorry I couldn't talk to you one last time. I tried. But hey, you're only ashes now anyway. And—

The air around her rippled like water. The car faded out of focus.

Then a moment of silence swept over or maybe *into* her. Gentle. Soft. Her racing heart began to slow. Her muscles began to relax, letting go of tension she hadn't even realized she'd been carrying.

Jake was sitting cross-legged in front of her, where the dashboard had been moments ago. "Hello, you. What's up?"

Jake! I'm so glad you're here!

"Son of a bitch, Liv!" Gabriel said. "What the hell are you doing?"

She felt Gabriel's hand on her arm and then the car slam to a stop. But it was like Gabriel and the world around her was fading further and further away into the distance.

"Heyyyy." Jake grabbed her hands. "What's going on?"

I'm talking to your ashes. My powers have kept growing. Like a lot.

She could tell her lips weren't moving and that she was only talking to him in her mind. But somehow it sounded as loud as if they were talking face to face.

"Yeah, I can tell." He looked almost worried. "It's like the size of the connection between where I am and you are has gone from small window a few days ago to like a giant hole in the wall."

Things have gotten really messed up, and I'm kind of in the middle of it. You know how someone killed your cousin? Well, now three more people have been attacked.

"I'm real sorry to hear that."

My friend Adam says he was with you the night Brett died?

"The guy they arrested? That's what you're here about?"

She nodded.

"Okay. Well, yeah he was with me. But he was drunk and kind of incoherent. He passed out in his car. I turned the engine off so he wouldn't drain the battery, left him to sleep it off and walked to a friend's cottage. What I should have done though is pocketed the keys instead of leaving them in the ignition. Brett and I weren't supposed to be having a party at Nana's cottage that weekend anyway. Nana was in Florida and we were under strict instructions not to let anyone over. I didn't find out Brett was dead until the next morning."

Is Brett there? You know, where you are?

"Nah, I've seen a bunch of people. But not him."

I tried asking Brett who killed him. Adam and I, we . . . we dug him up. And he . . . Tears were building in her eyes. *It was beyond horrible. I was trapped there.*

And these people from school were attacking me, saying things that—

"Shhhhh." Jake squeezed her hands. "You've got to promise me you'll stop doing this to yourself, okay? Stop listening to people like Brett. Stop caring what bullies and assholes say. Alright? They're lying. The truth about you is you're amazing." His fingers tapped her forehead. "This is *your* brain. You get to choose who to listen to, and what to believe about who you are."

He leaned forward and hugged her tight. "Thanks for all the time you spent talking and listening to me after I died. And thanks for this."

His image rippled. "You've got so many people who love you. You seriously need to wake up and see that."

Suddenly other faces were flickering around her. She could see her mom opening her arms for a hug. Then Gabriel looking at her with that sly smile that said he knew she was crazy and it was just fine with him. Tony sticking out his chest while he defended her to the police.

And Adam. . .

In the morgue trying to protect her from opening a new connection to Cynn—

Yanking her up out of Brett's grave—

Standing shirtless in the barn—

"Wow, there sure is a lot of him in here. I get why you'd want to help him."

Really? She didn't even know anymore.

Tears were streaming down her face now. The images were fading.

"Where did those come from?" Liv asked. "Did you do that?"

Jake nodded. "Yeah, I did. And it wasn't that hard to do. I think when you open your mind, it's kind of a two-way street. You can pull me in. But I can push my way into your mind too. A week ago it was like you just had this tiny space in your mind for me to step into. But now it's like your brain is a house and you've left the door unlocked, and anyone can walk in and rearrange the furniture. So promise me you'll be careful who you talk to. I'm really holding myself back because I'm afraid to touch anything or I could do you some major damage. Plus there's some weird stuff in here too, like someone's been actively trying to move their own crap into your brain. You have to stop letting them. Just tell the liars to shut the hell up. Haters don't have the right." He let her go and sat back. "I have to go now. Please don't take it personally, but I'm not coming back like this again. I got somewhere else better to be. So if you call me again, just know it won't work. I don't even know how you brought me back this time—"

"Your ashes. I broke into your cottage and kind of stole some."

"Seriously? You're lucky my Nana didn't shoot you."

His image faded. The echo of his laughter lingered in her mind.

Chapter Thirty

The vehicle faded back into focus. They were parked at the side of the road. Gabriel was sitting beside her on the driver's side. His arms were braced against the steering wheel.

"Hey . . ."

He flinched. "Don't, 'hey' me. Do you want to tell me what the hell you were doing?"

"I wasn't doing anything—"

"The hell you weren't. You were all tranced out and glowing."

What? Gabriel had been able to see her do that? Adam hadn't been able to see her do anything. And Tony had walked in on her chatting with Jake's corpse and not noticed. Were her powers growing? Or was Gabriel special?

"Did you see only me?"

He cut her a sideways glance. "Yeah . . . was there somebody else here?"

"I was talking to Jake's ghost. Inside a mental connection. That's what I wanted his ashes for. But I didn't know if it would work." She leaned her head back against the seat. "Look, this isn't exactly how I wanted to tell you, but, the day after we saw Brett murdered, I, uh, well . . . Okay, I know how crazy this is probably going to sound, but . . ." Liv took a deep breath. "I started being able to talk to the corpses. Just a little bit at first. Like I could hear their thoughts and see them projected. I'm really, really sorry I didn't tell you before."

Gabriel didn't speak.

She wanted him to yell. She wanted him to argue.

She wanted him to bang his hands down on the steering wheel and shout. Because then she could shout back and at least they'd be communicating.

Somehow his silence was far worse.

"I've only talked to a few dead people," she kept going. "Not very many. I'm still figuring out what I'm able to do. Basically, I touch them, and I see a projected image of them, and we talk."

Gabriel started the engine again and pulled back onto the road. His hands gripped the steering wheel at ten and two exactly.

"You're mad," she said. "I get it. Go ahead and yell at me if you need to, but believe me—I wanted you to know."

He slid a pair of sunglasses from his pocket and put them on.

"I'm glad you know now," she added. "Really. Jake couldn't tell me anything, but now I'm wondering if there's some connection between all that antique jewellery and the necklace Eddy stole from Cynn's corpse. We came up here to try to talk to Brett's ghost actually. And when I tried connecting with Brett's corpse—"

"*We*." He barked out a laugh that was more of a snarl. "Oh, so you didn't tell me but goddamn Adam Clay knew you could talk to the dead, didn't he? And you agreed to help him dig up his buddy Brett for a chat." He looked at her over his sunglasses. "Hell, he probably used you to chat with Cynn's corpse too."

"Gabe! What's the matter with you? I just told you I can talk to dead people. Corpses. Ghosts. Whatever. They talk to me. I talk to them. And all you can think about is that I was with Adam?"

"Oh, I'm sorry, I didn't know there was a specific way I'm supposed to deal with finding out my best friend never bothered telling me she has supernatural abilities—"

"It's not like I—"

"And that you're using them to help the *same people* who made our lives a living hell!" His voice rose. "It's like telling me you won the lottery and in the same breath adding that you're donating it to the Rosewood Bully Party Fund."

"That's not—"

"What the hell is the matter with you? We didn't

take enough crap from these people while they were alive, so you have to go dig them up for a second helping?"

"Look, I didn't exactly plan this—"

"You know, I actually tried to be the bigger man after Adam saved me from Brett that one time. I went and got the money to pay him back. And Adam asked if you were mine or if you belonged to someone else. *Belonged*, Liv. Like you were an object. Not like he liked you. Not like he respected you. Like you were some *thing* he'd decided he wanted to have just because he wanted it. Just like he had everything else."

No wonder Gabriel had flipped on out him. Hot tears pressed against her eyelids. "I'm sure he didn't mean it like *that*."

Adam couldn't have. Could he? Sure, he might be thoughtless and selfish sometimes, but—

Gabriel shook his head, like he was either too disgusted or too tired to fight. "It was supposed to be you and me against the world, Liv."

"It still is."

He slid his glasses back on and turned back to the road. "No, it isn't."

"Gabe—"

"Don't. Okay? Just give me some time to get my head around all of this."

"This?"

"You talking to the dead. You being in cahoots with Adam. You. Not. Trusting. Me."

She leaned back. Trees and signs passed. Numbers on the clock cycled through. The white lines of the highway went on and on and on.

He dropped her off at the apartment.

Liv paused, her hand on the car door. "You're still my best friend—even if we don't always tell each other everything."

Gabriel drove off without looking back.

Mom wasn't home and Adam had driven off with Liv's keys, so she got the building super to let her in. The apartment was empty and dark, but there was a fresh loaf of bread on the table. Someone had torn off a chunk and left crumbs on the counter. The button on the answering machine blinked. She still hadn't called the police or figured out how to tell her mom that her car had been stolen.

God, she was a mess.

Liv stripped off her filthy clothes, stepped into the shower and let the water run over her body. Her mind buzzed like a wasp trapped inside her skull. She got out and stared at herself in the mirror.

There was something wrong with her face. Her lips looked red. Deep red, like someone had painted them. Her cheeks seemed longer, her jaw thinner.

And her hair . . .

Her hair almost looked like it was moving.

Music was playing. Weird. Distorted. Like a stereo underwater. Long wet strands of black and purple hair slid and curved up the sides of her face. Twisted. Turned. Piled on top of her head.

Something shimmered, hovered, in the air above her. It landed on her head and bit in hard with metal teeth.

A tiara.

The front door clicked and the jangle of keys fell onto the table. Liv blinked. The image was gone. She grabbed a T-shirt and a pair of boxers from the dryer and pulled them on.

Her mom was waiting for her in the hallway. "You didn't tell me you wanted to borrow the car."

Crap.

"Although I must say, I'm impressed you brought it back with a full tank of gas and a carwash. Very thoughtful."

So, Adam had left her behind but brought the car back? Liv couldn't even begin to guess what that meant.

"You weren't here when I got in this morning," her mom added, "and I haven't heard from you all day."

"Yeah, sorry. I left early. I've been with Gabriel all day. The last week of school has been kind of crazy, plus there's work."

She turned to go, but her mom caught her under the chin and tilted her face toward her.

"What's going on?"

"Nothing. I'm fine, Mom. Just really, really tired."

That at least wasn't a lie.

Her Mom headed into the bathroom and a few moments later, Liv heard her running the shower. She walked into her bedroom and shut the door, not even bothering to turn on the light. Reaching for her bed, she pulled back the covers and slid under the cool, soft sheets.

And brushed up against a warm body.

Chapter Thirty-One

Liv sat up and smacked the light on.

Adam mumbled something and rolled over. His shoulders were bare. She lifted the covers. Well, at least he'd left his jeans on.

"How the hell could you just leave me like that?"

He didn't move.

"You obviously used my keys to get in. Where the hell is my stuff?"

She rolled him onto his back. Eyes still closed, he reached out and wrapped his arms around her. His mouth brushed against her face.

"Wake up," she hissed.

Adam's eyes fluttered open, then closed again.

"Oh, hey." He smiled at her. "When did you get here?"

"What the hell happened?"

"I was waiting for you. Guess I fell asleep."

"Yeah, because *that's* what I meant. I don't actually

care that you snuck out on me in the middle of the night, stole my stuff and left me in the middle of goddamn nowhere!"

He sat up and shook the hair out of his eyes.

"Hey, don't be like that!" He rubbed his eyelids. "I'm sorry. Really, really sorry. Your stuff is all there on the dresser and I returned the car. Even ran it through a carwash."

She sat up and crossed her arms. "Well aren't you a saint."

"So, you're mad."

"Oh, I'm more than mad."

She could still hear the sound of Mom's shower running. Liv reached past Adam to the MP3 player on her bedside table and turned on music to drown out the sound of their conversation even further.

"Hey, I'm trying to apologize! I had no intention of leaving you. You were asleep, so I went for a drive to see if I could find a Wi-Fi signal and check my e-mail. Nothing to write on, so no note. Speaking of—get this, I got an e-mail from DeathFetishGirl99. She's sorry she hasn't been in touch. She—"

"Or he."

"—or he. Whatever! Anyway, she says Felix's stabbing really threw her for a loop, but she's ready to help now. She wanted me to meet her at Bloor and Spadina this afternoon."

"So you ditched me and went."

"No! Well, sort of. But then, I realized I should drive

back, so I did. When I got there, I saw you and Gabriel at a truck stop. With his arms around you. I tried to wave at you, but you didn't see me. And I wasn't exactly going to run over and break you guys up, since you looked so *cozy*. So I went back to the graveyard and threw some dirt back in the hole, which fortunately had half filled in with mud thanks to the rainstorm anyway. I figured I'd meet up with you later."

"Adam! I met up with Gabriel *hours* after you ditched me. Does this mean you no longer think Gabe's a psycho, or were you just willing to risk it?"

"Why are you acting like this?"

"You took all my stuff and left me in a barn in the middle of nowhere!"

"I already said I was sorry for that. And I *am* sorry for that. I wasn't thinking."

"You weren't thinking. Of course."

She shook her head. What difference did it make what he said he *felt* about her. She still came second to chasing whatever random thought went running through his brain.

"But then I came back," he said, "and saw you with Gabriel—"

"Oh, now who sounds jealous?"

"*And* I returned your mother's car and your stuff. And I put you before my meeting with DeathFetish when I tried to go back for you, all right? But I apparently missed her. The good news is I've finally got everything sorted." He leaned back against her pillow. "I talked to DeathFetish online this afternoon. She emailed me back. We chatted back and forth for over an hour, and she explained everything—"

"Like her name? Or *his* name?"

"*She* didn't want to tell me, and that's cool. Her life is already in danger, and I don't want to make it any worse. She was at the party the night Brett was killed, though. She saw someone playing around with a knife. Then later she saw it lying all bloody in the grass."

"Who?" Liv asked. "What kind of knife?"

"I don't know. Anyway, she was going to grab it but then the police showed up and everything was total chaos. She'd always suspected her friend still had it. Then a couple weeks ago she confirmed for sure that the exact same person had the exact same knife." He sat back against the pillow. "See, she always suspected I was innocent, but once she saw a friend of hers with the knife, she knew for sure."

"And did she go to the police with any of this?" asked Liv.

"The person who has the knife was a really close friend of hers and she's kind of conflicted. Nobody wants to believe a friend could be a murderer. Plus, she's scared of them now and thinks her life might be in danger. I told her to go to the police, but I can't force her to. I get the impression she's kind of timid and needs help. So, we're going to meet up tomorrow, I'll get the knife and turn it over to police. And I'll try to convince her to come with me to talk to the cops and tell them everything she knows. "

"And you believe her."

Unbelievable.

"I believe she's in trouble," he said. "I believe she's scared. I'm not saying she's done anything close to the right thing. But yeah, not all people are strong like you. Some actually get scared and need someone to step up and help them make the right decision."

Strong like her.

Strong enough that you can just ignore them all year and they'll bounce back. Strong enough to survive digging up a grave, and getting attacked by the scary undead thing that used to be Brett, and being stranded in a barn in the middle of nowhere—

"Why are you scrunching up your face like that? I meant it as a compliment."

"Oh come *on*. She's been playing you from the beginning. Being all weak. Being all helpless. Needing you. Making you her knight in shining armour . . ."

"And what's wrong with someone coming to me for help? What's wrong with me wanting to help someone? She wrote me for weeks. Do you have any idea how much that meant to me to have someone write me emails like that?"

Yup. And you developed a crush on a stranger because she made you feel good about yourself. And you assumed she was me.

"I don't like it." Liv leaned back against the wall. "Nobody writes to some guy locked up in a youth facility, begging him for help when she could just step up and do the right thing herself. She could've gotten the knife without you. She could've gone to the police without you taking her by the hand and leading her there. This isn't some chick flick. She's not the damsel in distress. You're not the big strong hero."

"If I didn't know any better, I'd say now you sound jealous." His arm slipped around her shoulders. "Do you want to come with me? Do you want to talk to her?"

"I don't want to go anywhere near this train wreck."

"Okay, look—I'll keep my eyes open tomorrow and if anything looks wrong, I'll bail. She doesn't know you've been helping me, for which I'm insanely thankful, because at least that keeps *you* safe. Believe it or not, it really matters to me that you're okay and that I don't get you even more mixed up in this than I already have." He leaned over, hesitated slightly and kissed her neck. "Yeah, she and I flirted some in the past. Yeah, I've done some dumb things. But this could be my last night on the run . . . and I'm here with you."

She turned toward him. Adam leaned toward her. His lips brushed over hers.

She pushed him back.

"Sorry." He looked at the floor. "I guess I really screwed things up this time."

"Yeah, you did. You ditched me, Adam. You can't fix it that easily."

"I said I was sorry . . ."

"How can you act like it's no big deal?"

"I'm not saying it's no big deal. I'm saying I screwed up and I'm sorry. Please, just tell me what I need to say or do to make this right?"

"So you can fool around with me tonight then move on again tomorrow?"

He sighed. "Why does it feel like you're intentionally misunderstanding me? I really thought you were smarter than that."

She shoved him hard.

He fell onto the floor.

"Livvy?" It was Mom. "Are you alright?"

Liv hadn't noticed the fact the shower had switched off again. Now her mother's voice rose over the sound of the music.

She got up and ran over to the door. "Yeah, Mom, I'm fine. I just dropped something."

Adam glared up at her. "What was that for? I might've done the wrong thing, but I didn't do it to hurt you. I did it to save my own ass!"

Right. Only she'd jumped in to save him, and now it felt like she was drowning. She crouched down. "I trusted you, and you ditched me. You're still that same guy now you were last fall. You're that guy who's so insanely focused on your own stuff you'd take off down the highway without waiting for me to wake up."

"I'm not going to keep apologizing for that." Adam stood up, grabbed his shirt off the floor and yanked it on. "I said I want to make things right. Apparently I messed up too huge this time. But I'm not apologizing for being focused on saving my life. I'm the one wanted for murder. I'm the one on the run from the police. So yeah, I'm going to do whatever it takes to keep my ass out of jail."

"And I've been risking everything for you. I lied to my boss. I lied to my Mom. I lied to Gabriel—and hurt my best friend. Hell, I broke the law for you." She crossed her arms over her chest. "I'm not saying you're wrong to be focused on staying out of jail. I get it. But my life matters too, and I've got to get focused on protecting *myself*. Right now I'm going to go distract my mom so you can slip out."

Liv took a deep breath and turned toward the door.

"You don't think I want to protect you, too?"

She didn't look back. *Maybe I don't want you protecting me.*

"Did you even ask Gabriel if I was telling the truth about what I told you?" Adam asked. "How I paid Brett off? How I told him I liked you?"

She stopped. "Liked me? Or wanted to know if I belonged to anyone?"

"Wanted to know if you were single. Wanted to get with. I don't know exactly what I said. Brett and Eddy were being dicks and interrupting me with stupid sex jokes. Gabriel was totally pissed off. And I was trying to act like it was no big deal and like I didn't like you as much as I did. Does it really matter what my exact words were?"

"No, it matters that you're standing there defending the fact you pretended not to like me because of your idiotic, bully friends." Her hand touched the doorknob. "You know, for all your complaining before about how your friends just used you and didn't treat you like a real person, you haven't seemed to learn a whole lot."

Adam sighed. But for once, she didn't care how frustrated he was

"And, heads up, Gabriel knows I've been helping you."

"Crap. Really?"

"Yeah, what else did you expect? And he thinks you're a total asshole, so I suggest you steer clear of him. But I'm still going to ask him to take another look at that video card you found, in case he can find something we didn't see. Then I'll turn it in to the police."

"Okay." He shrugged. "Probably doesn't matter much now anyway."

"Alright." She waited and watched his face. "Take care of yourself."

She stepped out into the hallway, closed the door behind her and willed herself not to cry.

Chapter Thirty-Two

Liv was at the school dance. She wore a long dress and an antique gold necklace. She held something in her hands.

Music played.

Images flashed.

Doors opened and closed.

People bled.

Someone offered her a drink.

"I can't hold it. My hands are full."

She looked down.

She was holding Gabriel's severed head—

Liv woke up, not feeling rested in the slightest. Tonight was prom. Hopefully one that was less of a bloodbath than in her dream.

She crawled out of bed, got dressed, then waited way too long in front of her building, just in case Gabriel decided to show up and walk her to school. He didn't.

She was late for school. Not that it mattered. Most teachers knew the only reason students bothered showing up on the last day was to sign each other's yearbooks, gossip about who'd be together at the dance later and discuss who'd be voted queen. With Cynn out of the running, things were getting frantic.

Sharona stood on the front steps shoving campaign flyers at anyone who got within reach. Good to see Eddy's death hadn't slowed her down.

Well, her thong was probably black.

"You're voting for me, right?"

The flyer hit Liv's chest.

She let it flutter to the ground. "In what world?"

"Excuse me?" Sharona stepped into her face. "You really want to start with me, bitch?"

"Sorry, don't have the time." She pushed past Sharona and into the school.

The prom committee was manning voting stations. The yearbook committee was handing out books. Various parent-types doled out swag bags filled with anything somebody could slap their company's name on.

"Did you order a yearbook?"

A girl in a tailored jacket and two braids waved her towards a table.

"No, thanks. I'm . . ." She looked up. "*Felix*?"

Out of the hospital and looking like she'd just escaped an Ivy league catalogue from the sixties.

"Hey." She smiled. At Liv. A realistic looking smile, even.

"Amazing. They actually let you out in time to campaign?"

"Actually, I'm throwing my support behind Sharona. She wants it more than me."

Liv snorted.

The smile didn't waver. Felix's eyes darted toward the corporate swag table, where a well-dressed man with a Vitesse name tag stood watching them.

So Felix had decided to try public niceness on for size and turn down a crappy prize to lock in her chances for something really worth having. Brilliant. "I'm really loving the personality transplant. You finally got that the whole super-bitch thing wasn't working for you?"

Felix sighed. "You really don't believe people can change, do you?"

"People, yes. You? No."

Felix shook her head and turned back toward the table.

"Do you think Brett and Cynn were fooling around?"

Might as well throw that out as a parting shot and see what kind of reaction she got.

She wasn't disappointed. Felix's spine couldn't have shot up straighter if she'd jammed a pole up her back.

Felix spun around, reached out and hugged her, hard—just casually enough to make it look real. The Vitesse rep smiled.

"You trying to hurt me?" Felix's mouth was practically pressed up against her ear. "My boyfriend died last month, I got stabbed and my best friend just died a few days ago. I'm trying to get my life together. Now you want to run around spreading nasty rumours about ancient history?"

Well, not *that* ancient . . .

"I promise you, if that happened between Brett and Cynn, *I* never caught them at it." Felix stepped back. Her eyes opened wide. "But maybe someone else did."

Felix smoothed down her skirt and went back to stacking yearbooks. The man from Vitesse said something to her. Felix laughed.

What did she mean by "someone"? Someone as in Adam? Like Adam knew Brett fooled around with Cynn, so he killed them both? Bullshit.

Music slipped out from under the auditorium door. The front of her head ached again.

Think, Liv.

Adam wasn't the only one there the night Cynn died. And Liv still had the video card in her bag.

If she hadn't given in to Adam's idiotic demands about keeping Gabriel out of it, he might have figured out who DeathFetishGirl99 was, she'd probably know who Cynn's killer was, and she wouldn't have hurt the one guy she could actually count on.

She took out her cell phone and dialled.

"Yeah?"

Thank God, Gabriel was answering, at least.

"I feel horrible. Please don't stay mad at me. I need us to be okay."

There was a pause. "I'm not mad."

"Can we talk?"

"We can."

"Are you in the sound booth?"

"At home. Taking a 'me' day. How about you come here?"

"I'm on my way."

Liv walked to the subway to take it two stations south. It stopped after one. A voice in the overhead speaker said something about a brief delay. The doors stood open for what felt like forever while she stared at the station walls.

Adam kissed her here, in this station. Maybe on this very train.

She missed him. Painfully. Stupidly.

Even though she knew there was no way on earth she'd ever give him another chance.

Had he slept in the funeral home last night? If she jumped off now and ran down the street, would he still be there?

Then what?

He'd slide his arms around her, kiss her like he meant it.

And hurt her.

Again.

Chapter Thirty-Three

Gabriel lived beside his father, and occasionally his mother, in a separate loft above their six-car garage. Their house was on a long street in one of the richest neighbourhoods of Toronto.

He'd left the door open for her. Liv followed the narrow staircase up to Gabriel's lair. The space was dark and cavernous. Blinds were pulled down over the windows. An unmade bed was up against a wall. A black-light hummed in a corner.

Gabriel sat at his computer, his back to her. His long hair was loose around his shoulders.

"Knock knock," she said.

He didn't turn.

There was a school mug in his hand. Smelled like beer.

"Hey?" She crossed the room and laid a hand on his shoulder.

He put the mug down and reached up for her hand. His fingers snaked through hers. "Hey." He looked at her. His black eye was purple.

She gave his hand a quick squeeze. "We good?"

"We're okay." He let her hand go. "I don't like the fact you've been keeping secrets and I'm going to need time to process everything you've told me. Are your super special powers really as simple as you made it sound?"

"Yeah. I touch dead bodies. I see a vision of them and hear them in my head."

"And it started after Brett died?"

"Right after."

"Anything else I don't know?"

"Adam showed up last night. Returned my stuff. I kicked him out. Somebody called DeathFetishGirl99 wrote him emails saying they know who the killer is and could help prove his innocence, so he's teamed up with them now. Adam thinks it's a girl—actually, he thought it was me at first. But whoever they are, they're playing up the whole frightened damsel in distress thing and have Adam convinced they need his help to get the knife, turn it over to the police and do the right thing."

Gabriel made a noise somewhere between a choke and a laugh then returned to his computer. There were three different browser windows open on different screens. The first two looked like official records of some sort. Rosewood's logo spun slowly on the third.

She tapped the first screen. "And these are?"

"First, we've got the initial police report from Eddy's murder. Looks like Brett, Cynn and Eddy could have all been killed with the same knife. And you're right. It was small. Like a mini box cutter. He was also drunk as a skunk when he died, and probably had drugs in his system too. Same as Brett."

Nothing they hadn't already suspected.

"Second, hospital records. Felix was either stabbed by someone very short and weak or wasn't really trying, or we're actually down one victim."

"Huh?"

He looked *really* pleased with himself. "Felix stabbed herself."

"Wow."

He laughed and turned back. "Thought it was weird she wasn't allowed visitors, so I looked into it. Doctor thought the wound was self-inflicted. Called it an 'attention-getting stunt.' Kind of thing that looks really bad but is hardly fatal. That's probably why your being questioned by the police ended so abruptly and they never followed up. They realized they were questioning you for a non-crime. Doctors stitched her up and kept her three days for observation. Would also explain why they didn't keep a guard on her door and why they didn't want her talking to the press. Trying to nip her attention-getting in the bud. And get this—she went missing from her room a couple of times. Couple of hours at a time. Just reappeared before they hit that time limit when they had to call police. Claimed she snuck out to the local Internet café to catch up on her e-mail, but who's to say she didn't sneak out Thursday morning, stab Eddy and pop back into bed?"

"But she's still injured—"

"Yeah, but not too badly to slit somebody's throat. Sure, you'd have to be some kind of evil genius to pull it off, and she'd probably have needed to find a way to incapacitate Eddy or even tie him up before she killed him. But it's not impossible. It's not exactly hard to talk Eddy into getting high or blackout drunk. And that guy's lusted after Felix a while now. She might have even talked him into letting her tie him up, like for some kind of kinky game. 'Get down on your knees, baby. Close your eyes. Okay, now I'm just going to slit your throat from behind real quick.' Like leading a lamb to the slaughter. Not that I've come up with a plausible motive why yet."

Liv's brain was buzzing, big-time. "Felix was at school today, telling everyone to vote for Sharona. You should've seen it. She's got this total sweetness and light thing going now. In a totally manipulative way. What if she just wanted to become, like, the new Cynn?"

"You mean a fake sweet person who manipulates everyone into thinking that they're super nice?" He shook his head. "That'd be a really stupid way to go about it. Plus she'd have no reason to. Cynn was just a popular high school girl. Felix wouldn't stab herself for that, let alone kill anyone."

"What if she did it to increase her chances of being voted prom queen?"

"For what, the sympathy vote? And then realized she didn't really want it?"

The buzzing was getting louder. So loud Liv could hardly think.

"What if she killed Brett for sleeping with Cynn," Gabriel asked, "then got Eddy or someone to kill Cynn? Though why she'd wait weeks to kill her makes no sense. Hell, I'd even be more likely to believe she stabbed herself for the *internship*, if I could think of any conceivable way that injuring yourself would actually help you get a job with an airline."

Liv shook her head. "Something in my gut is telling me Felix is irrelevant here. She was always jealous of Cynn and this could have been her latest stunt to hog the limelight."

"I think your gut is being idiotic. It's like you've got this prom queen nonsense stuck in your brain and you've stopped thinking straight. Are you sure you're alright?"

Out of the corner of her eye, the Rosewood logo spun on the middle of the computer screen. Around. Around. Around. There was something almost hypnotic about it. Her temples ached.

All that matters is being prom queen. All that matters is being queen.

What? No! Where did that thought even *come* from? It didn't matter. None of that stuff mattered. Not to her, anyway. "Are we going to the dance together tonight?"

"You serious?" Gabriel turned back and stood. "After everything that happened yesterday I never figured you'd still want to go."

She couldn't read his expression. "I think I need to be there."

I think I'm going to be queen.

"Really?" He took a step toward her. His fingers slipped against hers, which for some reason felt weird. "You do know you're not going to get me out on the dance floor."

"Of course not." She stepped closer. "But we can hide out in the booth and keep our eyes peeled for potential psycho killers."

She was staring at Gabriel's mouth. His lips turned up at the corners.

Hang on. Was she actually thinking about kissing him now?

Gabriel smiled, but there was this want in his eyes, a desire, that made her breath feel almost painful in her lungs. Had she suspected that he wanted her before? Maybe. But she'd never seen it so clearly in his eyes before. Or maybe she'd just refused to see it?

And what was she doing? If they each took just one step closer, and tilted their chins, their lips would touch and she'd be risking the most important friendship she'd ever had. And why? Because she still felt hurt over Adam? Because her head felt so full of static she couldn't think straight?

She stepped back. No. She couldn't do it. Not now. Not like this. "We'd be going as friends, right? Just friends."

"Of course." His shoulders twitched in a casual shrug.

"Got something for you. And it's totally your kind of thing." She reached into her pocket and pulled out the high definition video card. "I told Adam I was going to turn it over to the police, but I figured you'd want to see it first."

He didn't touch it. He just looked at it, like it was some poisonous animal about to strike.

"You got this from Adam?" asked Gabriel.

"Yeah. Cynn's stalker filmed her in her underwear."

His face was still. With this weird calm she'd never seen before.

"I'm guessing whoever made this video is the same psycho that stripped and sliced Cynn. Probably Brett and Eddy, too."

Gabriel's hand shot out before she could react. He snatched the card from her hand.

She yanked her hand back. "What the *hell*?"

"You think just because someone was filming Cynn in her panties they must've *murdered* her too?"

"Well, it's a pretty logical—"

"Because filming someone is the same as raping and killing them?"

"No, but it's still like sexual assault. It's a serious violation."

He held the card up in her face. "Who else knows about this?"

"No one. Just Adam and me."

"Have you shown it to the police yet?"

"No."

He dropped the card on the floor and stomped on it until it cracked.

She felt sick as it dawned on her. "Oh, hell no. You were the creep in the bushes."

"Liv—"

"You lose it with me for not telling you all *my* business, then I find out you've been sneaking around outside Cynn's window, filming her like some pervert?"

"It's nothing like that."

"Oh, really?"

"Yeah! And it wasn't just her." His fingers jabbed the keyboard. He pointed at the Rosewood logo on the computer screen. "Look."

The logo stopped spinning. Trumpets played. The screen showed velvet curtains lifting.

"I don't—"

"Watch the damn screen."

The final tassel faded from view. Then the crap hit the screen, in living colour. Sharona dancing around drunk. Felix looking both totally crappy and pissed off in her hospital bed. Emma cheating on a test. Eddy throwing someone in a dumpster. And much, much more.

Liv's hand rose to her throat. "You made this . . . this—"

"I did."

There was a new look on his face now. One she'd never seen before. Strong. Proud.

Defiant.

"This is the video yearbook?"

The screen switched again, and now two overweight kids were going at it in the back of a car, to the tune of "Pop Goes the Weasel."

"You know how sick this thing is."

His smile had teeth. "Hell yeah, it's sick."

"No, Gabe! It's *seriously* sick."

She held down the power button. The screen went dark.

"You can't show this."

"Cynn's not even in it now, so no one can prove I was ever there the night she died."

"But—"

"I've timed it. It'll take the chaperones at least six minutes to cross the floor, climb the stairs to the sound booth and try to get in—the door will be locked, of course. I'll simultaneously upload it online to every social media and website I can, as well as e-mail it to everyone with a Rosewood e-mail address.

Even alumni. Plus, factor in the attention this'll get on the internet. And with the huge email list I got off setting up that website, too. And the production value. This thing will go viral. By the time the curtain falls tomorrow night, the whole world will have a chance to log online and see this."

"No, I mean you can't show *this*."

His face went white.

"Look. I know you want to get back at the people who've treated you—"

"Treated *us*."

"Us. Treated us like garbage. I get it. I really do. But you can't do this."

"I *can't*?"

Liv forgot sometimes how tall Gabriel was. She took another step back and bumped into his armchair. Wait a minute. He was her *best friend*. She *knew* him.

Didn't she?

"It's wrong," said Liv.

"Everything about that school is wrong."

"Not everyone in that school is a bully! Some are just nice, ordinary kids!"

"Right, like all the ones who just let it happen."

Gabriel reached for her hands, enveloping them in his. His voice dropped. "High school never ends, Liv. Not really. Bullies just go find bigger, more important ways to push people around. They need to have their lives ruined before they get that chance."

"But this'll ruin your life too."

"Oh, please. What's the worst they can do? Community service? A few weeks in some facility like Meadowhurst?"

Liv squeezed his hands. "Gabe, you know even better than I do how hard it is to scrub something off the internet. Once you upload this and it goes viral this thing will be online *forever*. People will be able to find it when they search your name. It'll always define you. As long as you live, you'll be known as that psycho-nerd who humiliated his classmates. Every university and college you apply to. Every prospective employer. Every time you ask someone out. This'll become who you are." She couldn't read his expression. "It's more than that. When I talked to Brett? His afterlife was seriously messed up. Badly. Like . . . infected with all this nasty stuff . . . You can't intentionally hurt people and not—"

"I am *nothing* like Brett!" He wrenched his hands away. "What the hell is the matter with you?"

"With *me*?"

"A week ago you hated everyone at this school as much as I did. Now some of them die and suddenly they're all your best buddies?"

"That's not fair—"

"Then answer me this. You think the Liv I knew last week would've told me not to do this?"

He crossed his arms in front of his chest.

She pressed her lips together. Of course she would have. Wouldn't she?

"I think you should go."

"But I—"

"I've got stuff to finish, and I'm not fighting about this anymore. For the sake of our friendship, I won't tell anyone you were helping Adam. But it's almost like I don't know who you are anymore. You've changed. So, if you try to screw this up for me, don't ever come running back to me begging for a favour again. I mean it, Liv."

"You're better than them. I know you, Gabe. You're not really this kind of guy."

He slid on his headphones and turned back to the computer.

Chapter Thirty-Four

Never Forget was quiet. Tony was sitting in the office.

He looked up when Liv walked in.

"The police say a medium named Madame Delilah claims we're harbouring a serial killer."

Oh.

Liv opened her mouth, hoping to come up with a believable lie.

Then she shut it again.

He sighed. "I told them to come back with a warrant. I can't handle one more prank right now."

She turned to walk into the display room. Tony's voice made her stop.

"Also, the police tell me that somebody left the storage cabinet in the embalming room open, which is how that thief was able to steal your friend's burial clothes and jewellery."

Crap.

"I'm really sorry, please don't fire me, I need this job—"

He held up his hand. "We all make mistakes and I guess it's partly my fault, asking you to work so many hours on top of school and everything else you've got going on. Your mother told me how late you've been coming home from here some nights." He sighed. "You're so good at this, I forget sometimes you should still have a life. I'm not going to fire you. But I have decided to bring someone else on. Not to take away any of your shifts, just so that when you want to go out, we've got things covered."

"I like working here." Liv shifted her weight from one foot to the other. "It's not like I've got anywhere else to be."

"Well, you should. Also, I'm going to make your job a real salaried one, where you get vacations and benefits."

"That would be . . ." She swallowed. "That would be great. But . . . you don't have to do that."

"Yes, I do." He crossed his arms in front of his chest. "You need to be able to take time off sometimes without worrying and have a real life outside this place. We've got enough lifeless corpses coming and going around here. We don't need one more shuffling around the halls."

He smiled at the attempted joke.

She looked at the floor and wondered what would happen if she tried to hug him.

He straightened his tie. "Now, the Maddox girl's paperwork is there on your desk. But if you don't want to do it, I'll understand."

"No problem. I want to."

At least this way she'd be doing her job, and it's not like Tony knew how to work the database. He still typed with two fingers.

Liv sat.

Adam was off chasing some mystery chick. Gabriel was imploding his life. Three classmates had died. She was doing paperwork.

Woot.

She transcribed Tony's notes from his chicken scrawl on paper into the computer.

Name: Cynthia Sarah Maddox. Age: 17. Address. Date of birth. Place of birth. Cause of death—

She stopped typing.

Tony thought that Cynn had died of a drug overdose.

What? But then how'd she ended up undressed and tied up?

It didn't make sense. But after looking at the body, Tony's best guess was that Cynn had ingested a huge amount of narcotics, passed out and never woken up again. No wonder she'd acted so weird in the video. Even explained why her post-death memory would be foggy.

Then someone had come along after she was unconscious, tied her to the bed so roughly her skin bruised and created a pretty blood bath out of her remains. Like a show.

Which meant her killer didn't have to be strong and definitely didn't have to be male. Could've been a scrawny bookworm or an ambitious bitchinista.

Could've been anyone.

She skimmed down the rest of the page. Cynn weighed more than she looked like she would. Didn't have any food in her system. Was—

Pregnant.

The kaleidoscope of information shifted inside Liv's head. "Paperwork's finished. I'm just going to go say some private good-byes."

The viewing room was already set for the funeral. Lines of chairs in sombre rows. An eruption of wreaths and flowers clustered around the casket. Cynn's hair was in golden ringlets. A tiara sat on her head.

She put her hand on Cynn's stomach.

"Hey. You there?"

Cynn's eyes fluttered open. Then she smiled.

"Hey, yourself. Where you been? I kind of missed you."

Liv nearly dropped the link. Well, this was . . . new. "How . . . are you feeling?"

Cynn pulled herself up onto her elbows. "Dead." She giggled.

The image sat up and swung her legs out of the casket. Then she climbed out entirely, her image brushing against Liv's body as she passed. It burned like ice.

Cynn paused. "I know I've been in a terrible mood recently." She tilted her head to the side and looked at her. "I feel *really* bad for how things went down between us when you brought Adam in to say hi." She glanced around the room. "He's not here now, is he?"

Alright, and why exactly was Cynn being nicer now?

Did Cynn want something? Could something actually be changing in Cynn now that she'd been dead a little longer? Or had she just realized she wasn't getting anywhere being rude and had decided to stop acting like a bitch to the one and only person she could still talk to?

Whatever the reason, Liv didn't actually care.

Let Cynn play nice. It would only make it easier to get information from her.

"Nah," Liv said. "Adam moved on."

"Sorry to hear it, but I'm not surprised. He's kind of like that. He tries to do the right thing, but he can be a bit of an idiot sometimes."

Yeah, that was a good way to put it.

"Well, that just gives us one more thing in common. I'm hoping we can start again. Friends?" Cynn reached out her hand.

Liv looked at it. "I'm actually using my right hand to keep the connection open between us. Just imagine I'm shaking your hand."

Cynn stretched her arms out and walked around in a circle like she was checking out the space. Could she actually see anything? This whole walking image thing was still new.

The buzzing in her brain was back again, like distorted music played off-key.

"Why didn't you tell me you were pregnant?"

Cynn tilted her head. "Who told you that?"

"Tony, my boss. He figured it out. He also thinks you could've died of an overdose. You were drinking a smoothie in the video I saw. Could someone have spiked it?"

Cynn dropped into a chair. "Guess that would explain why it's all so hazy." She pulled her knees up into her chest and wrapped her arms around herself. "I've been trying so hard to remember, but it's like the images come and go. My brain is just a mess right now and I can't make sense of things." Her lower lip quivered. "It's been awful."

Liv still wasn't sure she was anywhere close to believing Cynn wasn't trying to manipulate her for her own agenda. But, sure, she could play along.

"Hey, it's okay." Liv kept one hand firmly on Cynn's body and reached her other hand out toward the projection of Cynn's spirit. But ghost Cynn was still too far away to touch. "How about you just tell me what you know, and we'll go from there. We can work together to figure it out."

"Oh God, thank you." A smile spread across Cynn's face. Tears sparkled in her eyes. "I do want to help—leave something worthwhile behind, you know? I just needed to believe I could trust you."

"Alright," Liv said, "how about you start by telling me whose baby you were pregnant with. Then we can try to untangle what happened the day you died."

"We're going to make this work, you and I." Cynn

raised a ghostly palm toward her. "Because of you my life doesn't need to be over." She held out her hand. "Deal?"

"Deal." Liv extended her left hand.

Cynn grabbed it and yanked. Liv yelped. Painful sparks shot through her palm and up into her arm. She tried to pull back. Cynn's fingers slid through hers and clenched. The room around them began to dissolve.

Liv jerked both her hands back. For a moment she thought the connection was going to somehow hold her, then the link snapped. The effect was like being hit in the face with cold water.

What the hell was that?

She looked at the corpse, her heart pounding hard in her chest.

Had Cynn done that? Or had she?

Gingerly, she touched the torso.

The image flickered back. Cynn's spirit was lying in the casket again.

"What'd you try to do to me?"

"I didn't do anything." Cynn scowled. "Whatever the hell is going on, it's on your end, freak show, not mine."

So much for the nice act.

As she watched, expressions flickered over Cynn's face like a slide show. She was furious. She was ecstatic. She was terrified. Then bold. Then shy.

Liv pressed her hand harder against the body and concentrated. The flickering stopped. Cynn glared at her—with that same hateful look Liv caught flashing across her face a thousand times before when no one else was looking.

"Guess it gets harder to fool people when you're dead."

"Go screw yourself." Cynn looked away but her body didn't move.

"What? You're done walking around?"

"I'm tired." Cynn's shoulders twitched, like she was trying to shrug but her body wouldn't let her. "Now why don't you just ask me whatever the hell you want to know and leave me alone."

Liv pushed herself deeper into the connection. "Who was the father of your baby?"

"None of your damn business."

Liv closed her eyes and focused on the story Cynn had told her. She was in the car with Adam, Cynn and Felix arguing, driving up to Brett's party. She watched them stumble around drunk in the cottage living room. Sketchy, jerky, like a badly drawn cartoon, but she saw them.

Cynn whimpered. "Stop it."

Liv pressed deeper. There was a boy there, or at least the outline of one. He was bigger than she was. She climbed onto his lap. She started kissing him. He kissed her back. She grabbed his chain. He grabbed her body.

"It's not what you think," Cynn said.

They were in the bedroom now. On the floor. Clothes

off. Rolling around. The images were beginning to run, like chalk drawings in the rain.

"It was Brett, wasn't it?"

"Maybe."

In the vision, Cynn stumbled out of the bedroom, leaving him passed out drunk. The images vanished.

"Maybe?" Liv said. "Maybe you fooled around with your best friend's boyfriend the night he died?"

"Don't be so naive. People get drunk. Things happen."

Again the image twitched, like Cynn was trying to show how little she cared, but her limbs weren't cooperating. Was she too tired from what happened before to project a moving image? Or had Liv simply learned how to maintain control of the link?

Either way, served her right.

"What about Adam?" Liv asked.

"What about him? You told me yourself he's gone chasing after some mystery girl."

No, she hadn't.

"After you had that magical night in the barn and everything," Cynn shook her head. Her voice grew fainter. "And he stole your car? You really were stupid to trust him, you know."

"How can you possibly know all that?"

Cynn shrugged.

"Whatever the hell you think you're doing, it's not going to work," Liv said. "Yeah, I had feelings for Adam, but I'm not the one stupid enough to think they can treat people however they want and it'll never catch up with them. I saw what was in Brett's grave. I know what's going to happen to you."

Something dangerous flickered in Cynn's eyes. Her lips moved. Her voice barely made a sound.

Liv leaned down. "I can't hear you."

"I said, just imagine what's going to happen to Gabriel then."

Her image grew fuzzy. Liv pressed harder and focused on the link.

"Two losers like you thinking you can take on Rosewood? With his little video and your pathetic investigation. It won't work, you know. You could singlehandedly save the whole school and everyone would still hate you."

She was right.

"Of course I'm right."

"Get the hell out of my brain and answer my questions. Or I'm dropping this link."

Cynn's fingertips dissolved. Strands of hair wisped around her face like smoke. "It was all *his* fault, you know."

Liv clenched her teeth and focused on keeping the link alive. "Whose?"

"Gabriel's. Everything they ever did to him. Getting his head shoved in the toilet. Getting kicked and hit and spit on . . ." She giggled. "And you, the loser freak creeping along the edges of the hallway with that pathetic 'Please don't kick me' look on your face.

Staring at *my* boyfriend like that. You made it easy. We just stepped up and gave you what you were asking for."

The link was beginning to hurt, with the same harsh, biting cold from before. Her stomach ached. Cynn's image was still fading, and Liv could barely hear her.

"You're no better than me . . . You'd be just the same if you had the chance." Her voice was so low Liv had to practically lean her whole body into the casket to catch her words. "Let yourself admit you're *glad* we're dead . . . that if you had the chance you'd do whatever it took to make sure you were the one . . . in *control* . . ."

"That's it. I'm done talking." Liv pulled her hands back and stepped away from the casket.

Screw this. She had better things to do than waste her time with—

A noise behind her made her turn.

Cynn stood there. Real. Vibrant. Strong. Bolder than any image she'd ever seen before.

Liv screamed. Cynn lunged at her. Knocked her down onto the floor and wrapped her fingers around her neck.

"I'M NOT GIVING UP! You hear me? I won't be dead. I don't deserve to be dead."

Liv grabbed for her throat, clawing at Cynn's hands. She opened her mouth and screamed for Tony, but they weren't in the funeral home anymore. They were at school. She was lying on her back on the floor of the auditorium. Music thumped through her body. Disco lights spun above her head. Cynn straddled her. Pinned her down.

"This is my prom. My day. My life." Cynn wore the Rosewood sash. A crown glistened on her head. "No one has the right to take it away from me, and I'm staying. Even if I have to move into your body to do so."

Liv's eyes filled with tears. Cold, freezing pain poured into her from every angle. The blackness seeped in again. There was no Adam this time. No one to grab her and pull her out.

"Give up and die, bitch!" Cynn screamed. "Nobody cares if you live or you die."

Not true.

They're lying.

Some people cared.

You choose what to believe. . . .

She poured the images she'd seen inside Jake's ashes into the front of her mind and projected them behind Cynn, like an army. Gabriel. Her mom. Tony. They all cared.

Even Adam cared. Yeah, he'd been stupid and selfish and wrong, but that didn't mean he'd never actually cared—

"Why won't you die?" Cynn banged Liv's head against the dance floor.

Liv thrashed from side to side, trying to shake her off. She pushed her hands up into Cynn's face.

Jake's voice trickled through her memory like music. *"Someone's been actively trying to move their own crap into your brain. . . . You've got so many people who love you. . . . You seriously need to wake up and see that."*

Wake up.

In that second she realized her hands weren't really fighting Cynn—her hands were still just pressed up against a cold, dead corpse. All she had to do was drop the link and wake up.

She threw her body backwards, away from the casket. The lid slammed. The image splintered like a mirror. Liv landed hard on the floor.

The fragment of a ghostly scream hung in the air. Then it was gone.

Chapter Thirty-Five

Liv lay sprawled on the floor for a moment, staring at the casket above her as everything that had happened in the past five days rushed through her brain like the recap of a movie she'd seen before but never really understood.

Adam. Gabriel. Jake. Felix. Brett. Eddy.

Cynn.

The buzzing and the headache were gone. Her brain felt clearer than it had in days.

Liv stood up slowly, opened the casket and looked down at Cynn's cold dead body.

She didn't open a link. Or even touch her.

What the hell did you do to me?

Liv's skin felt clammy. She ran both hands through her hair. It was soaked with sweat.

She dialled Gabriel and got a click.

He was there. Not speaking. Just breathing.

"You don't have to talk if you don't want to. Just

listen. Okay Gabe? Please."

"If it's about the video, don't bother. I'm still showing it."

"No, it's not about that." She looked down at the body in the casket. "You said I haven't been myself, right?"

"No. You really haven't." He sounded pissed.

Liv's eyes ran over Cynn's corpse. In a weird way, the corpse looked more dead than it had before. Waxier. Faker. Like an embalmed thing. That just used to be a person.

"I think I've been a little bit possessed."

"Aren't we all?"

"Not this way. I think Cynn somehow got deep inside my brain and messed things up. When we first connected there was this weird static, and her voice echoed, and then I started getting headaches. My powers have been growing and Jake warned me that the connection is a two-way street, and I needed to learn how to protect myself from letting people get too far inside. And the crazy dead priest I met at the hospital told me I wasn't being safe. And then I'd catch myself saying or thinking these crazy things about popularity and prom that sounded more like Cynn than me. . . ."

Liv's voice trailed off.

"Well, Cynn was always a master manipulator," Gabriel said. Liv could almost hear him shrugging. "She always knew how to use people. Charm, manipulate, and exploit any weakness she could find. And you gave her direct access to your brain."

Liv shut the casket and then slid the clasp in place.

Yeah, well, she'd had just about enough of being used.

Liv turned her back on the casket.

"Anyway, we were wrong about Cynn's death," she said. "She was pregnant and she died of a drug overdose. The whole slashing part came later."

There was a long pause.

"Wow, okay, I did not see that coming. But, I think I'm done playing detectives—"

"I know," she said. "Me too. But I'm still coming to the dance tonight. Please don't play that video until I get there."

"You really can't talk me out of this."

"I know, but if you're going through with it, I'm going to be there."

"Why?"

"Because you're my best friend, and you actually matter."

She hung up, took a deep breath and looked back at the casket. "And maybe so do I."

She took Kiara's dress down off its hook. All she had in her purse was eyeliner and an empty tube of lip gloss. It was way too late to even think about finding a hairdresser.

"So you *are* going to the dance?" Tony stood behind her.

"I'll pop in, anyway. I need to talk to someone who's going to be there."

He nodded as if he understood something more than what she'd just said. "What would you say if I did your hair and makeup? I've got some real stuff in my kit for the top layer. It's been a while since I've done anyone living, but I'm pretty sure I remember how."

Liv's mouth opened.

Tony's hand shot up, palm out. "Now I know you're going to say you don't think about stuff like that. You don't care all your classmates wasted hundreds of dollars having some salon hack slap too much shellac on their head and paint them up like a plastic doll. But everyone knows who the best hairdresser and makeup artist is in this city, and I'm not ruining my good name by having my assistant walk in there not looking like she works for the master."

"I don't know what to say."

"Thank you will do."

She smiled. "Thank you."

"Welcome. Can't have you looking worse than the dead girls." He snorted. "Oh, and I already called my nephew's limo company, just in case you decided to go. He's sending a stretch for you. Got to uphold my reputation, after all."

The limo pulled up in front of the school. The driver got out and opened Liv's door. She stepped out into a flurry of flashbulb lights. Looked like the notoriety of the Rosewood serial killer had raised some press interest in the prom. Some reporter was asking her who designed her stilettos. Someone else asked how much the jewels around her neck were worth. She waved them away. If Gabriel went through with that video, what a waitress's daughter wore was going to be the last thing anyone cared about.

Her first stop was the ladies' room, where she checked herself out in the mirror. There stood a girl in a gorgeous silver gown. Glittering fabric caressed her curves. Long strands of black and violet hair were twisted artfully behind her head, save for a few delicate strands around her face. Smoky lines framed her eyes.

She actually looked . . . well, beautiful.

A reluctant smile turned up the corners of her lips. Liv walked into the auditorium, head held high. Strobes flashed from every corner. Mirrored balls sent down cascades of shimmering light.

People stared as she stepped out onto the dance floor—damn-who-*is*-that looks, followed by the jaw drop as they recognized her.

She smiled. Her shoulders relaxed.

She had this.

Sharona stood by the punch bowl in a bouffant dress, sneering. Liv could practically see the insult forming on her tongue.

Her eyes met Sharona's.

You think I'm going to let you tear me down?

Sharona looked away.

Liv laughed. She glanced toward the sound booth. The top of Gabriel's head just barely showed in the window, bowed toward the console. There was practically no cell reception in the gym, but she pressed his number on speed dial anyway to let him know she was here. The phone read "connecting" but didn't start ringing. She wove her way through the dancers until she reached the door to the stairs.

Good. The door was unlocked.

She shoved it open—

Oh God no.

Adam was hanging from the staircase. Blood streamed down his chest. A note pinned to his chest.

I'm sorry. I killed them all.

Chapter Thirty-Six

She ran up the stairs toward Adam. Thin metal wire looped around his neck. His throat was severed.

No no no no no no no. Adam couldn't be dead. He just couldn't.

She glanced up the stairs. She could probably scream at the top of her lungs and Gabriel would never hear her.

"GAABRIIIEEL . . ."

Worth a try.

Her fingers grabbed at the railing where the metal wire twisted around the staircase, holding Adam's body aloft. She pulled and yanked at the wire, trying to wrest Adam free, until her fingers bled.

His head slipped through the wire. His body fell.

She ran back down the stairs, dropped to the floor and pulled his head into her lap.

He wasn't breathing. She couldn't find a pulse.

But she couldn't open a connection to his spirit, either.

"Wow, so Adam finally killed himself." Felix stood in the doorway. "Fitting, really. First he slit his victims' throats. Then hung himself with wire so thin he slit his own neck."

"You kidding me? This isn't a suicide. Somebody tried to murder him. And they'll succeed if we can't get him to a hospital fast."

Adam's was bleeding all over her lap. Her hands were smeared with his blood, mingling with her own from where she'd cut her fingers trying to free him. She couldn't let him go. As long as she didn't feel his ghost maybe there was still hope.

Liv looked down at her cellphone. Still almost no bars. The minute counter was running as if her call to Gabriel had somehow connected for a moment but the line seemed dead.

"You've got to call the police. Don't run outside screaming and causing chaos because you'll tip off the killer and they'll get away again before the cops show up. Just run upstairs to the sound booth. Gabriel's there. He'll call 911."

Felix nodded slowly. She shut the door. A gold bodice hugged her body, erupting in a spray of purple and gold around her hips. Dark purple gloves ran from fingertips up over her elbows. An antique pendant hung around her neck.

It was funny how sometimes, when the world was collapsing, your mind locked focus on the smallest random thing.

"You're wearing Cynn's necklace?"

"It's mine." Felix's hand rose to her throat. "It's an antique. Brett said it belonged to his grandmother."

"But Cynn had it when she died. Then Eddy stole it." Felix's eyes narrowed.

"Look, I don't care," Liv said. "Adam needs our help. And there's a killer on the loose."

Felix crossed the room until she was standing right beside Liv. She looked down at the body.

"I guess Adam's going to have to kill you."

"What the f—"

Felix pulled off her necklace. A long thin blade shot out of the pendant.

Before Liv could even blink, Felix pressed the tip to Liv's throat.

"Toss your phone."

Crap.

Liv slid the phone across the floor.

"So that's how you walked out of Brett's cottage with the murder weapon. You wore it around your neck like a goddamn trophy."

Liv didn't know whether to be more disgusted or impressed. Police probably searched Felix and didn't find a thing.

"Guess I'll fix it so Adam kills you before hanging himself." Felix sighed. "Can't believe you're going to make me hang him back up again. It was hard enough the first time."

"Hey, look, I know Cynn fooled around with Brett

and got pregnant," Liv said. "And that was not cool. Serious betrayal. So if you snapped and killed them, everyone would understand."

Felix tilted her head to the side.

"Only I'm guessing you caught Brett passed out, and didn't know for sure who he'd been making out with. Then what? You dragged his sorry ass outside to teach him a lesson?"

What might have been a smile curled on Felix's lips. "Adam's car was parked right there with the keys in the ignition. I was just going to drive Brett down the highway and leave him somewhere. Make him hitchhike home."

"Totally understandable and, hey, maybe you didn't even know there was a knife in the pendant until you tried to take it off him. Accidents happen. Like slicing him so viciously you nearly decapitated him."

Felix's eyes darkened. "Hands up. And if you try anything I'll cut your throat."

Yeah, only she was probably going to do that anyway if Liv didn't think of some way to stop her.

"So, how's this for a theory?" Liv let go of Adam's body and gently let him slid onto the floor. "You found out that Cynn was the one who screwed Brett. So when you went over in the afternoon to try on prom dresses, you drugged her, thinking that after she passed out you'd get Eddy to pop by and slice her up for you—I mean, considering how he chased you around like a stupid, lustful puppy, you might as well use him for something, right? Then you stabbed yourself for an alibi and framed Adam, again. Total evil genius stuff. After all, if something went wrong when Eddy came over to commit murder for you, he'd be the one who'd likely get arrested. Bet you weren't counting on Eddy losing your funky knife and it ending up with Cynn's things at my work, so he had to break in to get it back for you."

Great how clear her mind was now that Cynn was no longer screwing with it. Too bad it hadn't been clear sooner. Maybe she wouldn't have ended up in a stairwell with a psycho set on killing her.

"How'd you get Eddy to help you, anyway? Money? Kinky sex?"

"Shut the hell up."

"So sex, then. Eew." Liv paused. "Figures. I'd rather have killed him than kept screwing him too."

"You have no idea." Felix snickered. Slowly she moved around behind Liv keeping the knife pressed to her throat.

"You must be DeathFetishGirl99, too. Did you email Adam to double check all your bases were covered? Or because gloating was so much fun? Wow, you really are full of yourself, aren't you?"

Felix punched Liv in the back of the head. Liv gritted her teeth and kept going. "Look, I get it. It's not fair how some of us have to work a hell of a lot harder than others to get by. Why throw it all away over a stupid, horny jerk like Brett who was probably going to cheat on you eventually, anyway?"

"Seriously? You think this is only about who he slept with? He got conscious after I got him in the car, you moron. Lost it big time. Told me he'd . . ." Felix bit her words back.

"Rat you out to the police on beating up your dad and trashing his car?" Liv asked. "Or leak some of your really kinky sex pics online? Ruin your reputation so bad no university would dare offer you a scholarship? Something even worse?"

"Maybe I snapped, okay. But this is *my* life. Mine. I made it. I deserve it. No one takes it away from me. Not some asshole boyfriend, not my father, not my pathetic mother. And definitely not some skank who was screwing my man.

"Some stupid toad in admin told me I'd gotten the Vitesse internship. Paperwork in progress. Then Cynn calls up Brett's mom and tells her she's going to be a grandmother. Suddenly they tell her she's getting my internship and they're delaying the announcement to work something out. She wasn't even going to keep the damn thing until she figured out she could use my dead boyfriend's baby to take my internship away. After all, it's a family company and the internship is basically a publicity thing being done in Brett's honour. His folks were so devastated at losing their only son that they practically jumped at the chance to do something nice for the mother of their grandkid and brand new baby heir. But, you can't get anywhere without a few sacrifices, right? So what if I killed Cynn. And Brett. And Eddy. And Adam. And you. I'm going to leave here and go on with my life. None of you matter."

The steady pulse of background music stopped cold and before Liv could even open her mouth to scream, a voice boomed: "Felix. Felix Almon. If Felix is in the building, could she please make her way to the stage?"

"Sounds like you're needed out there," Liv said.

"Don't be stupid."

"Ladies and gentleman. I'm thrilled to announce Felix Almon is Rosewood's new prom queen. As winner of this year's crown, Felix has just won a five *thousand* dollar shopping spree at Yorkdale." The voice was loud and had an official sportscaster ring to it. It sounded exactly like Gabriel trying really hard not to sound like himself, and doing a pretty damn good job of it.

"Guess I better make this quick."

"Don't be stupid. You can't cut me bad enough to kill without getting blood all over yourself."

"Good point."

Then before she could think to move, Liv felt the thick gold chain drop around her neck. With one hand Felix gripped the chain, twisted it hard and pulled back, cutting off Liv's air. With the other, she shoved Liv's head toward the ground.

Pain filled Liv's lungs.

Felix was strangling her.

She couldn't breathe.

Frantically Liv grabbed at the chain and twisted her body sideways, trying to break it.

Felix press her knee into Liv's back.

"Don't fight it," Felix hissed. "You're never going to win."

The urge to breathe filled through her body. It was excruciating.

"Who knew Rosewood alumni could be so generous?" Gabriel's voice echoed in the distance. "Let's all start chanting her name now! Felix! Felix! Felix!"

Thanks Gabriel. But it's too late.

Darkness swept over her.

For a second, there was nothing.

Then, there was a crack. A rustle. The smell of damp in the air.

Liv opened her eyes. She was lying in a forest.

Chapter Thirty-Seven

Liv stretched her limbs and stood. It was raining. Drops pattered on the leaves above. Fog drifted between the grey trees.

So, this was death?

Standing alone in a bloody prom dress surrounded by grey and damp?

Well, if so, the afterlife really sucked.

She shivered. There were goose bumps on her arms.

Brett's afterlife had been a total horror show. Jake had seemed really happy with his.

And hers was, what, exactly? A soggy empty forest?

Whatever it was, she was in no mood to put up with it now.

Liv started walking. Pushing back tree branches.

"Hello? Jake? Anybody?"

Then she saw him. There was a figure sitting on the ground at the base of a tree wearing a plain grey hoody.

"Adam!"

She ran toward him. Her feet stumbled on roots and she tripped through the underbrush. Liv dropped down to the ground beside Adam and grabbed his hands with both of hers.

"Thank God I found you."

She leaned forward until her forehead was against his.

"I'm sorry," Adam said. "You were right about not trusting DeathFetishGirl99. It was Felix and she killed me. I acted like an idiot, and now I'm dead."

"I think we're both dead. And that sucks, big time. But I'm not sure exactly where we are or what's happening."

Adam sat back and looked into her face. His eyes were now the same grey as the world around them. "I don't understand why you're here though. Why are you dead?"

The ground pulsed. Shockwaves ran through her limbs. Her skin tingled.

"What do you mean, why am I dead?" Her voice seemed to be growing stronger, louder. "I'm dead because Felix jumped me in the stairwell too and then she strangled me."

Wind rushed past them. Hard. Tugging her hair free from her up-do and sending it flying around her face. Then the wind changed course and rushed back in the direction it had come from.

"I mean, *you* shouldn't be dead."

"Hey, I don't want to be dead," Liv said. "I really,

really don't want to be dead, and I don't know how to get us out of here. But I think we should fight this. We need to fight against this place, wherever it is. Cynn seemed to think she could come back. She tried to use my body to do it, but maybe there's another way."

Adam looped his fingers through hers.

"I can't fight this," he said. "I'm done. I don't know how to explain it, but this is it for me."

"Of course you can! We'll fight it together."

Another earthquake shook the ground.

Like something was pushing her out of here.

And something was pulling her back.

She squeezed Adam's hands and held on tightly.

"I don't know if this works," Liv added. "Or even if it *will* work. But I do know you can either surrender to all the stupid crap, or you can fight it and try to be something better. And I'm tired of not fighting. I should have fought against what those assholes at Rosewood were doing to me months ago. I should have stood up for myself sooner. But I'm here now and I'm going to fight this. I'm going to fight this, right now, with everything I've got. And focus all my energy, all my will and determination to getting myself out of this place and back into my body. I want to be alive. Maybe I didn't get how much I wanted to be alive before. But I do and I will." She looked down at their hands. Bright red blood from Adam's corpse still covered her body, mingled with hers from where she'd cut her fingers trying to free him. But his skin was so ashen he was almost grey. "And I'm bringing you back with me."

More wind. Harder this time pulling her body backward. Yanking her out of this place.

The trees above disappeared. The staircase floated before her eyes.

She tightened her grip on Adam's hands like an anchor in a tornado. Her arms ached like her shoulders were being pulled from their sockets.

The wind stopped. She fell forward against Adam's chest.

The forest was back.

"No, you're not taking me with you." Adam pulled his hands away from hers. "You're going to let go of me and go back on your own."

"I don't want to let you go!"

"You can't hold onto me if I won't hold onto you." Adam stood up. "I don't want to be the thing keeping you somewhere dead!"

"Hang on, let's just stop and think about this—"

"Yeah, stopping to think has never been my strong suit." He chuckled. "And I don't think you have time."

Fresh blood trickled down from the cut to his throat. Faint blue flickered like a flame in his eyes.

"But look at you!" She jumped up. "It's working. You're becoming stronger, more alive. Somehow."

Adam paused. He looked down at his hands

and turned them over slowly. Their colour was growing warmer. Like sepia tint in a black and white photograph.

Then he laughed like he was remembering a joke he'd heard a long time ago. "So, maybe I've got some life left in me. Good."

"Yeah, good! Now you can use it to come back."

He shook his head. "No, Liv. Then I can use it to help push you out of here."

Gently he took her face in his hands. She looked up into his face. Warmth filled her body.

But it felt like he was giving something up. Giving something away.

Like he was draining whatever little bit of his life or spirit there was left of him.

"Hang on," she said. "I honestly don't know what's going to happen to you if you do this. You can still go have an amazing existence even if you're dead. Jake seemed really super happy with his afterlife. What if doing this seriously screws up your dead world somehow? There are way worse places to be than stuck in some rain and trees."

He shrugged. "Guess I'm going to find out."

The colour was disappearing from his skin. The blue was fading from his eyes. Adam's blood ran grey.

"But I was going to save you."

"I know." His lips brushed her face. "And that means more to me than I've got words to tell you. Nobody ever cared about me enough to try to save me before.

But you can't save me by killing yourself. I don't want you to. And besides, you deserve better than that."

The ground was pulsing beneath them again.

"But I don't want to say goodbye to you forever." Tears were building in her eyes. "I'm seriously going to miss you. I—"

"Yeah, and I'll miss you too." Adam leaned forward. His lips touched hers.

The wind blew past.

The trees shook.

She let Adam go.

And focused every bit of her strength into throwing herself backward into the wind.

She was falling.

Concrete hit her back.

"If you don't start breathing, I'm going to kill you," said Gabriel.

Chapter Thirty-Eight

Liv was lying on her back in the stairwell. Gabriel was kneeling over her. His hands pressed her chest. His mouth came down toward hers. She sat up so quickly they bumped heads.

"You were performing CPR on me?"

She touched her neck. What the hell? She'd have thought her windpipe would be crushed after being strangled to death, but her throat felt okay. And the air in her lungs felt surprisingly strong. Weirdly so.

As if whatever she'd harnessed inside her to fight her way back from the dead had made her come back a bit different. Somehow.

Gabriel's face was pale. "You're alive."

"Yeah, I'm alive."

She stood up. Her legs felt stronger too.

Almost like there was more life flowing around

inside her veins now than there usually was. Funny. She'd spent all this time trying to figure out how to use her abilities to help dead people like Cynn move around in ghost form and pretend to be alive, she never even thought about what it would be like to somehow harness that inside herself.

"But . . . But that shouldn't have worked." Gabriel was still sitting on the floor. "I mean, I tried—of course I tried—because I didn't know what else to do. And I couldn't just sit here and do nothing. You didn't have a pulse. You weren't breathing."

"I know. I was dead. I was in the afterlife. It was really shitty. I decided to come back. I don't know how to explain it, so I'm not even going to try. But I'm good. And I think maybe instead of just letting ghosts like Cynn drain my abilities, I can actually focus them inside myself to make me more alive. Somehow. That probably sounds weird. I haven't quite figured it all out, myself. But anyway, I felt you trying to bring me back and it gave me something to latch onto. So thank you. Now, come on."

She tapped him on the shoulder. He looked up. And it was only then she saw the streaks of tears running down his cheek. He'd actually been crying?

"Oh God, Gabe!" She leaned down and hugged him. "Look, it's okay. I'm alive. See!"

"I'm sorry I yelled at you. I'm sorry I made that goddamn video. I thought I was never going to get the chance to tell you, that you were right and—"

She kissed the top of his head. "I forgive you. And I need you. Now come on."

Then she grabbed his hand and pulled him up. Adam's corpse was still lying beside the stairs. She couldn't bear to look at it or think about him right now. "Tell me you called the police and they're about to bust in here any minute and arrest Felix."

"I called the police," Gabriel said, sounding a lot more like himself again. "Average police response time is twelve minutes. When they get here they'll find Adam's body looking like a suicide, shut the party down and question everyone. Then it becomes a matter of 'we said, she said' while police decide whether or not to arrest Felix and if there's enough evidence to press charges. Right now the only evidence that defends Adam or accuses Felix is what you and I've got to say. And I gotta say, it's going to be kinda hard to convince anyone that Felix just tried to kill you when you've got that whole super healthy glow thing going on again."

Right. Or they could just conclude that Adam-the-psycho-killer committed suicide and dismiss what Liv and Gabriel had to say as just the rantings of bitter outsiders.

"Unless we had serious proof," she said.

"We don't have proof."

"Then we've got twelve minutes to figure out how to get some."

She ran up the stairs to the sound booth. Gabriel followed.

He reached the top of the stairs and paused and looked down. "Are we going to talk about what just happened to Adam?"

She took a deep breath. "Nope. We're going to stop his killer."

Gabriel locked the door behind them then slid into a chair.

"Do we know where Felix is?" she asked.

He glanced at the monitors. "On stage making her acceptance speech. Moment of personal genius, might I add."

"She didn't win?"

"Not by a long shot, but it'll take time for them to figure out what to do about it. And the prize was greatly exaggerated." His smile faded. "I'm really sorry I wasn't heroic earlier. When I got your phone call, I heard you guys talking and spent ages flipping through the security camera feeds looking for you. I'm guessing Felix disabled the security camera in the stairwell because it wasn't switched on. Then I rushed out the door and saw your body."

"You did just fine."

Liv looked through the window. The dance floor was packed. Security guards flanked the sides of the hall.

"Does Felix still have the knife on her or did she ditch it?"

"I don't know," Gabriel said. "Where did she have the knife?"

"It's in her necklace."

He laughed.

"What the hell's so funny?"

"She's wearing the murder weapon. Now, that takes serious guts. No wonder she managed to smuggle it out of the party after killing Brett. . . ."

Liv shot Gabriel a dirty look. "Don't sound so impressed."

He raised his palms. "Sorry."

"The problem is, I soaked the damn thing in acetone to get Adam's prints off it. We can't even prove it was used to kill Cynn or Brett. Just Eddy."

"Nah." Gabriel rolled his chair up to the console. "The real problem is that when the cops bust in here they'll have over three hundred people to sort through and we're the only people who know there's even a knife in the necklace. It's not like the cops are going to strip search everyone here once they find a dead body. Felix already walked out of one crime scene wearing it—Brett's. And there were only like a dozen people at that party. Sure, we can tell the cops that Felix has a knife hidden in her necklace and trust that this time they'll find it. The problem is, what happens if she figures out you're not dead? Will she just find a way to dump the necklace before the cops get to her? It'll be pandemonium once the cops burst through. And the knife is small enough to flush down a toilet or drop down a sewer grate. Hell, she could drop it in between the crack of the platform and the stage and let it get lost in the gears of the machinery that raises the platform. I know that's what I would do. It's not like the police are going to dismantle the place and tear Rosewood into pieces on the word of two losers who claim they saw a tiny knife in an antique necklace."

"What if she gets into a major, public fistfight with someone at the prom? What if when the cops burst in she's actually in the process of trying to publically kill someone?"

"As her victim screams out at the top of their lungs that she's a killer?" Gabriel let out a laugh and practically spluttered. "Well, yeah obviously then she'd be restrained by Rosewood's rent-a-cops before she had a chance to ditch the knife. But it's not like you or I are going to be able to get through the crowd and anywhere near the podium. Especially you." He waved a hand over her bloody dress. "No offense, but you look like something out of a horror movie."

"None taken. And there's more than one way to get to Felix." Liv pressed her palm against the sound booth window. It slid open. She looked down. The auditorium balcony was only about three feet below the sound booth, and the balcony ran all the way around the auditorium in almost a complete circle.

"That platform she's standing on can be raised, right? Like almost all the way up to the balcony?"

"Yeah."

"How fast can you lower it back down?"

"Safely? Fifteen seconds."

"Unsafely?"

"Five."

Liv pulled off her stilettos. "I'll climb down to the balcony. You raise her up as high as you can. I'll jump down and give her the fight of her life."

"Promise me you're not going to die again."

"I'm not going to die again, because you'll be in total control of the platform. How much damage do you think she can do to me in five seconds? And besides, the cops should be here soon."

"I can only move the platform a few feet sideways. How do you expect to get from the balcony to the centre of the stage?"

"I'll climb across the lighting rig."

He opened his mouth to protest.

She stared him down until he shut it again.

"Don't even *try* to tell me it won't hold my weight. I've seen you do it plenty of times. Plus, if I happen to fall, you can open the safety net underneath. Whatever happened to me when I died and came back, I feel stronger than I ever have in my life. You honestly think you can stop me?"

Gabriel's face paled. "You get how insane this is? You're going to climb across a lighting rig and get into a fistfight with a serial killer, just so you can make sure she gets arrested with the murder weapon, and found guilty? Liv, Felix *killed* you."

"Yeah, she did." Liv's arms crossed. "Felix killed me. And that's kind of the point, isn't it? Felix and her friends beat us down for months—*and we took it*. Then she murdered me. And I let her."

"That wasn't your fault. None of it was. You were the victim."

"Not anymore." She slid her hand down his arm until her fingers grabbed his. "But when I was dead . . . It's hard to explain . . . It's like I realized I hadn't fought for myself. I'd let stuff just happen to me. I needed to choose to be alive and fight for me. I need to confront her. Myself. Face to face." She squeezed his hand tightly. "Please Gabe, I know how badly you want hurt the people who hurt you. Yup, you were unbelievably wrong to make that video. But you weren't wrong to want to find some way to stand up for yourself. To stand up for us. Don't deny me the one chance I might ever get to smack down the person who killed me."

Now she couldn't tell if he was laughing or fighting the urge to cry. Maybe both.

"Fine. I think you're insane. But, if somebody killed me I'd want to beat the crap out of them too. So if this is what you want to do, I've got your back. You going to take a weapon? There's not much around here, but remember she has the knife."

"I'm going to need my hands to climb. I hardly have pockets in a prom dress. But I'm not about to give her a chance to get that knife open."

Gabriel fished around inside his pocket and pulled out a wireless microphone headset with an earpiece. "Wear this. I'll keep a channel open between us the whole time. Anything goes wrong, you just say the word and I'll bring the platform right down."

She took the headset and slid it on.

"Now, you better go fast before I change my mind."

She put her arms on Gabriel's shoulders and rested her chin on top of his head. "You are incredible. I hope you know that. I'm always going to love you."

"Yeah, I know. BFFs. Now go."

Liv climbed up onto the window ledge and jumped.

She hit the balcony and paused for a moment to catch her breath. Below her Felix's platform started to rise. Felix looked surprised, but she seemed to be going with it. The crowd was cheering. Probably thrilled someone had cut off her speech.

Problem was now everyone was looking up.

Liv crouched low and scrambled around the side of the balcony until she reached the lighting rig. She tapped her radio mic.

"Hey. How about a distraction?"

"On it."

The stage lights dropped. Music started pounding. Strobes flashed. A few hundred balloons fell from the ceiling. She gritted her teeth and climbed from the balcony onto the lighting rig. It swayed.

Alrighty then. It was just like climbing a jungle gym in the playground. Simple as that. Except thirty feet in the air, in a prom dress, with lights screwing up your vision, balloons bouncing off of you and freaking loud music making the bars vibrate. Yeah, just like a jungle gym.

She crawled across the lighting rig and slid down through the bars until she was just above Felix.

Then she jumped.

She landed on the hydraulic platform.

Felix glared at her. "What the hell? I thought you were dead!"

"I was. Didn't like it." Liv punched her in the face as hard as she could. Felix stumbled back. Liv raised her fist and prepared to keep swinging. "Okay, Gabe. You can lower the platform any time now."

The power went out and everything went dark. The crowd groaned.

"Hey, Livvy?" Gabriel was trying to sound calm, but it wasn't quite working. "I gotta run downstairs to the fuse box. You just—"

Felix hit her from behind. The earpiece went dead.

Chapter Thirty-Nine

Felix grabbed the back of Liv's head. She smashed her face into the railing. "I am so going to make you pay."

The platform wasn't moving. No power meant no safety net.

Liv thrashed and managed to break Felix's grasp. She spun toward the sound of Felix's voice.

"What?" Liv said. "You didn't factor me into your plans?"

Fingernails flew into Liv's face, scratching and clawing like an animal trying to rip her eyes out. Liv tightened her fist, punched again and made contact with Felix's nose. A satisfying gush of blood poured over her knuckles.

Felix stopped her attack.

Liv readied her fists to fight.

She could hear Felix breathing but couldn't tell where she was.

Then Felix managed to get hold of her from behind.

They struggled, both flailing at each other, neither able to connect properly. Until Felix kicked Liv's legs out from under her. Liv fell hard against the metal platform floor, with Felix landing hard on top of her. Her head swam. Liv pressed her palms into the platform and struggled to shake Felix off. Felix pressed her weight down even harder on Liv's back. Air rushed out of her lungs. She opened her mouth to scream but couldn't make a sound.

Then Liv felt the tip of the knife pressing against her neck.

"You don't get it do you, you demented skank?" Felix hissed. "You're as good as dead. You'll never prove Adam wasn't a killer and the cops are going to find out you were helping him and hiding him. You have no proof I killed Brett or Cynn. All your little stunt up here is going to do is make you look even guiltier. You think I'm going to sit in jail one day when there's a creep like you to pin this on? All I have to do is kill you and tell everyone that you brought the knife up here to kill me. Maybe they'll even thank me for ridding the world of one more ugly, worthless freak."

A new voice suddenly filled the darkness. "Damn Felix, you always were a demented, shallow, selfish ass."

It was Adam—so close it was like he was crouching down beside her. Liv's heart beat so hard it felt like it would jump out of her chest. Adam's hand was on her shoulder. Felix's grip on her body loosened. Liv turned her head toward the sound of Adam' voice, but couldn't see him in the darkness.

"Look, I know I'm an idiot. And a moron. But even I get that Liv is stronger, and smarter, and braver—and yeah, hotter—than someone like you could ever hope to be," Adam said. "You know, as much as I regret not getting the chance to pound your head into the ground, Felix, I'm so damn happy to know that Liv is going to destroy you."

"What the hell?" Felix's voice quavered in the darkness. "What the hell is happening here?"

"You're losing." Liv reared back, throwing Felix off her. "That's what's happening."

Liv leapt to her feet. The lights came on. She turned toward Felix.

They were alone on the platform.

Liv lunged for Felix's throat and shoved her all the way to the edge. She bent Felix backward over the empty space with her hand on her throat. Torn hair extensions hung from Felix's head. Her dress was shredded. Her face was bloody.

Voices shouted below them. Police ran into the building.

"Help me!" Felix screamed. "Police! Please! Liv has me trapped. She's been working with Adam. She killed him in the staircase. Now she's trying to kill me. Help me. Please—"

Trumpets blared. The lights cut off again. A screen unfurled. A spotlight shone. The Rosewood logo spun.

What? Gabriel was showing the video yearbook *now*?

But the image that flickered onto the screen was security footage from the stairwell—Adam stepped inside the door. Felix came up from behind, hit him over the head and wrapped a wire around his neck.

The crowd gasped.

Felix's face went white. "How did you do this? I thought I'd killed the security camera feed."

Liv stepped back and crossed her arms. "Guess it didn't stay dead either."

"This is my life." Felix's recorded voice filled the air. *"No one takes it away from me."*

Gabriel had even managed to pick up audio. All of it, right through to the confession while she held Liv at knifepoint.

"So what if I killed Cynn. And Brett. And Eddy. And Adam. And you. I'm going to leave here and go on with my life. None of you matter."

"I don't know how you've done this," Felix stepped backwards up onto the railing. "But this is my life. I'd rather die than let you take it from me. So, good luck proving you didn't murder me."

Felix dove backwards over the railing. Her screams filled the air.

She fell through the air toward the stage, arms outstretched.

Felix was committing suicide, in the school auditorium, in front of an audience.

And there was nothing Liv could do save her. Nor, to be honest, was she entirely sure she wanted to.

Except, the difference between someone like her and someone like me is that I'd still try—

The trap door opened.

Felix fell into the safety net.

Police swarmed around her.

The earpiece crackled to life again.

"Catch," Gabriel said. He chuckled.

"Nicely done." Liv sat down and leaned back against the railing.

"Thanks."

The platform started to lower slowly.

"Any reason why you didn't tell me earlier about your funky stairwell video thing?"

"Didn't know I had it," Gabriel said. "Honestly. The feed was totally dead. It came back to life when the power came back on."

Liv looked down at the remnants of her bloody dress. Her hands were a mess of cuts. She couldn't figure out how much of the blood on her was Adam's and how much was hers. She glanced back up toward the ceiling. Tears filled her eyes.

Where are you, Adam? When I heard your voice in the darkness I thought maybe you weren't completely gone.

The platform was almost at the ground now. Liv looked up. Police were everywhere, herding people toward the door.

Then a figure broke through the crowd and bolted

across the auditorium floor toward her, dodging the officer trying to stop him.

"Gabriel!" Liv jumped off the platform and ran toward him.

"Hey, you!" Gabriel caught her in a bear hug and pulled her into his chest. "Welcome back."

"Tell me you'll never show that other video," she whispered.

"After all this? It would be anticlimactic." His arms tightened around her. "Besides, this way I get to be a hero."

Police were swarming them. Gabriel slipped one arm around Liv's shoulder and raised the other over his head.

"No, need to arrest us!" Gabriel called loudly. "We're totally underage and we're coming willingly. When you call our folks be sure to mention Liv just did something insanely heroic and I helped her catch a psycho killer."

His head leaned against hers.

"Hey, I'm sorry about Adam," Gabriel's voice dropped again. "I mean, I still think he was a total prick and he really wasn't good enough for you, but . . ."

"But you helped me catch his killer. And you had my back."

He grinned. "Anytime."

Epilogue

Liv pulled the sheet back slowly and looked down at the body on the embalming table. The corpse was in her late twenties. With high cheekbones and a long, multi-coloured mohawk. The drummer of an up-and-coming indie band, she'd drowned saving two kids whose boat had collapsed in Lake Ontario. Liv brushed a hand over her shoulder.

I'm sure you have stories to tell.

Liv pulled the sheet back over the body.

But I'm not in the right headspace for listening.

It had been three weeks since Adam had been murdered and Felix had been arrested. Liv still hadn't let a corpse back into her brain yet. Sometimes when she walked into the embalming room or helped Tony with a body, she could feel their voices buzzing in the back of her mind, like a song playing in the far distance or a mosquito begging to be swatted.

But she always pushed their voices back before they managed to get inside her.

Because my brain is tired. I'm tired. And keeping my life together is more important than letting strangers rent space in my mind.

Besides, she was still getting used to the weird feeling of having extra life inside her body. It was hard to explain, no matter how many times Gabriel asked her to. It was like there was more air in her lungs or adrenaline in her system than there had been before she'd died.

In a really good way.

She switched off the lights and opened the back door. Muggy summer air swept into the prep room. Thunder rumbled above her. She stood in the doorway and leaned her back against the open door and stared out at the night. Her eyes closed.

She felt the warmth of a body standing in front of her before she heard his voice.

"But you know," Adam said, "If you don't close the door completely, someday someone is going to find their way in."

She jumped. Two hands landed on her shoulders. Familiar. Comforting. She wanted to open her eyes. She wanted to leap out of her skin. But she didn't move a muscle in case he disappeared.

"You're a dumbass," Liv said. "You could have come back and still you disappeared for weeks?"

She could hear him laughing. She reached out for

him and felt his chest against her palms. Her hands slid up his body and around the back of his neck. Her fingers played with his hair.

"Well, maybe I'm just a slow learner and it took me some time to figure out how to make this happen." Adam's hands slid onto her waist. "Damn, I've missed you."

His lips brushed her neck.

"Good." A sob was building in the back of her throat. Liv didn't know whether she was about to laugh or cry. She pulled his body against hers and felt his breath on her face. "How are you even here?"

"You left a connection open between us I could use to pull myself back."

"But that's not possible." She shook her head. Tears were pushing their way to the corner of her eyes. "I tried. I really tried. I mean, I thought I heard you up on the platform when I was fighting Felix. But when the lights came on, you were gone. Then the police took your corpse away before I could try to talk to you. Your body didn't come to my funeral home. Your parents had a private family funeral. I couldn't get to your corpse. I couldn't get your ashes. I couldn't get any piece of you to hold onto. I couldn't even find out where your body was buried—"

"Hey. It's okay." Adam's fingers brushed her cheeks. "Maybe my blood somehow got into your veins when you tried to save me. Or maybe something happened inside your brain when our spirits connected in the afterlife. Heck, I don't know if this is a blood thing, or a mental thing, or some emotional heart ... something ... whatever."

"A something whatever?" Eyes still closed, Liv shook her head. "How can you possibly have gotten even worse at explaining things since being murdered?"

"Hey, I never claimed to know exactly how things work." His hands settled back around her waist. "All I know is I went crazy in the afterworld without you. You made me want to return. You gave me a reason to fight to come back. You made me want to be alive."

I love you too, Adam. But I'm afraid you're not real. I'm afraid that you're not really here. I'm afraid to open my eyes, because when I open my eyes I'll be alone again and you'll be gone.

"Are you sure about that, Liv?" Adam whispered. "Maybe you should open your eyes."

Then Adam kissed her, pulling her up against his body and clutching her to him like a lifeline.

And Liv opened her eyes.

ABOUT THE AUTHOR

Mags Storey is an award-winning novelist and journalist. She used to travel the world. Now she lives in the GTA. She's occasionally mistaken for a zombie. But hey, this is Toronto.

ACKNOWLEDGEMENTS

One hot summer night I fell asleep as a thunderstorm raged outside. I dreamt. Of a subway. A kiss. A bloody body. And when I woke up, Liv had moved into my mind.

Thank you to everyone who helped this book become a reality. Including Andy Meisenheimer who introduced me to Renni Brown of *The Editorial Department*, who used this very first draft of this book to help me learn how to be a better writer. And Conor McCreery of *Kill Shakespeare*, who introduced me to Peter Chiykowski of *Rock Paper Cynic*, who introduced me to Sandra Kasturi of ChiZine who helped me expand the novel in many weird and wonderful ways, and who along with Brett Savory brought *Dead Girls Don't* to life. The power of geek network is strong with this one.

Also thanks to everyone at Starbucks near the 404 who keeps me caffeinated and puts up with my mutterings. And to all the funeral home staff, nurses, doctors, security guards, transit workers and police officers who advised me on both killing people and handling dead bodies. (Yes, lots of the facts in this book are true. Except for all those which aren't . . . Well, would you expect me to tell how to actually get away with murder?)

Thanks especially Cooper Solicitors who were willing to help defend Adam against murder charges, even though he was fictional.

Thanks also to all of the friends whose fingerprints made their way onto these pages, including but not limited to, Jason Brow, Ian Campbell, Len Hayes, Heather Medhurst, Arwen and Dee Nicholson and Jenn Whinnem. Also Andrea Fort and Sunny M. Hope of Cerberus, Sally Christensen and John Torres, Phil Gotfried, and everyone else at the incomparable Nerd Mafia.

Thank you to Michael, Big Bug, Little Bug and Small Dog for making this life worth living, and helping me live fearlessly.

Toronto, I love you. Please forgive me for making my alternative version of you so dirty, dingy, broken and susceptible to both the undead and corruption. It's only fiction. Don't make this weird. Well, weird*er*.

And finally, thanks to you for reading.

In the words of *Rock, Paper, Cynic*: Fill your mind with awesome things.

UNLEASH YOUR WEIRD

DID YOU ENJOY THIS BOOK? CHECK OUT OUR OTHER CHITEEN TITLES!

THE GOOD BROTHER
E.L. CHEN

Tori Wong is starting over. She's fled her parents' strict home to live out of the shadow of her overachieving brother, to whom her parents always compare hereven though he's dead. But during Yu Lan, or The Festival of Hungry Ghosts, when traditional Chinese believe that neglected spirits roam the earth, Tori's vengeful brother Seymour returns to haunt her. And soon, Tori begins to despair that she too is a hungry ghost and has more in common with Seymour than she'd thought. . . .

AVAILABLE NOW
978-1-77148-345-2

ALSO AVAILABLE FROM CHITEEN

THE FLAME IN THE MAZE
CAITLIN SWEET

The Flame in the Maze picks up the thread of the tale begun in *The Door in the Mountain*. The Princess Ariadne is scheming to bring her hated half-brother Asterion to ultimate ruin; Asterion himself, part human, part bull, is grappling with madness and pain in the labyrinth that lies within a sacred mountain; Chara, his childhood friend, is trying desperately to find him. In a different prison, Icarus, the bird-boy who cannot fly, plans his escape with his father, Daedalus—and plots revenge upon the princess he once loved. All of their paths come together at last, drawn by fire, hatred, love and hope—and all of them are changed.

OCTOBER 2015
978-1-77148-326-1

THE DOOR IN THE MOUNTAIN
CAITLIN SWEET

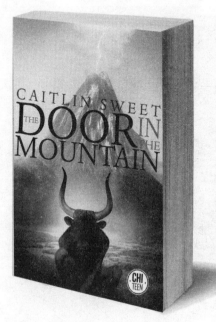

Lost in time, shrouded in dark myths of blood and magic, *The Door in the Mountain* leads to the world of ancient Crete: a place where a beautiful, bitter young princess named Ariadne schemes to imprison her godmarked half-brother deep in the heart of a mountain maze . . .

. . . where a boy named Icarus tries, and fails, to fly . . .

. . . and where a slave girl changes the paths of all their lives forever.

AVAILABLE NOW
978-1-77148-191-5

ALSO AVAILABLE FROM CHITEEN

FLOATING BOY AND THE GIRL WHO COULDN'T FLY

P.T. JONES

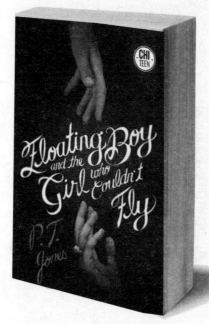

Things Mary doesn't want to fall into: the river, high school, her mother's life.

Things Mary does kind of want to fall into: love, the sky.

This is the story of a girl who sees a boy float away one fine day. This is the story of the girl who reaches up for that boy with her hand and with her heart. This is the story of a girl who takes on the army to save a town, who goes toe-to-toe with a mad scientist, who has to fight a plague to save her family.

It's all up in the air for now, though, and falling fast. . . .

AVAILABLE NOW
978-1-77148-173-1

CHITEEN.COM

THE CHOIR BOATS
DANIEL A. RABUZZI

London, 1812 | What would you give to make good on the sins of your past? For merchant Barnabas McDoon, the answer is: everything.

When emissaries from a world called Yount offer Barnabas a chance to redeem himself, he accepts their price—to voyage to Yount with the key that only he can use to unlock the door to their prison. But bleak forces seek to stop him: Yount's jailer, a once-human wizard who craves his own salvation, kidnaps Barnabas's nephew. A fallen angel—a monstrous owl with eyes of fire—will unleash Hell if Yount is freed. And, meanwhile, Barnabas's niece, Sally, and a mysterious pauper named Maggie seek with dream-songs to wake the sleeping goddess who may be the only hope for Yount and Earth alike.

AVAILABLE NOW
978-0-98094-107-4

ALSO AVAILABLE FROM CHITEEN

THE INDIGO PHEASANT
DANIEL A. RABUZZI

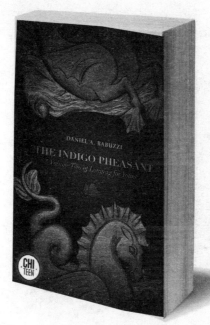

London 1817. Maggie Collins, born into slavery in Maryland, whose mathematical genius and strength of mind can match those of a goddess, must build the world's most powerful and sophisticated machine—to free the lost land of Yount from the fallen angel Strix Tender Wurm. Sally, of the merchant house McDoon, must choose either to help Maggie or to hinder her. Together—or not—Maggie and Sally drive to conclusion the story started in The Choir Boats—a story of blood-soaked song, family secrets, sins new and old in search of expiation, forbidden love, high policy and acts of state, financial ruin, betrayals intimate and grand, sorcery from the origins of time, and battle in the streets of London and on the arcane seas of Yount.

AVAILABLE NOW
978-1-92746-909-5

CHITEEN.COM

PICKING UP THE GHOST
TONE MILAZZO

Living in St. Jude, a 110-year-old dying city on the edge of the Mississippi, is tough. But when a letter informs fourteen-year-old Cinque Williams of the passing of the father he never met, he is faced with an incomplete past and an uncertain future. A curse meant for his father condemns Cinque to a slow death even as it opens his eyes to the strange otherworld around him. With help from the ghost Willy T, an enigmatic White Woman named Iku, an African Loa, and a devious shape-shifter, Cinque gathers the tools to confront the ghost of his dead father. But he will learn that sometimes too much knowledge can be dangerous—and the people he trusts most are those poised to betray him.

AVAILABLE NOW
978-1-92685-135-8

ALSO AVAILABLE FROM CHITEEN